D1327831

THE CLASSIC CRIME SERIES

Eric Ambler **The Mask of Dimitrios**
with an introduction by Robert Harris

Francis Iles **Malice Aforethought**
with an introduction by Colin Dexter

Nicholas Blake **The Beast Must Die**
with an introduction by P. D. James

Eric Ambler **Journey Into Fear**
with an introduction by Robert Harris

Christianna Brand **Green for Danger**
with an introduction by Lindsey Davis

Edmund Crispin **Love Lies Bleeding**
with an introduction by Jonathan Gash

Forthcoming titles for autumn 1999
Francis Iles **Before the Fact**
Eric Ambler **Epitaph for a Spy**
Cyril Hare **Tragedy at Law**
Hillary Waugh **Last Seen Wearing . . .**

THE MASK OF DIMITRIOS

Eric Ambler began his writing career in the early 1930s, and quickly established a reputation as a thriller writer of extraordinary depth and originality. He is often credited as the inventor of the modern political thriller and John Le Carré once described him as 'the source on which we all draw'.

Ambler began his working life at an engineering firm, then as a copywriter at an advertising agency, while in his spare time he worked on his ambition to become a playwright. His first novel was published in 1936 and as his reputation as a novelist grew he turned to writing full time. During the war he was seconded to the Army Film Unit, where he wrote, among other projects, *The Way Ahead* with Peter Ustinov.

He moved to Hollywood in 1957 and during his eleven years there scripted some memorable films, including *A Night to Remember* and *The Cruel Sea*, which won him an Oscar nomination.

In a career spanning over sixty years, Eric Ambler wrote nineteen novels. He was married to Joan Harrison, who wrote or co-wrote many of Alfred Hitchcock's screenplays – in fact Hitchcock organized their wedding. Eric Ambler died in London in October 1998.

Robert Harris is the author of the bestselling novels *Fatherland*, *Enigma* and *Archangel*.

By the same author

The Dark Frontier
Uncommon Danger
Epitaph for a Spy
Cause for Alarm
Journey Into Fear
Judgement on Deltchev
The Schirmer Inheritance
The Night-Comers
Passage of Arms
The Light of Day
A Kind of Anger
The Ability to Kill and Other Pieces
Dirty Story
The Intercom Conspiracy
The Levanter
Dr Frigo
Send No More Roses
The Care of Time
Here Lies (Autobiography)
The Story So Far (Memories and other fictions)

Eric Ambler

The **Mask** of **Dimitrios**

with an introduction by
Robert Harris

MACMILLAN

*Macmillan would like to thank
H.R.F. Keating, John McLaughlin, Ralph Spurrier,
Lisanne Radice and Peters, Fraser and Dunlop
for their help in compiling this series.*

First published 1939 by Hodder & Stoughton

This edition published 1999 by Macmillan
an imprint of Macmillan Publishers Ltd
25 Eccleston Place, London SW1W 9NF
Basingstoke and Oxford

Associated companies throughout the world

ISBN 0 333 74604 X

Phototypeset by Intype London Ltd
Printed and bound in Great Britain by
Mackays of Chatham plc, Chatham, Kent

Introduction
by **Robert Harris**

Eric Ambler is a writer who really shouldn't need any introduction. His early novels were so good, his fame so great
and his influence so far-reaching, that none of his contem-
poraries would have dreamed that within his lifetime his
work would disappear from the bookshops. But it did, and
a whole generation – my generation, as it happens – has
grown up knowing almost nothing about him.

He was born in London in 1909, trained as an engineer
and worked as an advertising copywriter before becoming
a novelist; he eventually ending up writing movies in Hollywood. He was a professional writer for half a century and
his work forms, I would argue, a key link in that chain of
twentieth-century English storytellers that starts with
Joseph Conrad, takes in Graham Greene, and is extended
into our own time by the novels of John Le Carré and Len
Deighton. The genre associated with these novelists travels
under various labels – crime, suspense, espionage, adven-
ture, thriller, 'entertainment' – but is stamped by certain
common characteristics: a strong narrative drive, intelligent
prose, a powerful sense of atmosphere and an engagement
with the wider politics of the contemporary world. These
are novels (to take a few of their titles at random) about
journeys into fear, guns for sale, secret agents, perfect spies
and funerals in Berlin.

It was, I suppose, Ambler's misfortune to have written

his most famous work by the time he was in his early thirties, and the three books reprinted in this series – *Epitaph for a Spy* (1938)*, *The Mask of Dimitrios* (1939) and *Journey Into Fear* (1940) – are probably the novels upon which his reputation will rest. His fictional world is the Europe of the dictators immediately before the outbreak of the Second World War: a world of crooked arms salesmen, secret policemen, jaded whores and 'displaced persons', the midnight whistle of crowded trains lurching towards shabby frontier posts, commercial travellers' hotels with bad drains and suspicious concierges, warm champagne served in seedy brothels, unregistered cargo ships that have seen better days, drunken captains, false passports, stolen blueprints – and always, in the background, reverberating from wirelesses and foreign newspapers, the encroaching menace of war.

So strong is this atmosphere that, on one level, these three novels can be read and enjoyed purely as period pieces. If you want to experience the feel of the Continent in the 1930s, you will find few better guides. But there is more to Ambler than that.

He was, for a start, a gifted creator of credible characters. His heroes are invariably anti-heroes: the lonely and anxious Hungarian language teacher, Josef Vadassy (*Epitaph for a Spy*), who takes his holiday photographs to be developed in a French chemist's and finds himself mistaken for a secret agent; the 'lecturer in political economy at a minor university', Charles Latimer (*The Mask of Dimitrios*), whose donnish hobby of writing detective stories sparks an idle interest in the identity of a washed-

* To be published in the Pan Classic Crime series in November 1999.

up body in Turkey; and the amiable and luckless engineer, Mr Graham (*Journey Into Fear*), who ends up being hunted across half Europe:

> He was always friendly. Nothing effusive; just friendly; a bit like an expensive dentist trying to take your mind off things. He looked rather like an expensive dentist, too . . .

This device – of having an unwitting bystander suddenly sucked through the surface of everyday life into a subterranean world of violence and danger – had, of course, been employed before: John Buchan's *The Thirty-Nine Steps* (1915) is the classic example. And it would be used again, especially in the movies; for instance in Hitchcock's *North by Northwest*, starring Cary Grant (Alfred Hitchcock, incidentally, was a witness at Ambler's second wedding). But Ambler's trick was to make his bystanders neither men of action nor handsome seducers, but ordinary figures: clumsy, dull and frightened.

This gives his work, for all its nostalgic charm, an unexpectedly modern tone. His stories are realistic. His characters do real jobs. The criminal conspiracies in which they become enmeshed (heroin smuggling, arms dealing) are real, too; indeed, they are not much changed today. Dimitrios turns out to be a cocaine addict.

Ambler's demotic prose style is also modern. He doesn't hang around. Almost every paragraph has some telling incidental detail (in a plush and gloomy Turkish restaurant the characters 'sat down in upholstered chairs which exuded wafts of stale scent'). But the reader barely has time to register the quality of the writing because the story moves so quickly. Like his leading characters, Ambler, you feel, is a practical fellow, set on getting the job done with a minimum of fuss, then heading for home and a whisky and soda.

Above all, in these three novels, Ambler anticipates the moral landscape of the Cold War thriller. 'Good did not triumph,' muses the refugee Vadassy in *Epitaph for a Spy*. 'Evil did not triumph. The two resolved, destroyed each other, and created new evils, new goods that slew each other in their turn.' We like to think that ours is the sophisticated, world-weary generation; the one which has learned that all political systems, at their core, have a seed of violence and corruption. It is almost a shock to find that Ambler got there more than half a century earlier. I particularly treasure this cynical, throwaway remark in *The Mask of Dimitrios*:

> In a dying civilization, political prestige is the reward not of the shrewdest diagnostician but of the man with the best bedside manner. It is the decoration conferred on mediocrity by ignorance . . .

I hope very much that the reissue of these three novels will enable a new generation of readers to discover the excitement, skill and wit of Eric Ambler. He himself was looking forward immensely to the prospect of seeing his work in print again, and I was nervously wondering how he would react to being 'introduced' by a mere whipper-snapper such as myself. Sadly, however, I shall never know, as he died peacefully in his sleep on 23 October 1998, in his ninetieth year, leaving behind these wonderful books.

The **Mask** of **Dimitrios**

To Alan and Felice Harvey

'But the iniquity of oblivion blindely scattereth her poppy, and deals with the memory of men without distinction to merit of perpetuity . . . Without the favour of the everlasting register, the first man had been as unknown as the last, and Methuselah's long life had been his only Chronicle.'

– Sir Thomas Browne: *Hydriotaphia*

Contents

1. Origins of an Obsession   9

2. The Dossier of Dimitrios   22

3. 1922   36

4. Mr Peters   56

5. 1923   73

6. Carte Postale   95

7. Half a Million Francs   118

8. Grodek   135

9. Belgrade, 1926   153

10. The Eight Angels   180

11. Paris, 1928–1931   198

12. Monsieur C. K.   226

13. Rendezvous   249

14. The Mask of Dimitrios   269

15. The Strange Town   286

1

Origins of an Obsession

A Frenchman named Chamfort, who should have known better, once said that chance was a nickname for Providence.

It is one of those convenient, question-begging aphorisms coined to discredit the unpleasant truth that chance plays an important, if not predominant, part in human affairs. Yet it was not entirely inexcusable. Inevitably, chance does occasionally operate with a sort of fumbling coherence readily mistakable for the workings of a self-conscious Providence.

The story of Dimitrios Makropoulos is an example of this.

The fact that a man like Latimer should so much as learn of the existence of a man like Dimitrios is alone grotesque. That he should actually see the dead body of Dimitrios, that he should spend weeks that he could ill afford probing into the man's shadowy history, and that he should ultimately find himself in the position of owing his life to a criminal's odd taste in interior decoration are breathtaking in their absurdity.

Yet, when these facts are seen side by side with the other facts in the case, it is difficult not to become lost in superstitious awe. Their very absurdity seems to prohibit the use of the words 'chance' and 'coincidence'. For the sceptic there remains only one consolation: if there should be such a thing as a superhuman Law, it is administered with sub-human inefficiency. The choice of Latimer as its instrument could have been made only by an idiot.

During the first fifteen years of his adult life, Charles Latimer became a lecturer in political economy at a minor English university. By the time he was thirty-five he had, in addition, written three books. The first was a study of the influence of Proudhon on nineteenth century Italian political thought. The second was entitled *The Gotha Programme of 1875*. The third was an assessment of the economic implications of Rosenberg's *Der Mythus des zwanzigsten Jahrhunderts*.

It was soon after he had finished correcting the bulky proofs of the last work, and in the hope of dispelling the black depression which was the aftermath of his temporary association with the philosophy of National Socialism and its prophet, Dr Rosenberg, that he wrote his first detective story.

A Bloody Shovel was an immediate success. It was fol-lowed by *'I,' said the Fly* and *Murder's Arms*. From the great army of university professors who write detective stories in their spare time, Latimer soon emerged as one of the shamefaced few who could make money at the sport. It was, perhaps, inevitable that, sooner or later, he would become a professional writer in name as well as in fact. Three things hastened the transition. The first was a dis-agreement with the university authorities over what he held to be a matter of principle. The second was an illness. The third was the fact that he happened to be unmarried. Not long after the publication of *No Doornail This* and following the illness, which had made inroads on his constitutional reserves, he wrote, with only mild reluctance, a letter of resignation and went abroad to complete his fifth detective story in the sun.

It was the week after he had finished that book's successor that he went to Turkey. He had spent a year in and near Athens and was longing for a change of scene. His health was much improved but the prospect of an English autumn was uninviting. At the suggestion of a Greek friend he took the steamer from the Piraeus to Istanbul.

It was in Istanbul and from Colonel Haki that he first heard of Dimitrios.

★

A letter of introduction is an uneasy document. More often than not, the bearer of it is only casually acquainted with the giver who, in turn, may know the person to whom it is addressed even less well. The chances of its presentation having a satisfactory outcome for all three are slender.

Among the letters of introduction which Latimer carried with him to Istanbul was one to a Madame Chávez, who lived, he had been told, in a villa on the Bosphorus. Three days after he arrived, he wrote to her and received in reply an invitation to join a four day party at the villa. A trifle apprehensively, he accepted.

For Madame Chávez, the road from Buenos Ayres had been as liberally paved with gold as the road to it. A very handsome Turkish woman, she had successfully married and divorced a wealthy Argentine meat broker and, with a fraction of her gains from these transactions, had purchased a small palace which had once housed minor Turkish royalty. It stood, remote and inconvenient of

Eric Ambler

access, overlooking a bay of fantastic beauty and, apart from the fact that the supplies of fresh water were insufficient to serve even one of its nine bathrooms, was exquisitely appointed. But for the other guests and his hostess's Turkish habit of striking her servants violently in the face when they displeased her (which was often), Latimer, for whom such grandiose discomfort was a novelty, would have enjoyed himself.

The other guests were a very noisy pair of Marseillais, three Italians, two young Turkish naval officers and their 'fiancées' of the moment, and an assortment of Istanbul businessmen with their wives. The greater part of the time they spent in drinking Madame Chávez's seemingly inexhaustible supplies of Dutch gin and dancing to a gramophone attended by a servant who went on steadily playing records whether the guests happened to be dancing at the moment or not. On the pretext of ill-health, Latimer excused himself from much of the drinking and most of the dancing. He was generally ignored.

It was in the late afternoon of his last day there and he was sitting at the end of the vine-covered terrace out of earshot of the gramophone, when he saw a large chauffeur-driven touring car lurching up the long, dusty road to the villa. As it roared into the courtyard below, the occupant of the rear seat flung the door open and vaulted out before the car came to a standstill.

He was a tall man with lean, muscular cheeks whose pale tan contrasted well with a head of grey hair cropped Prussian fashion. A narrow frontal bone, a long beak of a nose and thin lips gave him a somewhat predatory air. He could not be less than fifty, Latimer thought, and studied

12

the waist below the beautifully cut officer's uniform in the hope of detecting the corsets.

He watched the tall officer whip a silk handkerchief from his sleeve, flick some invisible dust from his immaculate patent-leather riding boots, tilt his cap raffishly and stride out of sight. Somewhere in the villa, a bell pealed.

Colonel Haki, for this was the officer's name, was an immediate success with the party. A quarter of an hour after his arrival, Madame Chávez, with an air of shy confusion clearly intended to inform her guests that she regarded herself as hopelessly compromised by the Colonel's unexpected appearance, led him on to the terrace and introduced him. All smiles and gallantry, he clicked heels, kissed hands, bowed, acknowledged the salutes of the naval officers and ogled the businessmen's wives. The performance so fascinated Latimer that, when his turn came to be introduced, the sound of his own name made him jump. The Colonel pump-handled his arm warmly.

'Damned pleased indeed to meet you, old boy,' he said.

'Monsieur le Colonel parle bien anglais,' explained Madame Chávez.

'Quelques mots,' said Colonel Haki.

Latimer looked amiably into a pair of pale grey eyes. 'How do you do?'

'Cheerio – all – the – best,' replied the Colonel with grave courtesy, and passed on to kiss the hand of, and to run an appraising eye over, a stout girl in a bathing costume.

It was not until late in the evening that Latimer spoke to the Colonel again. The Colonel had injected a good deal of boisterous vitality into the party; cracking jokes, laughing loudly, making humorously brazen advances to the wives and rather more surreptitious ones to the unmarried women. From time to time his eye caught Latimer's and he grinned deprecatingly. 'I've got to play the fool like this – it's expected of me,' said the grin; 'but don't think I like it.' Then, long after dinner, when the guests had begun to take less interest in the dancing and more in the progress of a game of mixed strip poker, the Colonel took him by the arm and walked him on to the terrace.

'You must excuse me, Mr Latimer,' he said in French, 'but I should very much like to talk with you. Those women – phew!' He slid a cigarette case under Latimer's nose. 'A cigarette?'

'Thank you.'

Colonel Haki glanced over his shoulder. 'The other end of the terrace is more secluded,' he said, and then, as they began to walk, 'You know, I came up here today specially to see you. Madame told me you were here and really I could not resist the temptation of talking with the writer whose works I so much admire.'

Latimer murmured a noncommittal appreciation of the compliment. He was in a difficulty, for he had no means of knowing whether the Colonel was thinking in terms of political economy or detection. He had once startled and irritated a kindly old don who had professed interest in his 'last book', by asking the old man whether he preferred his corpses shot or bludgeoned. It sounded affected to ask which set of books was under discussion.

Colonel Haki, however, did not wait to be questioned. 'I get all the latest *romans policiers* sent to me from Paris,' he went on. 'I read nothing but *romans policiers*. I would like you to see my collection. Especially I like the English and American ones. All the best of them are translated into

French. French writers themselves, I do not find sympathetic. French culture is not such as can produce a *roman policier* of the first order. I have just added your *Une Pelle Ensanglantée* to my library. Formidable! But I cannot quite understand the significance of the title.'

Latimer spent some time trying to explain in French the meaning of 'to call a spade a bloody shovel' and to translate the play on words which had given (to those readers with suitable minds) the essential clue to the murderer's identity in the very title.

Colonel Haki listened intently, nodding his head and saying, 'Yes, I see, I see it clearly now,' before Latimer had reached the point of the explanation.

'Monsieur,' he said when Latimer had given up in despair, 'I wonder whether you would do me the honour of lunching with me one day this week. I think,' he added mysteriously, 'that I may be able to help you.'

Latimer did not see in what way he could be helped by Colonel Haki but said that he would be glad to lunch with him. They arranged to meet at the Pera Palace Hotel three days later.

It was not until the evening before it that Latimer thought very much more about the luncheon appointment. He was sitting in the lounge of his hotel with the manager of his bank's Istanbul branch.

Collinson, he thought, was a pleasant fellow but a monotonous companion. His conversation consisted almost entirely of gossip about the doings of the English and American colonies in Istanbul. 'Do you know the Fitzwilliams,' he would say. 'No? A pity, you'd like them. Well, the other day . . .' As a source of information about Kemal Ataturk's economic reforms he had proved a failure.

Eric Ambler

'By the way,' said Latimer after listening to an account of the goings-on of the Turkish-born wife of an American car salesman, 'do you know of a man named Colonel Haki?'

'Haki? What made you think of him?'

'I'm lunching with him tomorrow.'

Collinson's eyebrows went up. '*Are* you, by Jove!' He scratched his chin. 'Well I know *of* him.' He hesitated. 'Haki's one of those people you hear a lot about in this place but never seem to get a line on. One of the people behind the scenes, if you get me. He's got more influence than a good many of the men who are supposed to be at the top at Ankara. He was one of the Gazi's own particular men in Anatolia in 1919, a deputy in the Provisional Government. I've heard stories about him then. Blood-thirsty devil by all accounts. There was something about torturing prisoners. But then both sides did that and I dare say it was the Sultan's boys that started it. I heard, too, that he can drink a couple of bottles of Scotch at a sitting and stay stone cold sober. Don't believe that, though. How did you get on to him?'

Latimer explained. 'What does he do for a living?' he added. 'I don't understand these uniforms.'

Collinson shrugged. 'Well, I've *heard* on good authority that he's the head of the secret police, but that's probably just another story. That's the worst of this place. Can't believe a word they say in the Club. Why, only the other day . . .'

It was with rather more enthusiasm than before that Latimer went to his luncheon appointment the following day. He had judged Colonel Haki to be something of a

16

ruffian and Collinson's vague information had tended to confirm that view.

The Colonel arrived, bursting with apologies, twenty minutes late, and hurried his guest straight into the restaurant. 'We must have a whisky soda immediately,' he said and called loudly for a bottle of 'Johnnie'.

During most of the meal he talked about the detective stories he had read, his reactions to them, his opinions of the characters and his preference for murderers who shot their victims. At last, with an almost empty bottle of whisky at his elbow and a strawberry ice in front of him, he leaned forward across the table.

'I think, Mr Latimer,' he said again, 'that I can help you.'

For one wild moment Latimer wondered if he were going to be offered a job in the Turkish secret service, but he said, 'That's very kind of you.'

'It was my ambition,' continued Colonel Haki, 'to write a good *roman policier* of my own. I have often thought that I could do so if I had the time. That is the trouble – the time. I have found that out. But ...' He paused impressively.

Latimer waited. He was always meeting people who felt that they could write detective stories if they had the time.

'But,' repeated the Colonel, 'I have the plot prepared. I would like to make you a present of it.'

Latimer said that it was very good indeed of him.

The Colonel waved away his thanks. 'Your books have given me so much pleasure, Mr Latimer. I am glad to make you a present of an idea for a new one. I have not the time to use it myself, and, in any case,' he added magnanimously, 'you would make better use of it than I should.'

Latimer mumbled incoherently.

'The scene of the story,' pursued his host, his grey eyes fixed on Latimer's, 'is an English country house belonging to the rich Lord Robinson. There is a party for the English weekend. In the middle of the party, Lord Robinson is discovered in the library sitting at his desk – shot through the temple. The wound is singed. A pool of blood has formed on the desk and it has soaked into a paper. The paper is a new will which the Lord was about to sign. The old will divided his money equally between six persons, his relations, who are at the party. The new will, which he has been prevented from signing by the murderer's bullet, leaves all to one of those relations. Therefore' – he pointed his ice cream spoon accusingly – 'one of the five other relations is the guilty one. That is logical, is it not?'

Latimer opened his mouth, then shut it again and nodded.

Colonel Haki grinned triumphantly. 'That is the trick.'

'The trick?'

'The Lord was murdered by none of the suspects, but by the butler, whose wife had been seduced by this Lord! What do you think of that, eh?'

'Very ingenious.'

His host leaned back contentedly and smoothed out his tunic. 'It is only a trick, but I am glad you like it. Of course, I have the whole plot worked out in detail. The *flic* is a High Commissioner of Scotland Yard. He seduces one of the suspects, a very pretty woman, and it is for her sake that he solves the mystery. It is quite artistic. But, as I say, I have the whole thing written out.'

'I should be very interested,' said Latimer with sincerity, 'to read your notes.'

'That is what I hoped you would say. Are you pressed for time?'

'Not a bit.'

'Then let us go back to my office and I will show you what I have done. It is written in French.'

Latimer hesitated only momentarily. He had nothing better to do, and it might be interesting to see Colonel Haki's office.

'I should like to go back with you,' he said.

★

The Colonel's office was situated at the top of what might once have been a cheap hotel, but which, from the inside, was unmistakably a government building, in Galata. It was a large room at the end of a corridor. When they went in a uniformed clerk was bending over the desk. He straightened his back, clicked his heels and said something in Turkish. The Colonel answered him and nodded a dismissal. Latimer looked round him. Besides the desk there were several small chairs and an American water-cooler. The walls were bare and the floor was covered with coconut matting. Long green sun lattices hanging outside the windows kept out most of the light. It was very cool after the heat of the car which had brought them.

The Colonel waved him to a chair, gave him a cigarette and began rummaging in a drawer. At last he drew out a sheet or two of typewritten paper and held it out.

'There you are, Mr Latimer. *The Clue of the Bloodstained Will*, I have called it, but I am not convinced that that is the best title. All the best titles have been used, I find. But I will think of some alternatives. Read it, and do not be afraid to say frankly what you think of it. If there are any details which you think should be altered, I will alter them.'

Latimer took the sheets and read while the Colonel sat on the corner of his desk and swung a long, gleaming leg.

Latimer read through the sheets twice and then put them down. He was feeling ashamed of himself because he had wanted several times to laugh. He should not have come. Now that he *had* come, the best thing he could do was to leave as quickly as possible.

'I cannot suggest any improvements at the moment,' he said slowly. 'Of course, it all wants thinking over; it is so easy to make mistakes with problems of this sort. There is so much to be thought of. Questions of British legal procedure, for instance . . .'

'Yes, yes, of course.' Colonel Haki slid off the desk and sat down in his chair. 'But you think you can use it, eh?'

'I am very grateful indeed for your generosity,' said Latimer evasively.

'It is nothing. You shall send me a free copy of the book when it appears.' He swung round in his chair and picked up the telephone. 'I will have a copy made for you to take away.'

Latimer sat back. Well, that was that! It could not take long to make a copy. He listened to the Colonel talking to someone over the telephone and saw him frown. The Colonel put the telephone down and turned to him.

'You will excuse me if I deal with a small matter?'

'Of course.'

The Colonel drew a bulky manila file towards him and began to go through the papers inside it. Then he selected one and glanced down it. As he did so the uniformed clerk rapped on the door and marched in with a thin yellow folder under his arm. The Colonel took the folder and put it on the desk in front of him; then, with a word of instruction, he handed over *The Clue of the Bloodstained Will* to the clerk, who clicked his heels and went out. There was silence in the room.

Latimer, affecting preoccupation with his cigarette, glanced across the desk. Colonel Haki was slowly turning the pages inside the folder, and on his face was a look that Latimer had not seen there before. It was the look of the expert attending to the business he understood perfectly. There was a sort of watchful repose in his face that reminded Latimer of a very old and experienced cat contemplating a very young and inexperienced mouse. In that moment he revised his ideas about Colonel Haki. He had been feeling a little sorry for him as one feels sorry for anyone who has unconsciously made a fool of himself. He saw now that the Colonel stood in need of no such consideration. As his long, yellowish fingers turned the pages of the folder, Latimer remembered a sentence of Collinson's: 'There was something about torturing prisoners.' He knew suddenly that he was seeing the real Colonel Haki for the first time. Then the Colonel looked up and his pale eyes rested thoughtfully on Latimer's tie.

For a moment Latimer had an uncomfortable suspicion that although the man across the desk appeared to be looking at his tie, he was actually looking into his mind. Then the Colonel's eyes moved upwards and he grinned slightly in a way that made Latimer feel as if he had been caught stealing something.

He said, 'I wonder if you are interested in *real* murderers, Mr Latimer.'

2
The Dossier of Dimitrios

Latimer felt himself redden. From the condescending professional he had been changed suddenly into the ridiculous amateur. It was a little disconcerting.

'Well, yes,' he said slowly. 'I suppose I am.'

Colonel Haki pursed his lips. 'You know, Mr Latimer,' he said, 'I find the murderer in a *roman policier* much more sympathetic than a real murderer. In a *roman policier* there is a corpse, a number of suspects, a detective and a gallows. That is artistic. The real murderer is not artistic. I, who am a sort of policeman, tell you that squarely.' He tapped the folder on his desk. 'Here is a real murderer. We have known of his existence for nearly twenty years. This is his dossier. We know of one murder he may have committed. There are doubtless others of which we, at any rate, know nothing. This man is typical. A dirty type, common, cowardly, scum. Murder, espionage, drugs – that is the history. There were also two affairs of assassination.'

'Assassination! That argues a certain courage, surely?'

The Colonel laughed unpleasantly. 'My dear friend, Dimitrios would have nothing to do with the actual shooting. No! His kind never risk their skins like that. They stay on the fringe of the plot. They are the professionals, the *entrepreneurs*, the links between the businessmen, the politicians who desire the end but are afraid of the means, and the fanatics, the idealists who are prepared to die for their convictions. The important thing to know about an assassination or an attempted assassination is not who fired the shot, but who paid for the bullet. It is the rats like Dimitrios who can best tell you that. They are always ready to talk to save themselves the inconvenience of a prison cell. Dimitrios would have been the same as any other. Courage!' He laughed again. 'Dimitrios was a little cleverer than some of them, I'll grant you that. As far as I know, no government has ever caught him and there is no photograph in his dossier. But we knew him all right, and so did Sofia and Belgrade and Paris and Athens. He was a great traveller, was Dimitrios.'

'That sounds as though he's dead.'

'Yes, he is dead.' Colonel Haki turned the corners of his thin mouth down contemptuously. 'A fisherman pulled his body out of the Bosphorus last night. It is believed that he had been knifed and thrown overboard from a ship. Like the scum he was, he was floating.'

'At least,' said Latimer, 'he died by violence. That is something very like justice.'

'Ah!' The Colonel leaned forward. 'There is the writer speaking. Everything must be tidy, artistic, like a *roman policier*. Very well!' He pulled the dossier towards him and opened it. 'Just listen, Mr Latimer, to this. Then you shall tell me if it is artistic.'

He began to read.

'Dimitrios Makropoulos.' He stopped and looked up. 'We have never been able to find out whether that was the surname of the family that adopted him or an alias. He was known usually as Dimitrios.' He turned to the dossier again. 'Dimitrios Makropoulos. Born 1889 in Larissa, Greece. Found abandoned. Parents unknown. Mother believed Rumanian. Registered as Greek subject and adopted by Greek family. Criminal record with Greek authorities. Details unobtainable.' He looked up at Latimer. 'That was before he came to our notice. We first heard of him at Izmir[1] in 1922, a few days after our troops occupied the town. A *deunme*[2] named Sholem was found in his room with his throat cut: he was a money lender and kept his money under the floorboards. These were ripped up and the money had been taken. There was much violence in Izmir at that time and little notice would have been taken by the military authorities. The thing might have been done by one of our soldiers. Then, another Jew, a relation of Sholem's, drew the attention of the military to a Negro named Dhris Mohammed, who had been spending money in the cafés and boasting that a Jew had lent him the money without interest. Inquiries were made and Dhris was arrested. His replies to the court martial were unsatisfactory and he was condemned to death. Then he made a confession. He was a fig-packer, and he said that one of his fellow workmen, whom he called Dimitrios, had told him of Sholem's wealth hidden under the floorboards of his room. They had planned the robbery together and had entered Sholem's room by night. It had been Dimitrios, he said, who had killed the Jew. He thought that Dimitrios, being registered as a Greek, had escaped and bought a passage on one of the refugee ships that waited at secret places along the coast.'

1. Smyrna.
2. Jew turned Moslem.

He shrugged. 'The authorities did not believe his story. We were at war with Greece, and it was the sort of story a guilty man might invent to save his neck. They found that there had been a fig-packer named Dimitrios, that his fellow workmen had disliked him and that he had disappeared.' He grinned. 'Quite a lot of Greeks named Dimitrios disappeared at that time. You could see their bodies in the streets and floating in the harbour. This Negro's story was unprovable. He was hanged.'

He paused. During this recital he had not once referred to the dossier.

'You have a very good memory for facts,' commented Latimer.

The Colonel grinned again. 'I was the president of the court martial. It was through that that I was able to mark down Dimitrios later on. I was transferred a year later to the secret police. In 1924 a plot to assassinate the Gazi was discovered. It was the year he abolished the Caliphate and the plot was outwardly the work of a group of religious fanatics. Actually the men behind it were agents of some people in the good graces of a neighbouring friendly government. They had good reasons for wishing the Gazi out of the way. The plot was discovered. The details are unimportant. But one of the agents who escaped was a man known as Dimitrios.' He pushed the cigarettes towards Latimer. 'Please smoke.'

Latimer shook his head. 'Was it the same Dimitrios?'

'It was. Now, tell me frankly, Mr Latimer. Do you find anything artistic there? Could you make a good *roman policier* out of that? Is there anything there that could be of the slightest interest to a writer?'

'Police work interests me a great deal – naturally. But what happened to Dimitrios? How did the story end?'

Colonel Haki snapped his fingers. 'Ah! I was waiting for you to ask that. I knew you would ask it. And my answer is this: it *didn't* end!'

'Then what happened?'

'I will tell you. The first problem was to identify Dimitrios of Izmir with Dimitrios of Edirné.[1] Accordingly we revived the affair of Sholem, issued a warrant for the arrest of a Greek fig-packer named Dimitrios on a charge of murder and, with that excuse, asked foreign police authorities for assistance. We did not learn much, but what we did learn was sufficient. Dimitrios had been concerned with the attempted assassination of Stambulisky in Bulgaria which had preceded the Macedonian officers' *putsch* in 1923. The Sofia police know very little but that he was known there to be a Greek from Izmir. A woman with whom he had associated in Sofia was questioned. She stated that she had had a letter from him a short time before. He had given no address, but as she had had very urgent reasons for wishing to get in touch with him she had looked at the postmark. It was from Edirné. The Sofia police obtained a rough description of him that agreed with that given by the Negro in Izmir. The Greek police stated that he had had a criminal record prior to 1922 and gave those particulars of his origin. The warrant is probably still in existence, but we did not find Dimitrios with it.

'It was not until two years later that we heard of him again. We received an inquiry from the Yugoslav Government concerning a Turkish subject named Dimitrios Talat.

1. Adrianople.

He was wanted, they said, for robbery, but an agent of ours in Belgrade reported that the robbery was the theft of some secret naval documents and that the charge the Yugoslavs hoped to bring against him was one of espionage on behalf of France. By the first name and the description issued by the Belgrade police we guessed that Talat was probably Dimitrios of Izmir. About the same time our Consul in Switzerland renewed the passport, issued apparently at Ankara, of a man named Talat. It is a common Turkish name, but when it came to entering the record of the renewal it was found from the number that no such passport had been issued. The passport had been forged.' He spread out his hands. 'You see, Mr Latimer? There is your story. Incomplete. Inartistic. No detection, no suspects, no hidden motives, merely sordid.'

'But interesting, nevertheless,' objected Latimer. 'What happened over the Talat business?'

'Still looking for the end of your story, Mr Latimer? All right, then. Nothing happened about Talat. It is just a name. We never heard it again. If he used the passport we don't know. It does not matter. We have Dimitrios. A corpse, it is true, but we have him. We shall probably never know who killed him. The ordinary police will doubtless make their inquiries and report to us that they have no hope of discovering the murderer. This dossier will go into the archives. It is just one of many similar cases.'

'You said something about drugs.'

Colonel Haki began to look bored. 'Oh, yes. Dimitrios made a lot of money once I should think. Another unfinished story. About three years after the Belgrade affair we heard of him again. Nothing to do with us but the available information was added to the dossier as a routine matter.'

He referred to the dossier. 'In 1929, the League of Nations Advisory Committee on the illicit traffic of drugs received a report from the French government concerning the seizure of a large quantity of heroin at the Swiss frontier. It was concealed in a mattress in a sleeping car coming from Sofia. One of the car attendants was found to be responsible for the smuggling, but all he could, or would, tell the police was that the drug was to have been collected in Paris by a man who worked at the rail terminus. He did not know the man's name and had never spoken to him, but he described him. The man in question was later arrested. Questioned, he admitted the charge but claimed that he knew nothing of the destination of the drug. He received one consignment a month which was collected by a third man. The police set a trap for this third man and caught him only to find there was a fourth intermediary. They arrested six men in all in connection with that affair and only obtained one real clue. It was that the man at the head of this peddling organization was a man known as Dimitrios. Through the medium of the Committee, the Bulgarian government then revealed that they had found a clandestine heroin laboratory at Radomir and had seized two hundred and thirty kilos of heroin ready for delivery. The consignee's name was Dimitrios. During the next year the French succeeded in discovering one or two other large heroin consignments bound for Dimitrios. But they did not get very much nearer to Dimitrios himself. There were difficulties. The stuff never seemed to come in the same way twice and by the end of the year, 1930, all they had to show in the way of arrests were a number of smugglers and some insignificant pedlars. Judging by the amounts of heroin they did find, Dimitrios must have been making huge sums for himself. Then, quite suddenly, about a year after that, Dimitrios went out of the drug business. The first news the police had of this was an anonymous letter which gave the names of all the principal members of the gang, their life histories and details of how evidence against every one of them might be obtained. The French police had a theory at the time. They said that Dimitrios himself had become a heroin addict. Whether that is true or not, the fact is that by December, the gang was rounded up. One of them, a woman, was already wanted for fraud. Some of them threatened to kill Dimitrios when they were released from prison, but the most any of them could tell the police about him was that his surname was Makropoulos and that he had a flat in the seventeenth *arrondissement*. They never found the flat and they never found Dimitrios.'

The clerk had come in and was standing by the desk.

'Ah,' said the Colonel, 'here is your copy.'

Latimer took it and thanked him rather absently.

'And that was the last you heard of Dimitrios?' he asked.

'Oh, no. The last we heard of him was about a year later. A Croat attempted to assassinate a Yugoslav politician in Zagreb. In the confession he made to the police, he said that friends had obtained the pistol he used from a man named Dimitrios in Rome. If it was Dimitrios of Izmir he must have returned to his old profession. A dirty type. There are a few more like him who should float in the Bosphorus.'

'You say you never had a photograph of him. How did you identify him?'

'There was a French *carte d'identité* sewn inside the lining of his coat. It was issued about a year ago at Lyons to Dimitrios Makropoulos. It is a visitor's *carte* and he is described as being without occupation. That might mean anything. There was, of course, a photograph in it. We've turned it over to the French. They say that it is quite genuine.' He pushed the dossier aside and stood up. 'There's an inquest tomorrow. I have to go and have a look at the body in the police mortuary. That is a thing you do not have to contend with in books, Mr Latimer – a list of regulations. A man is found floating in the Bosphorus. A police matter, clearly. But because this man happens to be on my files, my organization has to deal with it also. I have my car waiting. Can I take you anywhere?'

'If my hotel isn't too much out of your way, I should like to be taken there.'

'Of course. You have the plot of your new book safely? Good. Then we are ready.'

In the car, the Colonel elaborated on the virtues of *The Clue of the Bloodstained Will*. Latimer promised to keep in touch with him and let him know how the book progressed. The car pulled up outside his hotel. They had exchanged farewells and Latimer was about to get out when he hesitated and then dropped back into his seat.

'Look here, Colonel,' he said, 'I want to make what will seem to you a rather strange request.'

The Colonel gestured expansively. 'Anything.'

'I have a fancy to see the body of this man Dimitrios. I wonder if it would be impossible for you to take me with you.'

The Colonel frowned and then shrugged. 'If you wish to come, by all means do so. But I do not see . . .'

'I have never,' lied Latimer quickly, 'seen either a dead

man or a mortuary. I think that every detective story writer should see those things.'

The Colonel's face cleared, 'My dear fellow, of course he should. One cannot write about that which one has never seen.' He signalled the chauffeur on. 'Perhaps,' he added as they drove off again, 'we can incorporate a scene in a mortuary in your new book. I will think about it.'

★

The mortuary was a small, corrugated-iron building in the precincts of a police station near the mosque of Nouri Osmanieh. A police official, collected en route by the Colonel, led them across the yard which separated it from the main building. The afternoon heat had set the air above the concrete quivering and Latimer began to wish that he had not come. It was not the weather for visiting corrugated-iron mortuaries.

The official unlocked the door and opened it. A blast of hot, carbolic-laden air came out, as from an oven, to meet them. Latimer took off his hat and followed the Colonel in.

There were no windows and light was supplied by a single high-powered electric lamp in an enamel reflector. On each side of a gangway which ran down the centre, there were four high, wooden trestle tables. All but three were bare. The three were draped with stiff, heavy tarpaulins which bulged slightly above the level of the other trestles. The heat was overpowering and Latimer felt the sweat begin to soak into his shirt and trickle down his legs.

'It's very hot,' he said.

The Colonel shrugged and nodded towards the trestles. 'They don't complain.'

The official went to the nearest of the three trestles,

leaned over it and dragged the tarpaulin back. The Colonel walked over and looked down. Latimer forced himself to follow.

The body lying on the trestle was that of a short, broad-shouldered man of about fifty. From where he stood near the foot of the table, Latimer could see very little of the face, only a section of putty-coloured flesh and a fringe of tousled grey hair. The body was wrapped in a mackintosh sheet. By the feet was a neat pile of crumpled clothing: some underwear, a shirt, socks, a flowered tie and a blue serge suit stained nearly grey by sea water. Beside this pile was a pair of narrow, pointed shoes, the soles of which had warped as they had dried.

Latimer took a step nearer so that he could see the face.

No one had troubled to close the eyes and the whites of them stared upwards at the light. The lower jaw had dropped slightly. It was not quite the face that Latimer had pictured; rather rounder, and with thick lips instead of thin, a face that would work and quiver under the stress of emotion. The cheeks were loose and deeply lined. But it was too late now to form any judgement of the mind that had once been behind the face. The mind had gone.

The official had been speaking to the Colonel. Now he stopped.

'Killed by a knife wound in the stomach, according to the doctor,' translated the Colonel. 'Already dead when he got into the water.'

'Where did the clothes come from?'

'Lyons, all except the suit and shoes which are Greek. Poor stuff.'

He renewed his conversation with the official.

Latimer stared at the corpse. So this was Dimitrios. This

was the man who had, perhaps, slit the throat of Sholem, the Jew turned Moslem. This was the man who had connived at assassinations, who had spied for France. This was the man who had trafficked in drugs, who had given a gun to a Croat terrorist and who, in the end, had himself died by violence. This putty-coloured bulk was the end of an odyssey. Dimitrios had returned at last to the country whence he had set out so many years before.

So many years. Europe in labour had through its pain seen for an instant a new glory, and then had collapsed to welter again in the agonies of war and fear. Governments had risen and fallen; men and women had worked, had starved, had made speeches, had fought, had been tortured, had died. Hope had come and gone, a fugitive in the scented bosom of illusion. Men had learned to sniff the heady dreamstuff of the soul and wait impassively while the lathes turned the guns for their destruction. And through those years, Dimitrios had lived and breathed and come to terms with his strange gods. He had been a dangerous man. Now, in the loneliness of death, beside the squalid pile of clothes that was his estate, he was pitiable.

Latimer watched the two men as they discussed the filling-in of a printed form the official had produced. They turned to the clothes and began making an inventory of them.

Yet at some time Dimitrios had made money, much money. What had happened to it? Had he spent it or lost it? 'Easy come, easy go,' they said. But had Dimitrios been the sort of man to let money go easily, howsoever he had acquired it? They knew so little about him! A few odd facts about a few odd incidents in his life, that was all the dossier amounted to! No more. It told you something. It told you that he had been unscrupulous, ruthless and treacherous. It told you that his way of life had been consistently criminal. But it did not tell you anything that enabled you to see the living man who had slit Sholem's throat, who had lived in a flat in Paris 17. And for every one of the crimes recorded in the dossier there must have been others, perhaps even more serious. What had happened in those two- and three-year intervals which the dossier bridged so casually? And what had happened since he had been in Lyons a year ago? By what route had he travelled to keep his appointment with Nemesis?

They were not questions that Colonel Haki would bother even to ask, much less to answer. He was the professional, concerned only with the unfanciful business of disposing of a decomposing body. But there must be people who knew of Dimitrios, his friends (if he had had any), and his enemies, people in Smyrna, people in Sofia, people in Belgrade, in Adrianople, in Paris, in Lyons, people all over Europe, who *could* answer them. If you could find those people and get the answers you would have the material for what would surely be the strangest of biographies.

Latimer's heart missed a beat. It would be an absurd thing to attempt, of course. Unthinkably foolish. If one did it one would begin with, say, Smyrna and try to follow one's man step by step from there, using the dossier as a rough guide. It would be an experiment in detection really. One would, no doubt, fail to discover anything new; but there would be valuable data to be gained even from failure. All the routine enquiries over which one skated so easily in one's novels one would have to make oneself. Not that any man in his senses would dream of going on such a wild goose chase – heavens no! But it was amusing to play with the idea and if one were a little tired of Istanbul . . .

He looked up and caught the Colonel's eye.

The Colonel grimaced a reference to the heat of the place. He had finished his business with the official. 'Have you seen all you wanted to see?'

Latimer nodded.

Colonel Haki turned and looked at the body as if it were a piece of his own handiwork of which he was taking leave. For a moment or two he remained motionless. Then his right arm went out, and, grasping the dead man's hair, he lifted the head so that the sightless eyes stared into his.

'Ugly devil, isn't he?' he said. 'Life is very strange. I've known about him for nearly twenty years and this is the first time I've met him face to face. Those eyes have seen some things I should like to see. It is a pity that the mouth can never speak about them.'

He let the head go and it dropped back with a thud on to the table. Then, he drew out his silk handkerchief and wiped his fingers carefully. 'The sooner he's in a coffin the better,' he added as they walked away.

3

1922

In the early hours of an August morning in 1922, the Turkish Nationalist Army under the command of Mustafa Kemal Pasha attacked the centre of the Greek army at Dumlu Punar on the plateau two hundred miles west of Smyrna. By the following morning, the Greek army had broken and was in headlong retreat towards Smyrna and the sea. In the days that followed, the retreat became a rout. Unable to destroy the Turkish army, the Greeks turned with frantic savagery to the business of destroying the Turkish population in the path of their flight. From Ala-shehr to Smyrna they burnt and slaughtered. Not a village was left standing. Amid the smouldering ruins the pursuing Turks found the bodies of the villagers. Assisted by the few half-crazed Anatolian peasants who had survived, they took their revenge on the Greeks they were able to overtake. To the bodies of the Turkish women and children were added the mutilated carcases of Greek stragglers. But the main Greek army had escaped by sea. Their lust for infidel blood still unsatisfied, the Turks swept on. On the ninth of September, they occupied Smyrna.

For a fortnight, refugees from the oncoming Turks had been pouring into the city to swell the already large Greek and Armenian populations. They had thought that the Greek army would turn and defend Smyrna. But the Greek army had fled. Now they were caught in a trap. The holocaust began.

The register of the Armenian Asia Minor Defence League had been seized by the occupying troops, and, on the night of the tenth, a party of regulars entered the Armenian quarters to find and kill those whose names appeared on the register. The Armenians resisted and the Turks ran amok. The massacre that followed acted like a signal. Encouraged by their officers, the Turkish troops descended next day upon the non-Turkish quarters of the city and began systematically to kill. Dragged from their houses and hiding places, men, women and children were butchered in the streets which soon became littered with mutilated bodies. The wooden walls of the churches, packed with refugees, were drenched with benzine and fired. The occupants who were not burnt alive were bayoneted as they tried to escape. In many parts looted houses had also been set on fire and now the flames began to spread.

At first, attempts were made to isolate the blaze. Then, the wind changed, blowing the fire away from the Turkish quarter, and further outbreaks were started by the troops. Soon, the whole city, with the exception of the Turkish quarter and a few houses near the Kassamba railway station, was burning fiercely. The massacre continued with unabated ferocity. A cordon of troops was drawn round the city to keep the refugees within the burning area. The streams of panic-stricken fugitives were shot down pitilessly or driven back into the inferno. The narrow, gutted streets became so choked with corpses that, even had the would-be rescue parties been able to endure the sickening stench that arose, they could not have passed along them.

Smyrna was changed from a city into a charnel-house.
Many refugees had tried to reach ships in the inner
harbour. Shot, drowned, mangled by propellers, their
bodies floated hideously in the blood-tinged water. But the
quayside was still crowded with those trying frantically to
escape from the blazing waterfront, buildings toppling
above them a few yards behind. It was said that the screams
of these people were heard a mile out at sea. *Giaur Izmir* –
infidel Smyrna – had atoned for its sins.

By the time that dawn broke on the fifteenth of September, over one hundred and twenty thousand persons
had perished; but somewhere amidst that horror had been
Dimitrios, alive.

★

As, sixteen years later, his train drew into Smyrna, Latimer
came to the conclusion that he was being a fool. It was not
a conclusion that he had reached hastily or without
weighing carefully all the available evidence. It was a conclusion that he disliked exceedingly. Yet there were two
hard facts that were inescapable. In the first place, he might
have asked Colonel Haki for assistance in gaining access to
the records of the court martial and confession of Dhris
Mohammed, and had not been able to think of a reasonable
excuse for doing so. In the second place, he knew so little
Turkish that, even assuming that he could gain access to
the records without Colonel Haki's help, he would be
unable to read them. To have set out at all on this fantastic
and slightly undignified wild goose chase was bad enough.
To have set out without, so to speak, a gun and ammu-
nition with which to make the killing was crass idiocy. Had
he not been installed within an hour of his arrival in an

excellent hotel, had his room not possessed a very comfortable bed and a view across the gulf to the sun-drenched, khaki hills that lay beyond it, and, above all, had he not been offered a dry Martini by the French proprietor who greeted him, he would have abandoned his experiment in detection and returned forthwith to Istanbul. As it was . . . Dimitrios or no Dimitrios, he might as well see something of Smyrna now that he was in the place. He partly unpacked his suitcases.

It has been said that Latimer possessed a tenacious mind. Perhaps it would have been more accurate to say that he did not possess the sort of mental airlock system which enables its fortunate owner to dispose of problems merely by forgetting them. Latimer might banish the problem from his mind but it would soon return to nibble furtively at his consciousness. He would have an uneasy feeling that he had mislaid something without being quite sure what that something was. His thoughts would wander from the business in hand. He would find himself staring blankly into space until, suddenly, there was the problem, back again. Useless to reason that, as he himself had created it, he should, therefore, be able to destroy it. Useless to argue that it was futile and that the solution of it did not matter anyway. It had to be tackled. On his second morning in Smyrna, he shrugged his shoulders irritably, went to the proprietor of his hotel and asked to be put in touch with a good interpreter.

Fedor Muishkin was a self-important little Russian of about sixty, with a thick, pendulous underlip which flapped and quivered as he talked. He had an office on the waterfront and earned his living by translating business documents and interpreting for the masters and pursers of foreign cargo vessels using the port. He had been a Mensh-evik and had fled from Odessa in 1919; but although, as the hotel proprietor pointed out sardonically, he now declared himself in sympathy with the Soviets, he had preferred not to return to Russia. A humbug, mind you, but at the same time a good interpreter. If you wanted an interpreter, Mui-shkin was the man.

Muishkin himself also said that he was the man. He had a high-pitched, husky voice and scratched himself a great deal. His English was accurate but larded with slang phrases that never seemed quite to fit their contexts. He said: 'If there is anything I can do for you just give me the wire. I'm dirt cheap.'

'I want,' Latimer explained, 'to trace the record of a Greek who left here in September, 1922.'

The other's eyebrows went up. '1922, eh? A Greek who left here?' He chuckled breathlessly. 'A good many of them left here then.' He spat on one forefinger and drew it across his throat. 'Like that! It was damn-awful the way those Turks treated those Greeks. Blood!'

'This man got away on a refugee ship. His name was Dimitrios. He was believed to have conspired with a Negro named Dhris Mohammed to murder a moneylender named Sholem. The Negro was tried by a military court and hanged. Dimitrios got away. I want to inspect, if I can, the records of the evidence taken at the trial, the confession of the Negro and the inquiries concerning Dimitrios.'

Muishkin stared. 'Dimitrios?'

'Yes.'

'1922?'

'Yes.' Latimer's heart jumped. 'Why? Did you happen to know him?'

The Russian appeared to be about to say something and then to change his mind. He shook his head. 'No. I was thinking that it was a very common name. Have you permission to examine the police archives?'

'No. I was hoping that you might be able to advise me as to the best way of getting permission. I realize, of course, that your business is only concerned with making translations, but if you could help me in this matter I would be very grateful.'

Muishkin pinched his lower lip thoughtfully. 'Perhaps if you were to approach the British Vice-Consul and request him to secure permission . . . ?' He broke off. 'But excuse me,' he said; 'why do you want these records? I ask, not because I cannot mind my own damn business, but that question may be asked by the police. Now,' he went on slowly, 'if it were a *legal* matter and quite above board and Bristol fashion, I have a friend with influence who might arrange the matter quite cheap.'

Latimer felt himself redden. 'As it happens,' he said as casually as he could, 'it *is* a legal matter. I could, of course, go to the Consul, but if you care to arrange this business for me then I shall be saved the trouble.'

'A pleasure. I shall speak to my friend today. The police, you understand, are damn-awful and if I go to them myself it will cost plenty. I like to protect my clients.'

'That's very good of you.'

'Don't mention it.' A faraway look came into his eyes. 'I like you British, you know. You understand how to do business. You do not haggle like those damn Greeks. When a man says cash with order you pay cash with order. A deposit? OK. The British play fair. There is a mutual confidence between all parties. A chap can do his best work under such circumstances. He feels . . .'

'How much?' interrupted Latimer.

'Five hundred piastres?' He said it hesitantly. His eyes were mournful. Here was an artist who had no confidence in himself, a child in business matters, happy only in his work.

Latimer thought for a moment. Five hundred piastres was less than a pound. Cheap enough. Then he detected a gleam in the mournful eyes.

'Two hundred and fifty,' he said firmly.

Muishkin threw up his hands in despair. He had to live. There was his friend, too. He had great influence.

Soon after, having paid over one hundred and fifty piastres on account of a finally agreed price of three hundred (including fifty piastres for the influential friend), Latimer left. It was understood that he would call in the following day to learn the result of the negotiations with the friend. He walked back along the quayside not unpleased with his morning's work. He would have preferred, it was true, to have examined the records himself and to have seen the translation done. He would have felt more like an investigator and less like an inquisitive tourist, but there it was. There was always the chance, of course, that Muishkin might have in mind the pocketing of an easy one hundred and fifty piastres, but somehow he did not think so. He was susceptible to impressions and the Russian had impressed him as being fundamentally, if not superficially, honest. And there could be no question of his being deceived by manufactured documents. Colonal Haki had told him enough about the Dhris Mohammed court martial to enable him to detect that sort of fraud. The only thing that could go wrong was that the friend would prove unworthy of his fifty piastres.

Muishkin's office was locked when he called the next day and although he waited for an hour on the filthy wooden landing outside it, the interpreter did not appear. A second call, later in the day, was equally abortive. He shrugged. It hardly seemed worth any man's while to embezzle five shillings worth of Turkish piastres. But he began to lose a little of his confidence.

It was restored by a note that awaited him at the hotel on his return. A page of wild handwriting explained that the writer had been called away from his office to interpret in a dispute between a Rumanian second-mate and the dock police over the death by crowbar of a Greek steve-dore, that he could pull out his own fingernails one by one for causing Mister Latimer inconvenience, that his friend had arranged everything and that he would deliver the translation himself the following evening.

He arrived, sweating profusely, very shortly before the time of the evening meal, and Latimer was drinking an aperitif. Muishkin came towards him waving his arms and rolling his eyes despairingly and, throwing himself into an armchair, emitted a loud gasp of exhaustion.

'What a day! Such heat!' he said.

'Have you got the translation?'

Muishkin nodded wearily, his eyes closed. With what seemed a painful effort he put his hand in his inside pocket and drew out a bundle of papers secured by a wire clip. He thrust them into Latimer's hands – the dying courier delivering his last dispatch.

'Will you have a drink?' said Latimer.

The Russian's eyes flickered open and he looked round

like a man regaining consciousness. He said: 'If you like. I will have an absinthe, please. *Avec de la glace.*'

The waiter took the order and Latimer sat back to inspect his purchase.

The translation was handwritten and covered twelve large sheets of paper. Latimer glanced through the first two or three pages. There was no doubt that it was all genuine. He began to read it carefully.

NATIONAL GOVERNMENT OF TURKEY
TRIBUNAL OF INDEPENDENCE

By order of the officer commanding the garrison of Izmir, acting under the Decree Law promulgated at Ankara on the eighteenth day of the sixth month of 1922 in the new calendar.

Summary of evidence taken before the Deputy President of the Tribunal, Major-of-Brigade Zia Haki, on the sixth day of the tenth month of 1922 in the new calendar.

The Jew, Zakari, complains that the murder of his cousin, Sholem, was the work of Dhris Mohammed, a Negro fig-packer of Buja.

Last week, a patrol belonging to the sixtieth regiment discovered the body of Sholem, a Duenme money-lender, in his room in an unnamed street near the Old Mosque. His throat had been cut. Although this man was neither the son of True Believers nor of good repu-tation, our vigilant police instituted inquiries and discovered that his money had been taken.

Several days later, the complainant, Zakari, informed the Commandant of Police that he had been in a café and seen the man Dhris showing handfuls of Greek money. He knew Dhris for a poor man and was sur-prised. Later, when Dhris had become drunk, he heard him boast that the Jew Sholem had lent him money without interest. At that time he knew nothing of the death of Sholem, but when his relations told him of it he remembered what he had seen and heard.

Evidence was heard from Abdul Hakk, the owner of the Bar Cristal, who said that Dhris had shown this Greek money, a matter of several hundreds of drachma, and had boasted that he had had it from the Jew Sholem without interest. He had thought this strange for Sholem was a hard man.

A dock-worker named Ismail also deposed that he had heard this from the prisoner.

Asked to explain how he came into possession of the money, the murderer first denied that he had had the money or that he had ever seen Sholem and said that as a True Believer, he was hated by the Jew Zakari. He said that Abdul Hakk and Ismail had also lied.

Questioned sternly by the Deputy-President of the Tribunal, he then admitted that he had had the money and that it had been given to him by Sholem for a service he had done. But he could not explain what this service had been and his manner became strange and agitated. He denied killing Sholem and in a blasphemous way called upon the True God to witness his innocence.

The Deputy-President then ordered that the prisoner be hanged, the other members of the Tribunal agreeing that this was right and just.

Latimer had come to the end of a page. He looked at Muishkin. The Russian had swallowed the absinthe and was examining the glass. He caught Latimer's eye. 'Absinthe,' he said, 'is very good indeed. So cooling.'

'Will you have another?'

'If you like.' He smiled and indicated the papers in Latimer's hand. 'That's all right, eh?'

'Oh yes, it looks all right. But they are a little vague about their dates, aren't they? There is no doctor's report either, and no attempt to fix the time of the murder. As for the evidence, it seems fantastically feeble to me. Nothing was proved.'

Muishkin looked surprised. 'But why bother to prove? This Negro was obviously guilty. Best to hang him.'

'I see. Well, if you don't mind, I'll go on glancing through it.'

Muishkin shrugged, stretched himself luxuriously and signalled to the waiter. Latimer turned a page and went on reading.

STATEMENT MADE BY THE MURDERER,
DHRIS MOHAMMED, IN THE PRESENCE OF THE
GUARD-COMMANDANT OF THE BARRACKS IN
IZMIR AND OTHER TRUE WITNESSES

It is said in the book that he shall not prosper who makes lies and I say these things in order to prove my innocence and to save myself from the gallows. I have lied, but now I will tell the truth. I am a True Believer. There is no god but God.

I did not kill Sholem. I tell you I did not kill him. Why should I lie now? Yes, I will explain. It was not I, but Dimitrios, who killed Sholem.

I will tell you about Dimitrios and you will believe me. Dimitrios is a Greek. To Greeks he is a Greek, but to True Believers he says that he is also a Believer and that it is only with the authorities that he is a Greek because of some paper signed by his foster-parents.

Dimitrios worked with others of us in the packing shed and he was hated by many for his violence and for his bitter tongue. But I am a man who loves other men as brothers and I would speak with Dimitrios some-times as he worked and tell him of the religion of God. And he would listen.

Then, when the Greeks were fleeing before the vic-torious army of the True God, Dimitrios came to my house and asked me to hide him from the terror of the Greeks. He said that he was a True Believer. So I hid him. Then, our Glorious army came to our aid. But Dimitrios did not go because he was, by reason of this paper signed by his foster-parents, a Greek and in fear of his life. So he stayed in my house and, when he went out, dressed like a Turk. Then, one day, he said certain things to me. There was a Jew Sholem, he said, who had much money, Greek pieces and some gold, hidden below the floor of his room. It was the time, he said, to take our revenge upon those who had insulted the True God and His Prophet. It was wrong, he said, that a pig of a Jew should have the money rightfully belonging to True Believers. He proposed that we should go secretly to Sholem, bind him and take his money.

At first I was afraid, but he put heart into me, reminding me of the book which says that whosoever fights for the religion of God, whether he be slain or victorious, will surely find a great reward. This is now my reward: to be hanged like a dog.

Yes, I will go on. That night after the curfew we went to the place where Sholem lived and crept up the stairs to his room. The door was bolted. Then Dimitrios knocked and called out that it was a patrol to search the house and Sholem opened the door. He had been in bed and he was grumbling at being woken from his sleep. When he saw us he called upon God and tried to close the door. But Dimitrios seized him and held him while I went in as we had arranged and searched for the loose board which concealed the money. Dimitrios dragged the old man across the bed and kept him down with his knee.

I soon found the loose board and turned round full of joy to tell Dimitrios. He had his back turned towards me and was pressing down on Sholem with the blanket to stifle his cries. He said that he himself would bind Sholem with rope which we had brought. I saw him now draw out his knife. I thought that he was meaning to cut the rope for some purpose and I said nothing. Then, before I could speak, he drove the knife into the old Jew's neck and pulled it across his throat.

I saw the blood bubble and spurt out as if from a fountain and Sholem rolled over. Dimitrios stood away and watched him for a moment, then looked at me. I asked him what he had done and he answered that it was necessary to kill Sholem for fear that he should point us out to the police. Sholem was still moving on the bed and the blood was still bubbling, but Dimitrios said that he was certainly dead. After that, we took the money.

Then, Dimitrios said that it was better that we should not go together, but that each should take his share and go separately. That was agreed. I was afraid then, for Dimitrios had a knife and I had none and I thought he meant to kill me. I wondered why he had told me of the money. He had said that he needed a companion to search for the money while he held Sholem. But I could see that he had meant from the first to kill Sholem. Why then had he brought me? He could have found the money for himself after he had killed the Jew. But we divided the money equally and he smiled and did not try to kill me. We left the place separately. He had told me the day before that there were Greek ships lying off the coast near Smyrna and that he had overheard a man saying that the captains of these ships were taking refugees who could pay. I think that he escaped on one of those ships.

I see now that I was a fool of fools and that he was right to smile at me. He knew that when my purse becomes full my head becomes empty. He knew, God's curses fall upon him, that when I sin by becoming drunk I cannot stop my tongue from wagging. I did not kill Sholem. It was Dimitrios the Greek who killed him. Dimitrios . . . (*here followed a stream of unprintable obscenities*). There is no doubt in what I say. As God is God and as Mohammed is His Prophet, I swear that I have said the truth. For the love of God, have mercy.

A note was appended to this, saying that the confession had been signed with a thumb print and witnessed. The record went on:

The murderer was asked for a description of this Dimitrios and said:

'He has the look of a Greek, but I do not think he is one because he hates his own countrymen. He is shorter than I am and his hair is long and straight. His face is very still and he speaks very little. His eyes are brown and tired-looking. Many men are afraid of him, but I do not understand this as he is not strong and I could break him with my two hands.'

N.B. The height of this man is 185 centimetres.

Inquiries have been made concerning the man Dimitrios at the packing sheds. He is known and disliked. Nothing has been heard of him for several weeks and he is presumed to have died in the fire. This seems likely.

The murderer was executed on the ninth day of the tenth month of 1922 in the new calendar.

Latimer returned to the confession and examined it thoughtfully. It rang true; there was no doubt about that. There was a circumstantial feeling about it. The Negro, Dhris, had obviously been a very stupid man. Could he have invented those details about the scene in Sholem's room? A guilty man inventing a tale would surely have embroidered it differently. And there was his fear that Dimitrios might have been going to kill him. If he himself had been responsible for the killing he would not have thought of that. Colonel Haki had said that it was the sort of story that a man might invent to save his neck. Fear did stimulate even the most sluggish imaginations, but did it stimulate them in quite that sort of way? The authorities obviously had not cared very much whether the story was or was not true. Their inquiries had been pitiably half-hearted; yet even so they had tended to confirm the Negro's story. Dimitrios had been presumed to have died in the fire. There was no evidence offered to support the presumption. It had, no doubt, been easier to hang Dhris Mohammed than to conduct, amidst all the terrible confusion of those October days, a search for a hypothetical Greek named Dimitrios. Dimitrios had, of course, counted on that fact. But for the accident of the Colonel's transfer to the secret police, he would never have been connected with the affair.

Latimer had once seen a zoophysicist friend of his build up the complete skeleton of a prehistoric animal from a fragment of fossilized bone. It had taken the zoophysicist nearly two years and Latimer, the economist, had marvelled at the man's inexhaustible enthusiasm for the task. Now, for the first time, he understood that enthusiasm. He had unearthed a single twisted fragment of the mind of Dimitrios and now he wanted to complete the structure. The fragment was small enough but it was substantial. The wretched Dhris had never had a chance. Dimitrios had used the Negro's dull wits, had played upon his religious fanaticism, his simplicity, his cupidity, with a skill that was terrifying. *We divided the money equally and he smiled and did not try to kill me.* Dimitrios had smiled. And the Negro had been too preoccupied with his fear of the man whom he could have broken with his two hands to wonder about that smile until it was too late. The brown, tired-looking eyes had watched Dhris Mohammed and understood him perfectly.

Latimer folded up the papers, put them in his pocket and turned to Muishkin.

'One hundred and fifty piastres, I owe you.'

'Right,' said Muishkin into his glass. He had ordered and was now finishing his third absinthe. He set down his glass and took the money from Latimer. 'I like you,' he said seriously. 'You have no *snobisme*. Now you will have a drink with me, eh?'

Latimer glanced at his watch. It was getting late and he had had nothing to eat. 'I'd be glad to,' he answered, 'but why not have some dinner with me first?'

'Good!' Muishkin clambered laboriously to his feet. 'Good,' he repeated, and Latimer saw that his eyes were unnaturally bright.

★

At the Russian's suggestion they went out to a restaurant, a place of subdued lights and red plush and gilt and stained mirrors, where French food was served. The room was full. Many of the men were ships' officers but the majority were in army uniforms. There were some unpleasant-looking civilians, but very few women. In one corner an orchestra of three laboured over a foxtrot. The atmosphere was thick with cigarette smoke. A waiter, who seemed very angry about something, found them a table and they sat down in upholstered chairs which exuded wafts of stale scent.

'*Ton*,' said Muishkin looking round. He seized the menu and after some deliberation chose the most expensive dish on it. With their food they drank a syrupy, resinous Smyrna wine. Muishkin began to talk about his life. Odessa, 1918. Stambul, 1919. Smyrna, 1921. Bolsheviks. Wrangel's army. Kiev. A woman they called The Butcher. They used the abattoir as a prison because the prison had become an abattoir. Terrible, damn-awful atrocities. Allied army of occupation. The English sporting. American relief. Bed bugs. Typhus. Vickers guns. The Greeks – God, those Greeks! Fortunes waiting to be picked up. Kemalists. His voice droned on while outside, through the cigarette smoke, beyond the red plush and the gilt and the white table-cloths, the amethyst twilight had deepened into night.

Another bottle of syrupy wine arrived. Latimer began to feel sleepy.

'And after so much madness, where are we now?'

demanded Muishkin. His English had been steadily deter-
iorating. Now, his lower lip wet and quivering with
emotion, he fixed Latimer with the unwavering stare of the
drunk about to become philosophical. 'Where now?' he
repeated and thumped the table.

'In Smyrna,' said Latimer and realized suddenly that he
had drunk too much of the wine.

Muishkin shook his head irritably. 'We grade rapidly to
damn-awful hell,' he declared. 'Are you a Marxist?'

'No.'

Muishkin leaned forward confidentially. 'Neither me.'
He plucked at Latimer's sleeve. His lip trembled violently.
'I'm a swindler.'

'Are you?'

'Yes.' Tears began to form in his eyes. 'I damn well
swindled you.'

'Did you?'

'Yes.' He fumbled in his pocket. 'You are no snob. You
must take back fifty piastres.'

'What for?'

'Take them back.' The tears began to course down his
cheeks and mingle with the sweat collecting on the point of
his chin. 'I swindled you, Mister. There was no damn
friend to pay, no permission, nothing.'

'Do you mean that you made up those records
yourself?'

Muishkin sat up sharply. '*Je ne suis pas un faussaire*,' he
asserted. He wagged a finger in Latimer's face. 'This type
came to me three months ago. By paying large bribes – '
the finger stabbed emphatically ' – large bribes, he had
obtained the permission to examine the archives for the
dossier on the murder of Sholem. The dossier was in the

old Arabic script and he brought photographs of the pages to me to translate. He took the photographs back, but I kept the translation on file. You see? I swindled you. You paid fifty piastres too much. Faugh!' He snapped his fingers. 'I could have swindled five hundred piastres, and you would have paid. I am too soft.'

'What did he want with this information?'

Muishkin looked sulky. 'I can mind my own damn nose in the business.'

'What did he look like?'

'He looked like a Frenchman.'

'What sort of a Frenchman?'

But Muishkin's head had sagged forward on to his chest and he did not answer. Then, after a moment or two, he raised his head and stared blankly at Latimer. His face was livid and Latimer guessed that he would very shortly be sick. His lips moved.

'*Je ne suis pas un faussaire,*' he muttered. 'Three hundred piastres, dirt cheap!' He stood up suddenly, murmured, '*Excusez-moi,*' and walked rapidly in the direction of the toilet.

Latimer waited for a time, then paid the bill and went to investigate. There was another entrance to the toilet and Muishkin had gone. Latimer walked back to his hotel.

From the balcony outside the window of his room, he could see over the bay to the hills beyond. A moon had risen and its reflection gleamed through the tangle of crane jibs along the quay where the steamers berthed. The searchlights of a Turkish cruiser anchored in the roadstead outside the inner port swung round like long white fingers, brushed the summits of the hills and were extinguished. Out in the harbour and on the slopes above the town pinpoints of light twinkled. A slight, warm breeze off the sea had begun to stir the leaves of a rubber tree in the garden below him. In another room of the hotel a woman laughed. Somewhere in the distance a gramophone was playing a tango. The turntable was revolving too quickly and the sound was shrill and congested.

Latimer lit a final cigarette and wondered for the hundredth time what the man who looked like a Frenchman had wanted with the dossier of the Sholem murder. At last he pitched his cigarette away and shrugged. One thing was certain: he could not possibly have been interested in Dimitrios.

4

Mr Peters

Two days later, Latimer left Smyrna. He did not see Muishkin again.

The situation in which a person, imagining fondly that he is in charge of his own destiny, is, in fact, the sport of circumstances beyond his control, is always fascinating. It is the essential element in most good theatre from the *Oedipus* of Sophocles to *East Lynne*. When, however, that person is oneself and one is examining the situation in retrospect, the fascination becomes a trifle morbid. Thus, when Latimer used afterwards to look back upon those two days in Smyrna, it was not so much his ignorance of the part he was playing, but the bliss which accompanied the ignorance that so appalled him. He had gone into the business believing his eyes to be wide open, whereas, actually, they had been tightly shut. That, no doubt, could not have been helped. The galling part was that he had failed for so long to perceive the fact. Of course, he did himself less than justice, but his self-esteem had been punctured; he had been transferred without his knowledge from the role of sophisticated, impersonal weigher of facts to that of active participator in a melodrama.

Of the imminence of that humiliation, however, he had no inkling when, on the morning after his dinner with Muishkin, he sat down with a pencil and a notebook to arrange the material for his experiment in detection.

Some time early in October 1922, Dimitrios had left Smyrna. He had had money and had probably purchased a passage on a Greek steamer. The next time Colonel Haki had heard of him he had been in Adrianople two years later. In that interim, however, the Bulgarian police had had trouble with him in Sofia in connection with the attempted assassination of Stambulisky. Latimer was a little hazy as to the precise date of that attempt, but he began to jot down a rough chronological table.

TIME		PLACE	REMARKS	SOURCE OF INFORMATION
1922	(October)	Smyrna	Sholem	Police Archives
1923	(early part)	Sofia	Stambulisky	Colonel Haki
1924		Adrianople	Kemal attempt	Colonel Haki
1926		Belgrade	Espionage for France	Colonel Haki
1926		Switzerland	Talat passport	Colonel Haki
1929–31 (?)		Paris	Drugs	Colonel Haki
1932		Zagreb	Croat assassin	Colonel Haki
1937		Lyons	*Carte d'identité*	Colonel Haki
1938		Istanbul	Murdered	Colonel Haki

The immediate problem, then, was quite clear-cut. In the six months following the murder of Sholem, Dimitrios had escaped from Smyrna, made his way to Sofia and become involved in a plot to assassinate the Bulgarian Prime Minister. Latimer found it a trifle difficult to form any estimate of the time required to become involved in a plot to kill a Prime Minister; but it was fairly certain that Dimitrios must have arrived in Sofia soon after his departure from Smyrna. If he had indeed escaped by Greek steamer he must have gone first to the Piraeus and Athens. From Athens he could have reached Sofia overland, via Salonika, or by sea, via the Dardenelles and the Golden Horn to Bourgaz or Varna, Bulgaria's Black Sea port.

Istanbul at that time was in Allied hands. He would have had nothing to fear from the Allies. The question was: what had induced him to go to Sofia?

However, the logical course now was to go to Athens and tackle the job of picking up the trail there. It would not be easy. Even if attempts had been made to record the presence of every refugee among the tens of thousands who had arrived, it was more than probable that what records still existed, if any, were incomplete. There was no point, however, in anticipating failure. He had several valuable friends in Athens and if there was a record in existence it was fairly certain that he would be able to get access to it. He shut up his notebook.

When the weekly boat to the Piraeus left Smyrna the following day, Latimer was among the passengers.

*

During the months following the Turkish occupation of Smyrna, more than eight hundred thousand Greeks returned to their country. They came, boatload after boatload of them, packed on the decks and in the holds. Many of them were naked and starving. Some still carried in their arms the dead children they had had no time to bury. With them came the germs of typhus and smallpox.

War-weary and ruined, gripped by a food shortage and starved of medical supplies, their motherland received them. In the hastily improvised refugee camps they died like flies. Outside Athens, on the Piraeus, in Salonika, masses of humanity lay rotting in the cold of a Greek winter. Then, the Fourth Assembly of the League of Nations, in session in Geneva, voted one hundred thousand gold francs to the Nansen relief organization for immediate use in Greece. The work of salvage began. Huge refugee settlements were organized. Food was brought and clothing and medical supplies. The epidemics were stopped. The survivors began to sort themselves into new communities. For the first time in history, large scale disaster had been halted by goodwill and reason. It seemed as if the human animal were at last discovering a conscience, as if it were at last becoming aware of its humanity.

All this and more, Latimer heard from a friend, one Siantos, in Athens. When, however, he came to the point of his enquiries, Siantos pursed his lips.

'A complete register of those who arrived from Smyrna? That is a tall order. If you had seen them come ... So many and in such a state . . .' And then followed the inevitable question: 'Why are you interested?'

It had occurred to Latimer that this question was going to crop up again and again. He had accordingly prepared his explanation. To have told the truth, to have explained that he was trying, for purely academic reasons, to trace the history of a dead criminal named Dimitrios would have been a long and uneasy business. He was, in any case, not anxious to have a second opinion on his prospects of success. His own was depressing enough. What had seemed a fascinating idea in a Turkish mortuary might well, in the bright, warm light of a Greek autumn, appear merely absurd. Much simpler to avoid the issue altogether.

He answered: 'It is in connection with a new book I am writing. A matter of detail that must be checked. I want to see if it is possible to trace an individual refugee after so long.'

Siantos said that he understood and Latimer grinned ashamedly to himself. The fact that one was a writer could

be relied upon to explain away the most curious extrava-
gances.

He had gone to Siantos because he knew that the man
had a Government post of some importance in Athens, but
now his first disappointment was in store for him. A week
went by and, at the end of it, Siantos was able to tell him
only that a register was in existence, that it was in the
custody of the municipal authorities and that it was not
open to inspection by unauthorized persons. Permission
would have to be obtained. It took another week, a week of
waiting, of sitting in *kafenios*, of being introduced to thirsty
gentlemen with connections in the municipal offices. At
last, however, the permission was forthcoming and the following day Latimer presented himself at the bureau in
which the records were housed.

The inquiry office was a bare tiled room with a counter
at one end. Behind the counter sat the official in charge.
He shrugged over the information Latimer had to give him.
A fig-packer named Dimitrios? October 1922? It was
impossible. The register had been compiled alphabetically
by surname.

Latimer's heart sank. All his trouble, then, was to go for
nothing. He had thanked the man and was turning away
when he had an idea. There was just a remote chance . . .

He turned back to the official. 'The surname,' he said,
'may have been Makropoulos.'

He was dimly aware, as he said it, that behind him a
man had entered the inquiry office through the door
leading to the street. The sun was streaming obliquely
into the room and for an instant a long, distorted
shadow twisted across the tiles as the newcomer passed
the window.

'Dimitrios Makropoulos?' repeated the official. 'That is better. If there was a person of that name on the register we will find him. It is a question of patience and organization. Please come this way.'

He raised the flap of the counter for Latimer to go through. As he did so he glanced over Latimer's shoulder.

'Gone!' he exclaimed. 'I have no assistance in my work of organization here. The whole burden falls upon my shoulders. Yet people have no patience. I am engaged for a moment. They cannot wait.' He shrugged. 'That is their affair. I do my duty. If you will follow me, please.'

Latimer followed him down a flight of stone stairs into an extensive basement occupied by row upon row of steel cabinets.

'Organization,' commented the official. 'That is the secret of modern statecraft. Organization will make a greater Greece. A new empire. But patience is necessary.' He led the way to a series of small cabinets in one corner of the basement, pulled open one of the drawers and began with his fingernail to flick over a series of cards. At last he stopped at a card and examined it carefully before closing the drawer. 'Makropoulos. If there is a record of this man we shall find it in drawer number sixteen. That is organization.'

In drawer number sixteen, however, they drew blank. The official threw up his hands in despair and searched again without success. Then inspiration came to Latimer.

'Try under the name of Talat,' he said desperately.

'But that is a Turkish name.'

'I know. But try it.'

The official shrugged. There was another reference to the main index. 'Drawer twenty-seven,' announced the official a little impatiently. 'Are you sure that this man came to Athens? Many went to Salonika. Why not this fig-packer?'

This was precisely the question that Latimer had been asking himself. He said nothing and watched the official's fingernail flicking over another series of cards. Suddenly it stopped.

'Have you found it?' said Latimer quickly.

The official pulled out a card. 'Here is one,' he said. 'The man was a fig-packer, but the name is Dimitrios Tala*dis*.'

'Let me see.' Latimer took the card. Dimitrios Taladis! There it was in black and white. He had found out something that Colonel Haki did not know. Dimitrios had used the name Talat before 1926. There could be no doubt that it *was* Dimitrios. He had merely tacked a Greek suffix on to the name. He stared at the card. And there were here some other things that Colonel Haki did not know.

He looked up at the beaming official. 'Can I copy this?'

'Of course. Patience and organization, you see. My organization is for use. But I must not let the record out of my sight. That is the regulation.'

Under the now somewhat mystified eyes of the apostle of organization and patience Latimer began to copy the wording on the card into his notebook, translating it as he did so into English. He wrote:

NUMBER T.53462
NATIONAL RELIEF ORGANIZATION
Refugee Section: ATHINAI

Sex: Male *Name:* Dimitrios Taladis. *Born:* Salonika, 1889. *Occupation:* Fig-packer. *Parents:* believed dead.

Identity Papers or Passport: Identity card lost. Said to
have been issued at Smyrna. *Nationality:* Greek. *Arrived:*
1 October 1922. *Coming from:* Smyrna. *On examination:*
Able-bodied. No disease. Without money. Assigned to
camp at Tabouria. Temporary identity paper issued.
Note: Left Tabouria on own initiative, 29th November,
1922. Warrant for arrest on charge of robbery and
attempted murder, issued in Athinai, 30th November,
1922. Believed to have escaped by sea.

Yes, that was Dimitrios all right. The date of his birth
agreed with that supplied by the Greek police (and based
on information gained prior to 1922) to Colonel Haki. The
place of birth, however, was different. According to the
Turkish dossier it had been Larissa. Why had Dimitrios
bothered to change it? If he were giving a false name, he
must have seen that the chances of its falsity being discovered by reference to the registration records were as
great for Salonika as for Larissa.

Salonika 1889! Why Salonika? Then Latimer remembered. Of course! It was quite simple. In 1889 Salonika had
been in Turkish territory, a part of the Ottoman Empire.
The registration records of that period would, in all prob-
ability, not be available to the Greek authorities. Dimitrios
had certainly been no fool. But why had he picked the
name Taladis? Why had he not chosen a typical Greek
name? The Turkish 'Talat' must have had some special
association for him. As for his identity card issued in
Smyrna, that would naturally be 'lost' since, presumably, it
had been issued to him in the name of Makropoulos by
which he was already known to the Greek police.

The date of his arrival fitted in with the vague allusions

to time made in the court martial. Unlike the majority of his fellow refugees, he had been able-bodied and free from disease when he had arrived. Naturally. Thanks to Sholem's Greek money, he had been able to buy a passage to the Piraeus and travel in comparative comfort instead of being loaded on to a refugee ship with thousands of others. Dimitrios had known how to look after himself. The fig-packer had packed enough figs. Dimitrios the man had been emerging from his chrysalis. No doubt he had had a substantial amount of Sholem's money left when he had arrived. Yet to the relief authorities he had been 'without money'. That had been sensible of him. He might other-wise have been forced to buy food and clothing for stupid fools who had failed to provide, as he had provided, for the future. His expenses had been heavy enough as it was; so heavy that another Sholem had been needed. No doubt he had regretted Dhris Mohammed's half share.

'Believed to have escaped by sea.' With the proceeds of the second robbery added to the balance from the first, he had no doubt been able to pay for his passage to Bourgaz. It would obviously have been too risky for him to have gone overland. He had only temporary identity papers and might have been stopped at the frontier, whereas in Bourgaz, the same papers issued by an international relief commission with considerable prestige would have enabled him to get through.

The official's much-advertised patience was showing signs of wearing thin. Latimer handed over the card, expressed his thanks in a suitable manner and returned thoughtfully to his hotel.

He was feeling pleased with himself. He had discovered some new information about Dimitrios and he had discovered it through his own efforts. It had been, it was true, an obvious piece of routine inquiry; but, in the best Scotland Yard tradition, it had called for patience and persistence. Besides, if he had not thought of trying the Talat name . . . He wished that he could have sent a report of his investigations to Colonel Haki, but that was out of the question. The Colonel would probably fail to understand the spirit in which the experiment in detection was being made. In any case, Dimitrios himself would by this time be mouldering below ground, his dossier sealed and forgotten in the archives of the Turkish secret police. The main thing was now to tackle the Sofia affair.

He tried to remember what he knew about postwar Bulgarian politics and speedily came to the conclusion that it was very little. In 1923 Stambulisky had, he knew, been head of a government of liberal tendencies, but of just how liberal those tendencies had been he had no idea. There had been an attempted assassination and later a military *coup d'état* carried out at the instigation, if not under the leadership of the IMRO; the International Macedonian Revolutionary Organization. Stambulisky had fled from Sofia, tried to organize a counter-revolution and been killed. That was the gist of the affair, he thought. But of the rights and wrongs of it (if any such distinction were possible), of the nature of the political forces involved, he was quite ignorant. That state of affairs would have to be remedied, and the place in which to remedy it would be Sofia.

That evening he asked Siantos to dinner. Latimer knew him for a vain, generous soul who liked discussing his friends' problems and was flattered when, by making judicious use of his official position, he could help them.

After giving thanks for the assistance in the matter of the municipal register, Latimer broached the subject of Sofia.

'I am going to trespass on your kindness still further, my dear Siantos.'

'So much the better.'

'Do you know anyone in Sofia? I want a letter of introduction to an intelligent newspaper man there who could give me some inside information about Bulgarian politics in 1923.'

Siantos smoothed his gleaming white hair and grinned admiringly. 'You writers have bizarre tastes. Something might be done. Do you want a Greek or a Bulgar?'

'Greek for preference. I don't speak Bulgarian.'

Siantos was thoughtful for a moment. 'There is a man in Sofia named Marukakis,' he said at last. 'He is the Sofia correspondent of a French news agency. I do not know him myself, but I might be able to get a letter to him from a friend of mine.' They were sitting in a restaurant, and now Siantos glanced round furtively and lowered his voice. 'There is only one trouble about him from your point of view. I happen to know that he has . . .' The voice sunk still lower in tone. Latimer was prepared for nothing less horrible than leprosy. ' . . . Communist tendencies,' concluded Siantos in a whisper.

Latimer raised his eyebrows. 'I don't regard that as a drawback. All the Communists I have ever met have been highly intelligent.'

Siantos looked shocked. 'How can that be? It is dangerous to say such things, my friend. Marxist thought is forbidden in Greece.'

'When can I have that letter?'

Siantos sighed. 'Bizarre!' he remarked. 'I will get it for you tomorrow. You writers . . .!'

★

Within a week the letter of introduction had been obtained, and Latimer, having secured Greek exit and Bulgarian ingress visas, boarded a night train for Sofia.

The train was not crowded and he had hoped to have a sleeping car compartment to himself, but five minutes before the train was due to start, luggage was carried in and deposited above the empty berth. The owner of the luggage followed very soon after it.

'I must apologize for intruding on your privacy,' he said to Latimer in English.

He was a fat, unhealthy-looking man of about fifty-five. He had turned to tip the porter before he spoke, and the first thing about him that impressed Latimer was that the seat of his trousers sagged absurdly, making his walk reminiscent of that of the hind legs of an elephant. Then Latimer saw his face and forgot about the trousers. There was the sort of sallow shapelessness about it that derives from simultaneous over-eating and under-sleeping. From above two heavy satchels of flesh peered a pair of pale blue, bloodshot eyes that seemed to be permanently weeping. The nose was rubbery and indeterminate. It was the mouth that gave the face expression. The lips were pallid and undefined, seeming thicker than they really were. Pressed together over unnaturally white and regular false teeth, they were set permanently in a saccharine smile. In conjunction with the weeping eyes above it, it created an impression of sweet patience in adversity, quite startling in its intensity. Here, it said, was a man who had suffered, who had been buffeted by fiendishly vindictive Fates as no other man had been buffeted, yet who had retained his humble faith in the essential goodness of man; here, it said, was a martyr who smiled through the flames – smiled yet who could not but weep for the misery of others as he did so. He reminded Latimer of a high church priest he had known in England who had been unfrocked for embezzling the altar fund.

'The berth was unoccupied,' Latimer pointed out; 'there is no question of your intruding.' He noted with an inward sigh that the man breathed very heavily and noisily through congested nostrils. He would probably snore.

The newcomer sat down on his berth and shook his head slowly. 'How good of you to put it that way! How little kindliness there is in the world these days! How little thought for others!' The bloodshot eyes met Latimer's. 'May I ask how far you are going?'

'Sofia.'

'Sofia. So? A beautiful city, beautiful. I am continuing to Bucaresti. I do hope that we shall have a pleasant journey together.'

Latimer said that he hoped so too. The fat man's English was very accurate, but he spoke it with an atrocious accent which Latimer could not place. It was thick and slightly guttural, as though he were speaking with his mouth full of cake. Occasionally, too, the accurate English would give out in the middle of a difficult sentence, which would be completed in very fluent French or German. Latimer gained the impression that the man had learned his English from books.

The fat man turned and began to unpack a small attaché case containing a pair of woollen pyjamas, some bed socks and a dog-eared paperback book. Latimer managed to see the title of the book. It was called *Pearls of Everyday Wisdom* and was in French. The fat man arranged these things carefully on the shelf and then produced a packet of thin Greek cheroots.

'Will you allow me to smoke, please?' he said, extending the packet.

'Please do. But I won't smoke just now myself, thank you.'

The train had begun to gather speed and the attendant came in to make up their beds. When he had gone, Latimer partially undressed and laid down on his bed.

The fat man picked up the book and then put it down again.

'You know,' he said, 'the moment the attendant told me that there was an Englishman on the train, I knew that I should have a pleasant journey.' The smile came into play, sweet and compassionate, a spiritual pat on the head.

'It's very good of you to say so.'

'Oh, no, that is how I feel.' His eyes bleared as smoke irritated them. He dabbed at them with one of the bedsocks. 'It is so silly of me to smoke,' he went on ruefully. 'My eyes are a little weak. The Great One in His wisdom has seen fit to give me weak eyes. No doubt He had a purpose. Perhaps it was that I might more keenly appreciate the beauties of His work – Mother Nature in all her exquisite raiment, the trees, the flowers, the clouds, the sky, the snowcapped hills, the wonderful views, the sunset in all its golden magnificence.'

'You ought to wear glasses.'

The fat man shook his head. 'If I needed glasses,' he said solemnly, 'the Great One would guide me to seek them.' He leaned forward earnestly. 'Do you not feel, my friend, that somewhere, above us, about us, within us, there is a power, a destiny, that directs us to do the things we do?'

'That's a large question.'

'But only because we are not simple enough, not humble enough, to understand. A man does not need a great education to be a philosopher. Let him only be simple and humble.' He looked at Latimer simply and humbly. 'Live and let live – that is the secret of happiness. Leave the Great One to answer the questions beyond our poor understanding. One cannot fight against one's Destiny. If the Great One wills that we shall do unpleasant things, depend upon it that He has a purpose even though that purpose is not always clear to us. If it is the Great One's will that some should become rich while others should remain poor, then we must accept His will.' He belched slightly and glanced up at the suitcases above Latimer's head. The smile became tenderly whimsical. 'I often think,' he said, 'that there is much food for thought in a train. Don't you? A piece of luggage, for instance. How like a human being! On its journey through life it will collect many brightly coloured labels. But the labels are only the outward appearances, the face that it puts upon the world. It is what is *inside* that is important. And so often –' he shook his head despondently – 'so very often, the suitcase is empty of the Beautiful Things. Don't you agree with me?'

This was nauseating. Latimer emitted a non-committal grunt. 'You speak very good English,' he added.

'English is the most beautiful language, I think. Shakespeare, H. G. Wells – you have some great English writers. But I cannot yet express all my ideas in English. I am, as you will have noticed, more at ease with French.'

'But your own language . . .?'

The fat man spread out large, soft hands on one of which twinkled a rather grubby diamond ring. 'I am a citizen of the world,' he said. 'To me, all countries, all languages are beautiful. If only men could live as brothers, without hatred, seeing only the beautiful things. But no! There are always Communists, etcetera. It is, no doubt, the Great One's will.'

Latimer said, 'I think I'll go to sleep now.'

'Sleep!' apostrophized his companion raptly. 'The great mercy vouchsafed to us poor humans. My name,' he added inconsequentially, 'is Mr Peters.'

'It has been very pleasant to have met you, Mr Peters,' returned Latimer firmly. 'We get into Sofia so early that I shan't trouble to undress.'

He switched off the main light in the compartment leaving only the dark blue emergency light glowing and the small reading lights over the berths. Then he stripped a blanket off his bed and wrapped it round him.

Mr Peters had watched these preparations in wistful silence. Now, he began to undress, balancing himself dexterously against the lurching of the train as he put on his pyjamas. At last he clambered into his bed and lay still for a moment, the breath whistling through his nostrils. Then he turned over on his side, groped for his book and began to read. Latimer switched off his own reading lamp. A few moments later he was asleep.

The train reached the frontier in the early hours of the morning and he was awakened by the attendant for his papers. Mr Peters was still reading. His papers had already been examined by the Greek and Bulgarian officials in the corridor outside and Latimer did not have an opportunity of ascertaining the nationality of the citizen of the world. A Bulgarian customs official put his head in the compartment, frowned at their suitcases and then withdrew. Soon the train moved on over the frontier. Dozing fitfully, Latimer saw the thin strip of sky between the blinds turn blue-black and then grey. The train was due in Sofia at seven. When, at last, he rose to dress and collect his belongings, he saw that Mr Peters had switched off his reading lamp and had his eyes closed. As the train began to rattle over the network of points outside Sofia, he gently slid the compartment door open.

Mr Peters stirred and opened his eyes.

'I'm sorry,' said Latimer, 'I tried not to waken you.'

In the semi-darkness of the compartment, the fat man's smile looked like a clown's grimace. 'Please don't trouble yourself about me,' he said. 'I was not asleep. I meant to tell you that the best hotel for you to stay at would be the Slavianska Besseda.'

'That's very kind of you, but I wired a reservation from Athens to the Grand Palace. It was recommended to me. Do you know it?'

'Yes. I think it is quite good.' The train began to slow down. 'Goodbye, Mr Latimer.'

'Goodbye.'

In his eagerness to get to a bath and some breakfast it did not occur to Latimer to wonder how Mr Peters had discovered his name.

5

1923

Latimer had thought carefully about the problem which awaited him in Sofia.

In Smyrna and Athens it had been simply a matter of gaining access to written records. Any competent private inquiry agents could have found out as much. Now, however, things were different. Dimitrios had, to be sure, a police record in Sofia; but, according to Colonel Haki, the Bulgarian police had known little about him. That they had, indeed, thought him of little importance was shown by the fact that it was not until they had received the Colonel's inquiry that they had troubled to get a description of him from the woman with whom he was known to have associated. Obviously it was what the police had *not* got in their records, rather than what they had got, which would be interesting. As the Colonel had pointed out, the important thing to know about an assassination was not who had fired the shot but who had paid for the bullet. What information the ordinary police had would no doubt be helpful, but their business would have been with shot-firing rather than bullet-buying. The first thing he had to find out was who had or might have stood to gain by the death of Stambulisky. Until he had that basic information it was idle to speculate as to the part Dimitrios had played. That the information, even if he did obtain it, might turn out to be quite useless as a basis for anything but a Communist pamphlet, was a contingency that he was not for the moment prepared to consider. He was beginning to like his experiment and was unwilling to abandon it easily. If it were to die, he would see that it died hard.

On the afternoon of his arrival he sought out Marukakis at the office of the French news agency and presented his letter of introduction.

The Greek was a dark, lean man of middle age with intelligent, rather bulbous eyes and a way of bringing his lips together at the end of a sentence as though amazed at his own lack of discretion. He greeted Latimer with the watchful courtesy of a negotiator in an armed truce. He spoke in French.

'What information is it that you need, Monsieur?'

'As much as you can give me about the Stambulisky affair of 1923.'

Marukakis raised his eyebrows. 'So long ago? I shall have to refresh my memory. No, it is no trouble, I will gladly help you. Give me an hour.'

'If you could have dinner with me at my hotel this evening, I would be delighted.'

'Where are you staying?'

'The Grand Palace.'

'We can get a better dinner than that at a fraction of the cost. If you like, I will call for you at eight o'clock and take you to the place. Agreed?'

'Certainly.'

'Good. At eight o'clock then. *Au 'voir.*'

He arrived punctually at eight o'clock and led the way in silence across the Boulevard Maria-Louise and up the Rue Alabinska to a small side-street. Halfway along it there was a grocer's shop. Marukakis stopped. He looked suddenly self-conscious. 'It does not look very much,' he said doubtfully, 'but the food is sometimes very good. Would you rather go to a better place?'

'Oh no, I'll leave it to you.'

Marukakis looked relieved. 'I thought that I had better ask you,' he said and pushed open the door of the shop. The door bell tinkled musically.

The interior of the shop was so crowded with stock that it seemed little larger than a telephone booth. On all sides rose scrubbed pinewood shelves crammed carelessly with bottles and curious-looking groceries. Festooned about the shelves and hanging in cascades from the ceiling like lush tropical fruits were sausages of almost every conceivable size and colour. In the midst of it all, leaning against a rampart of meal sacks behind the scales, was a stout woman nursing a baby. She grinned and said something to them. Marukakis answered and, motioning Latimer to follow him, skirted some crocks of pickled cucumbers, dived under a string of goats'-milk cheeses and pushed open a door leading into a passage. At the end of the passage was the restaurant.

It was very little larger than the shop but by some extraordinary means five tables had been arranged in it. Two of the tables were occupied by a group of men and women noisily eating soup. They sat down at a third. A moustachioed man in shirt sleeves and a green baize apron lounged over and addressed them in voluble Bulgarian.

'I think you had better order,' said Latimer.

Marukakis said something to the waiter who twirled his moustache and lounged away shouting at a dark opening in the wall that looked like the entrance to the cellar. A voice could be heard faintly acknowledging the order. The man returned with a bottle and three glasses.

'I have ordered vodka,' said Marukakis. 'I hope you like it.'

'Very much.'

'Good.'

The waiter filled the three glasses, took one for himself, nodded to Latimer and, throwing back his head, poured the vodka down his throat. Then he walked away.

'*A votre santé*,' said Marukakis politely. 'Now,' he went on as they set their glasses down, 'that we have drunk together and that we are comrades, I can be frank.' He pressed his lips together and frowned. 'I cannot stand it,' he burst out suddenly, 'when people are not straight-forward with me. I am a Greek and a Greek can smell a lie. That is why Greek businessmen are so successful in France and England. As soon as I read the letter you brought to me I smelt a lie. But more than a lie. It is an insult to the intelligence to suggest that the information for which you are asking could be of any possible use in a *roman policier*.'

'I am sorry,' said Latimer uncomfortably. 'The real reason why I want this information from you is so peculiar that I hesitated to give it.'

'The last person to whom I gave information in this way,' said Marukakis dourly, 'was writing a popular guide to European politics *à l'Americaine*. I was ill for a week when I finally read it. Ill you understand, not in the body but in the mind. I have a respect for facts and this book was very painful to me.'

'I'm not writing a book.'

Marukakis smiled. 'You English are so self-conscious.

Look! I will make a bargain with you. I will give you the information and then you shall tell me this peculiar reason of yours. Does that go?'

'It goes.'

'Very well then.'

Soup was put before them. It was thick and highly spiced and mixed with sour cream. As they ate it Marukakis began to talk.

*

In a dying civilization, political prestige is the reward not of the shrewdest diagnostician, but of the man with the best bedside manner. It is the decoration conferred on mediocrity by ignorance. Yet there remains one sort of political prestige that may still be worn with a certain pathetic dignity; it is that given to the liberal-minded leader of a party of conflicting doctrinaire extremists. His dignity is that of all doomed men: for, whether the two extremes proceed to mutual destruction or whether one of them prevails, doomed he is, either to suffer the hatred of the people or to die a martyr.

Thus it was with Monsieur Stambulisky, leader of the Bulgarian Peasant Agrarian Party, Prime Minister and Minister for Foreign Affairs. The Agrarian Party, faced by organized reaction, was immobilized, rendered powerless by its own internal conflicts. It died without firing a shot in its own defence.

The end began soon after Stambulisky returned to Sofia early in January 1923, from the Lausanne Conference.

On 23rd January, the Yugoslav (then Serbian) Government lodged an official protest in Sofia against a series of armed raids carried out by Bulgarian *comitadji* over the

Yugoslav frontier. A few days later, on 5th February, during a performance celebrating the foundation of the National Theatre in Sofia at which the King and Princesses were present, a bomb was thrown into the box in which sat several government ministers. The bomb exploded. Several persons were injured.

Both the authors and objects of these outrages were readily apparent.

From the start, Stambulisky's policy towards the Yugoslav Government had been one of appeasement and conciliation. Relations between the two countries had been improving rapidly. But an objection to this improvement came from the Macedonian Autonomists, represented by the notorious Macedonian Revolutionary Committee, which operated both in Yugoslavia and in Bulgaria. Fearing that friendly relations between the two countries might lead to joint action against them, the Macedonians set to work systematically to poison those relations and to destroy their enemy Stambulisky. The attacks of the *comitadji* and the theatre incident inaugurated a period of organized terrorism.

On 8th March, Stambulisky played his trump card by announcing that the Narodno Sobranie would be dissolved on the thirteenth and that new elections would be held in April.

This was disaster for the reactionary parties. Bulgaria was prospering under the Agrarian Government. The peasants were solidly behind Stambulisky. An election would have established him even more securely. The funds of the Macedonian Revolutionary Committee increased suddenly.

Almost immediately an attempt was made to assassinate

Stambulisky and his Minister of Railways, Atanassoff, at
Haskovo on the Thracian frontier. It was frustrated only
at the last moment. Several police officials responsible for
suppressing the activities of the *comitadji*, including the
Prefect of Petrich, were threatened with death. In the face
of these menaces, the elections were postponed.

Then, on 4th June, the Sofia police discovered a plot to
assassinate not only Stambulisky but also Muravieff, the
War Minister, and Stoyanoff, the Minister of the Interior.
A young army officer, believed to have been given the job
of killing Stoyanoff, was shot dead by the police in a gun
fight. Other young officers, also under the orders of the
terrorist Committee, were known to have arrived in Sofia,
and a search for them was made. The police were beginning to lose control of the situation.

Now was the time for the Agrarian Party to have acted,
to have armed their peasant supporters. But they did not
do so. Instead, they played politics among themselves. For
them, the enemy was the Macedonian Revolutionary Committee, a terrorist gang, a small organization quite incapable
of ousting a government entrenched behind hundreds of
thousands of peasant votes. They failed to perceive that the
activities of the Committee had been merely the smoke-
screen behind which the reactionary parties had been
steadily making their preparations for an offensive. They
very soon paid for this lack of perception.

At midnight on 8 June all was calm. By four o'clock on
the morning of the ninth, all the members of the Stambulisky Government, with the exception of Stambulisky
himself, were in prison and martial law had been declared.
The leaders of this *coup d'état* were the reactionaries

Zankoff and Rouseff, neither of whom had ever been connected with the Macedonian Committee.

Too late, Stambulisky tried to rally his peasants to their own defence. Several weeks later he was surrounded with a few followers in a country house some hundreds of miles from Sofia and captured. Shortly afterwards and in circumstances which are still obscure, he was shot.

★

It was in this way that, as Marukakis talked, Latimer sorted out the facts in his own mind. The Greek was a fast talker but liable, if he saw the chance, to turn from fact to revolutionary theory. Latimer was drinking his third glass of tea when the recital ended.

For a moment or two he was silent. At last he said: 'Do you know who put up the money for the Committee?'

Marukakis grinned. 'Rumours began to circulate some time after. There were many explanations offered, but, in my opinion, the most reasonable and, incidentally, the only one I was able to find any evidence for, was that the money had been advanced by the bank which held the Committee's funds. It is called the Eurasian Credit Trust.'

'You mean that this bank advanced the money on behalf of a third party?'

'No, I don't. The bank advanced the money on its own behalf. I happened to find out that it had been badly caught owing to the rise in the value of the *Lev* under the Stambulisky administration. In the early part of 1923 before the trouble started in earnest, the *Lev* doubled its value in two months. It was about eight hundred to the pound sterling and it rose to about four hundred. I could look up the actual figures if you are interested. Anyone who had been selling the *Lev* for delivery in three months or more, counting on a fall, would face huge losses. The Eurasian Credit Trust was not, nor is for that matter, the sort of bank to accept a loss like that.'

'What sort of a bank is it?'

'It is registered in Monaco which means not only that it pays no taxes in the countries in which it operates, but also that its balance sheet is not published and that it is impossible to find out anything about it. There are lots more like that in Europe. Its head office is in Paris, but it operates in the Balkans. Amongst other things it finances the clandestine manufacture of heroin in Bulgaria for illicit export.'

'Do you think that it financed the Zankoff *coup d'état?*'

'Possibly. At any rate it financed the conditions that made the *coup d'état* possible. It was an open secret that the attempt on Stambulisky and Atanassoff at Haskovo was the work of foreign gunmen imported and paid by someone specially for the purpose. A lot of people said, too, that although there was a lot of talking and threatening the trouble would have died down if it had not been for foreign *agents provocateurs*.'

This was better than Latimer had hoped.

'Is there any way in which I can get details of the Haskovo affair?'

Marukakis shrugged. 'It is over fifteen years old. The police might tell you something but I doubt it. If I knew what you wanted to know . . .'

Latimer made up his mind. 'Very well, I said I would tell you why I wanted this information and I will.' He went on hurriedly. 'When I was in Stambul some weeks ago I had lunch with a man who happened to be the chief of the

Turkish Secret Police. He was interested in detective stories and wanted me to use a plot he had thought of. We were discussing the respective merits of real and fictional murderers when, to illustrate his point, he read me the dossier of a man named Dimitrios Makropoulos or Dimitrios Talat. The man had been a scoundrel and a cut-throat of the worst sort. He had murdered a man in Smyrna and arranged to have another man hanged for it. He had been involved in three attempted assassinations including that of Stambulisky. He had been a French spy and he had organized a gang of drug peddlers in Paris. The day before I heard of him he had been found floating dead in the Bosphorus. He had been knifed in the stomach. For some reason or other I was curious to see him and persuaded this man to take me with him to the mortuary. Dimitrios was there on a table with his clothes piled up beside him.

'It may have been that I had had a good lunch and was feeling stupid, but I suddenly had a curious desire to know more about Dimitrios. As you know, I write detective stories. I told myself that if, for once, I tried doing some detecting myself instead of merely writing about other people doing it, I might get some interesting results. My idea was to try to fill in some of the gaps in the dossier. But that was only an excuse. I did not care to admit to myself then that my interest was nothing to do with detection. It is difficult to explain, but I see now that my curiosity about Dimitrios was that of the biographer rather than of the detective. There was an emotional element in it, too. I wanted to explain Dimitrios, to account for him, to understand his mind. Merely to label him with disapproval was not enough. I saw him not as a corpse in a mortuary, but as a man, not as an isolate, a phenomenon, but as a unit in a disintegrating social system.'

He paused. 'Well, there you are, Marukakis! That is why I am in Sofia, why I am wasting your time with questions about things that happened fifteen years ago. I am gathering material for a biography that will never be written, when I ought to be producing a detective story. It sounds unlikely enough to me. To you it must sound fantastic. But it is my explanation.'

He sat back feeling very foolish. It would have been better to have told a carefully thought out lie.

Marukakis had been staring at his tea. Now he looked up.

'What is your own private explanation of your interest in this Dimitrios?'

'I've just told you.'

'No. I think not. You deceive yourself. You hope *au fond* that by rationalizing Dimitrios, by explaining him, you will also explain that disintegrating social system you spoke about.'

'That is very ingenious; but, if you will forgive my saying so, a little over-simplified. I don't think that I can accept it.'

Marukakis shrugged. 'It is my opinion.'

'It is very good of you to believe me.'

'Why should I not believe you? It is too absurd for disbelief. What do you know of Dimitrios in Bulgaria?'

'Very little. He was, I am told, an intermediary in an attempt to assassinate Stambulisky. That is to say there is no evidence to show that he was going to do any shooting himself. He left Athens, wanted by the police for robbery and attempted murder, towards the end of November

1922. I found that out myself. I also believe that he came to Bulgaria by sea. He was known to the Sofia police. I know that because in 1924 the Turkish secret police made enquiries about him in connection with another matter. The police here questioned a woman with whom he was known to have associated.'

'If she were still here and alive it would be interesting to talk to her.'

'It would. I've traced Dimitrios in Smyrna and in Athens, where he called himself Taladis, but so far I have not talked to anyone who ever saw him alive. Unfortunately, I do not even know the woman's name.'

'The police records would contain it. If you like I will make inquiries.'

'I cannot ask you to take the trouble. If I like to waste my time reading police records there is nothing to prevent my doing so, but there is no reason why I should waste your time too.'

'There is plenty to prevent your wasting your time reading police records. In the first place, you cannot read Bulgarian and in the second place, the police would make difficulties. I am, God help me, an accredited journalist working for a French news agency. I have certain privileges. Besides –' he grinned – 'absurd as it is, your detecting intrigues me. The baroque in human affairs is always interesting, don't you think?' He looked round. The restaurant had emptied. The waiter was sitting asleep with his feet on one of the tables. Marukakis sighed. 'We shall have to wake the poor devil to pay him.'

★

On his third day in Sofia, Latimer received a letter from Marukakis.

The time had passed agreeably enough. He had looked at pictures and at the statue of Alexander the Second, he had sat in cafés and wandered through the streets, he had climbed Sofia's mountain, Vitocha, he had been to the theatre and to a cinema where he had seen a German film with Bulgarian subtitles. Intentionally, he had thought very little about Dimitrios and a great deal about the new book he had to write. It had irritated him only mildly to find that the former intention had proved more difficult to carry out than the latter.

Marukakis's letter swept the new book out of his mind completely.

> My dear Mr Latimer, [he wrote in French]
>   Here, as I promised, is a précis of all the information about Dimitrios Makropoulos which I have been able to obtain from the police. It is not, as you will see, complete. That is interesting, don't you think! Whether the woman can be found or not, I cannot say until I have made friends with a few more policemen. Perhaps we could meet tomorrow.
>   Assuring you of my most distinguished sentiments.
>   N. Marukakis.

Attached to this letter was the précis:

POLICE ARCHIVES, SOFIA 1922–4

Dimitrios Makropoulos. *Citizenship:* Greek. *Place of birth:* Salonika. *Date:* 1889. *Trade:* Described as fig-packer. *Entry:* Varna, 22nd December 1922, off Italian steamer *Isola Bella. Passport or Identity Card:* Relief Commission Identity Card No. T53462.

Eric Ambler

At police inspection of papers in Café Spetzi, rue Perotska. Sofia, 6th June 1923, was in company of woman named Irana Preveza, Greek-born Bulgar. D. M. known associate of foreign criminals. Proscribed for deportation, 7th June 1923. Released at request and on assurances of A. Vazoff, 7th June 1923.

In September 1924 request received from Turkish Government for information relating to a fig-packer named 'Dimitrios' wanted on a charge of murder. Above information supplied a month later. Irana Preveza when questioned reported receiving letter from Makropoulos at Adrianople. She gave following description:

Height: 182 centimetres. *Eyes:* brown. *Complexion:* dark, clean-shaven. *Hair:* dark and straight. *Distinguishing marks:* none.

At the foot of this *précis*, Marukakis had added a handwritten note.

> N.B. This is an ordinary police dossier only. Reference is made to a second dossier on the secret file, but it is forbidden to inspect this.

Latimer sighed. The second dossier contained no doubt, the details of the part played by Dimitrios in the events of 1923. The Bulgarian authorities had evidently known more about Dimitrios than they had been prepared to confide to the Turkish police. To know that the information was in existence, yet to be unable to get at it was really most irritating.

However, there was much food for thought in what information was available. The most obvious titbit was that on board the Italian steamer *Isola Bella* in December 1922, between the Piraeus and Varna in the Black Sea, the Relief Commission Identity Card number T53462 had suffered an alteration. 'Dimitrios Taladis' had become 'Dimitrios Makropoulos'. Either Dimitrios had discovered a talent for forgery or he had met and employed someone with such a talent.

Irana Preveza! A real clue that and one that would have to be followed up very carefully. If she were still alive there must surely be some way of finding her. For the moment, however, that task would have to be left to Marukakis. Incidentally, the fact that she was of Greek extraction was suggestive Dimitrios would probably not have spoken Bulgar.

'Known associate of foreign criminals,' was distinctly vague. What sort of criminals? Of what foreign nationality? And to what extent had he associated with them? And why had attempts been made to deport him just two days before the Zankoff *coup d'état?* Had Dimitrios been one of the suspected assassins for whom the Sofia police had been searching during that critical week? Colonel Haki had pooh-poohed the idea of his being an assassin at all. 'His kind never risk their skins like that.' But Colonel Haki had not known everything about Dimitrios. And who on earth was the obliging A. Vazoff who had so promptly and effectively intervened on behalf of Dimitrios? The answers to those questions were, no doubt, in that secret second dossier. Most irritating!

As for the description, it might, like most other tabulated descriptions, have fitted tens of thousands of men. With most persons, recognition, even of an intimate, was based on the perception of vague, half-observed quantities which together formed a caricature significant more in its relation to the observer than to the observed. A short man, conscious of his lack of height, would describe a man of medium height as tall. For the ordinary business of hating and loving and getting from the cradle to the deathbed with the least possible discomfort, such caricatures were, no doubt, satisfactory. But he, Latimer, needed more. He needed a portrait of Dimitrios, a portrait by an artist, an arrangement of accented lines infused by some alchemy with the spirit of the sitter. And if that were not available he must make his own portrait of Dimitrios from what crude daubs he could find in police dossiers, superimposing them on one another in the hope that two dimensions might eventually become three. The Negro, for instance, out of his fear, had given a description not wholly without significance. But there was nothing in the woman's description to add to his few vague brush strokes. Probably the police had bullied her. '*No lies now! Describe him. How tall was he? What was the colour of his eyes? His hair? You knew him well enough. We know that. You'd better be honest with us . . .*' And so on.

Yet it was odd that, with that second dossier on file, police had neither description nor photograph of their own. Dimitrios had been in custody, possibly for several hours, before A. Vazoff had come to the rescue.

And there was another thing that was odd. How could the woman have known his exact height to a centimetre? It was not the sort of thing you knew about even the most intimate friends. Often you did not know it about yourself.

An idea began to develop in Latimer's mind. Supposing Colonel Haki's little trick to secure information about Dimitrios (and the plot to assassinate Kemal) without seeming to be doing so, had not been as successful as he had thought. Supposing the Bulgarian authorities had seen through it. According to the Colonel, the Sofia police had known very little about Dimitrios. Yet the existence of the second dossier suggested that they had known a great deal that they had not been anxious to communicate to the Colonel.

Then why let him know anything at all? There had been a dozen ways of disposing of his circulated request for information. A regretful declaration that Dimitrios was unknown would have been the simplest. Then, Latimer remembered a phrase Colonel Haki had used: 'Some people in the good graces of a neighbouring friendly government' were behind it. Might not 'a neighbouring friendly government' have been anxious to appear helpful in the circumstances? It was not unreasonable to suppose so. And if for 'some people in the good graces of' you wrote 'Eurasian Credit Trust and A. Vazoff', the thing began to look interesting. Perhaps the same people who had wanted Stambulisky killed had also the 'good reasons for wishing the Gazi out of the way'. Perhaps Dimitrios . . .

Latimer shrugged. It was all the wildest supposition. There was no way, there could be no way, of substantiating any of it without access to the inaccessible second dossier. He returned reluctantly to his new book.

★

He had sent a note to Marukakis, and on the following morning received a telephone call from him. They arranged to meet again for dinner that evening.

'Have you got any farther with the police?'

'Yes. I will tell you everything when we meet this evening. Goodbye.'

By the time the evening came, Latimer was feeling very much as he had once used to feel while waiting for examination results: a little excited, a little apprehensive and very much irritated at the decorous delay in publishing information which had been in existence for several days. He smiled rather sourly at Marukakis.

'It is really very good of you to take so much trouble.'

Marukakis flourished a hand. 'Nonsense, my dear friend. I told you I was interested. Shall we go to the grocer's shop again? We can talk there quietly.'

From then until the end of the meal he talked incessantly about the position of the Scandinavian countries in the event of a major European war. Latimer began to feel as baleful as one of his own murderers.

'And now,' said the Greek at last, 'as to this question of your Dimitrios, we are going on a little trip tonight.'

'What do you mean?'

'I said that I would make friends with some policeman and I have done so. As a result I have found out where Irana Preveza is now. It was not very difficult. She turns out to be very well known – to the police.'

Latimer felt his heart begin to beat a little faster. 'Where is she?' he demanded.

'About five minutes' walk away from here. She is the proprietress of a *Nachtlokal* called *La Vièrge St Marie*.'

'*Nachtlokal*?'

He grinned. 'Well, you could call it a nightclub.'

'I see.'

'She has not always had her own place. For many years she worked either on her own or for other houses. But she grew too old. She had money saved, and so she started her own place. About fifty years of age, but looks younger. The police have quite an affection for her. She does not get up until ten in the evening, so we must wait a little before we try our luck at talking to her. Did you read her description of Dimitrios? No distinguishing marks! That made me laugh.'

'Did it occur to you to wonder how she knew that his height was exactly one hundred and eighty-two centimetres?'

Marukakis frowned. 'Why should it?'

'Very few people know even their own heights exactly.'

'What is your idea?'

'I think that that description came from the second dossier you mentioned, and not from the woman.'

'And so?'

'Just a moment. Do you know who A. Vazoff is?'

'I meant to tell you. I asked the same question. He was a lawyer.'

'Was?'

'He died three years ago. He left much money. It was claimed by a nephew living in Bucaresti. He had no relations living here. What are you thinking of?'

Latimer produced his theory a trifle apologetically.

Marukakis frowned over it. 'Perhaps you are right,' he said when Latimer had finished. 'I do not know. There is, as you say, no way of proving it. Kemal was always against the financiers, especially the international variety. He mistrusted them, and with reason. For years he would accept no foreign loans, and to a financier that is a blow in the face. You need not be so nervous of your idea, my friend. It is good. International big business has made revolutions before now to safeguard its interests. At one time it made them, as Necker made the French Revolution, in the name of Liberty, Equality and Fraternity. Now, with Socialism to fight, it makes them in the name of Law and Order and Sound Finance. Assassination? If an assassination is going to be good for business, then there will be an assassination. Not in Paris, of course, nor in London or New York. Oh, dear me, no! And the assassin will not steal forth from a board meeting. The method is simple. "How nice," someone will say, "if that man so-and-so, that scoundrel, that disruptive influence, that menace to peace and prosperity, were to go." That is all. A wish expressed. But, my friend, it is expressed in the hearing of a man whose business it is to hear such things and to take note of them, to issue instructions and to take the responsibility for them, to procure the ends yet never speak of the means. Your international financier needs good luck, and if Fate is a little forgetful, then Fate's elbow must be jogged.'

'That being left to Dimitrios!'

'Oh, no. I think not. The elbow-jogger-in-chief is an important man. He knows the very best people. He is a polite fellow with a beautiful wife and an income reported to come from the choicest securities. He is away from time to time in connection with vague business deals about which his friends are far too well-bred to question him. He has a foreign decoration or two which he wears at the more useful diplomatic receptions.' The Greek's voice grated suddenly. 'But he also knows men like Dimitrios, the dangerous class, the political hangers-on, the grafters and the undercover men, the social scum, that passively rotting mass thrown off by the lowest layers of an old society. He himself has no political convictions. For him there is no other nexus between man and man than naked self-interest. He believes in the survival of the fittest and the gospel of tooth and claw because he makes money by seeing that the weak die before they can become strong and that the law of the jungle remains the governing force in the affairs of the world. And he is all about us. Every city in the world knows him. He exists because big business, his master, needs him. International big business may conduct its operations with scraps of paper, but the ink it uses is human *blood*!'

He brought his fist down with a bang on the table as he uttered the last word. Latimer, who, as an Englishman, could never quite overcome his distaste for other people's rhetoric, had been staring at his plate. Now he raised his head. For a moment he considered mentioning the fact that he had recognized one or two phrases as coming from the Communist Manifesto, but decided not to do so. The Greek, after all, was being very helpful.

'That's a very purple patch,' he remarked. 'Don't you think you may be exaggerating a little?'

For a moment Marukakis glared at him, then suddenly he grinned. 'Of course I was exaggerating. But it is agreeable sometimes to talk in primary colours even if you have to think in greys. But, you know, I was not exaggerating as much as you might think. There are such men about.'

'Indeed?'

'One of them used to be on the board of directors of the Eurasian Credit Trust. His name was Anton Vazoff.'

'Vazoff!'

The Greek chuckled delightedly. 'I was keeping that as a little surprise for you later, but you may have it now. I found out from the files. Eurasian Credit Trust was not registered in Monaco until 1926. The list of directors prior to that date is still in existence and open to inspection if you know where to find it.'

'But,' spluttered Latimer, 'this is most important. Don't you see what . . .'

Marukakis interrupted him by calling for the bill. Then he glanced at Latimer slyly. 'You know,' he said, 'you English are sublime. You are the only nation in the world that believes that it has a monopoly of ordinary common sense.'

6

Carte Postale

La Vièrge St Marie was situated, with somewhat dingy logic, in a street of houses behind the church of *Sveta Nedelja*. The street was narrow, sloping and poorly lit. At first it seemed unnaturally silent. But behind the silence there were whispers of music and laughter – whispers that would start out suddenly as a door opened and then be smothered as it closed again. Two men came out of a doorway ahead of them, lit cigarettes and walked quickly away. The footsteps of another pedestrian approached and then stopped as their owner went into one of the houses.

'Not many people about now,' commented Marukakis. 'Too early.'

Most of the doors were panelled with translucent glass and had dim lights showing through them. On some of the panels the number of the house was painted; painted rather more elaborately than was necessary for ordinary purposes. Other doors bore names. There was *Wonderbar, OK, Jymmies Bar, Stambul, Torquemada, Vitocha, Le Viol de Lucrece* and, higher up the hill, *La Vièrge St Marie*.

For a moment they stood outside it. The door looked less shabby than some of the others. Latimer felt to see if his wallet was safe in his pocket as Marukakis pushed open the door and led the way in. Somewhere in the place an accordion band was playing a *paso-doble*. They were in a narrow passage between walls coated unevenly with red distemper. The floor was carpeted. Facing them at the end of the passage was a small *vestiaire*. When they had entered it had been empty except for a few hats and coats, but now a pallid man in a white jacket took his place behind the counter and grinned a welcome. He said: '*Bonsoir, Messieurs,*' took their hats and coats and indicated with a flourish a staircase leading down to the right in the direction of the music. It was labelled: BAR–DANCING–CABARET.

They found themselves in a low-ceilinged room about thirty feet square. At regular intervals round the pale blue walls were placed oval mirrors supported by *papier-mâché* cherubims. The spaces between the mirrors were decorated haphazardly with highly stylized pictures painted on the walls, of monocled men with straw-coloured hair and nude torsoes, and women in tailor-made costumes and check stockings. In one corner of the room was a minute bar; in the opposite corner the platform on which sat the band – four listless Negroes in white 'Argentine' blouses. Near them was a blue plush curtained doorway. The rest of the wall space was taken up by small cubicles which rose to the shoulder height of those sitting at the tables set inside them. A few more tables encroached on the dancefloor in the centre.

When they came in there were about a dozen persons seated in the cubicles. The band was still playing and two girls who looked as though they might presently form part of the cabaret were dancing solemnly together.

'Too early,' repeated Marukakis disappointedly. 'But it will pick up soon.'

A waiter swept them to one of the cubicles and hurried

away, to reappear a moment or two later with a bottle of champagne.

'Have you got plenty of money with you?' murmured Marukakis. 'We shall have to pay at least two hundred leva for this poison.'

Latimer nodded. Two hundred leva was about ten shillings.

The band stopped. The two girls finished their dance, and one of them caught Latimer's eye. They walked over to the cubicle and stood smiling down. Marukakis said something. Still smiling, the two shrugged their shoulders and went away. Marukakis looked doubtfully at Latimer.

'I said that we had business to discuss, but that we would entertain them later. Of course, if you don't want to be bothered with them . . .'

'I don't,' said Latimer firmly and then shuddered as he drank some of the champagne.

Marukakis sighed. 'It seems a pity. We shall have to pay for the champagne. Someone may as well drink it.'

'Where is La Preveza?'

'She will be down at any moment now, I should think. Of course,' he added thoughtfully, 'we could go up to her.' He raised his eyes significantly towards the ceiling. 'It is really quite refined, this place. Everything seems to be most discreet.'

'If she will be down here soon there seems to be no point in our going up.' He felt an austere prig and wished that the champagne had been drinkable.

'Just so,' said Marukakis gloomily.

But an hour and a half passed by before the proprietress of *La Vièrge St Marie* put in an appearance. During that time things certainly did become livelier. More people

97

arrived, mostly men, although among them were one or two peculiar-looking women. An obvious pimp, who looked very sober, brought in a couple of Germans who looked very drunk and might have been commercial travellers on the spree. A pair of rather sinister young men sat down and ordered Vichy water. There was a certain amount of coming and going through the plush-curtained door. The cubicles were all occupied and extra tables were set up on the dancefloor which soon became a congested mass of swaying, sweating couples. Presently, however, the floor was cleared and a number of the girls who had disappeared some minutes before to replace their clothes with a bunch or two of artificial primroses and a great deal of suntan lotion, did a short dance. They were followed by a youth dressed as a woman who sang songs in German; then they reappeared without their primroses to do another dance. This concluded the cabaret and the audience swarmed back on to the dancefloor. The atmosphere thickened, and became hotter and hotter.

Through smarting eyes Latimer was idly watching one of the sinister young men offering the other a pinch of what might have been snuff, but which was not, and wondering whether he should make another attempt to slake his thirst with the champagne, when suddenly Marukakis touched his arm.

'That will be her,' he said.

Latimer looked across the room. For a moment a couple on the extreme corner of the dancefloor obstructed the view; then the couple moved an inch or two, and he saw her standing motionless by the curtained door by which she had entered.

She possessed that odd blousy quality that is independent of good clothes and well-dressed hair and skilful maquillage. Her figure was full but good and she held herself well; her dress was probably expensive, her thick, dark hair looked as though it had spent the past two hours in the hands of a hairdresser. Yet she remained, unmistakably and irrevocably, a slattern. There was something temporary, an air of suspended animation, about her. It seemed as if at any moment the hair should begin to straggle, the dress slip down negligently over one soft, creamy shoulder, the hand with the diamond cluster ring which now hung loosely at her side reach up to pluck at pink silk shoulder straps and pat abstractedly at the hair. You saw it in her dark eyes. The mouth was firm and good-humoured in the loose, raddled flesh about it, but the eyes were humid with sleep and the carelessness of sleep. They made you think of things you had forgotten, of clumsy gilt hotel chairs strewn with discarded clothes and of grey dawn light slanting through closed shutters, of attar of roses and of the musty smell of heavy curtains on brass rings, of the sound of the warm, slow breathing of a sleeper against the ticking of a clock in the darkness. Yet now the eyes were open and watchful, moving about while the mouth smiled a greeting here and there. Latimer watched her turn suddenly and go towards the bar.

Marukakis beckoned to the waiter and said something to him. The man hesitated and then nodded. Latimer saw him weave his way towards where Madame Preveza was talking to a fat man with his arm round one of the cabaret girls. The waiter whispered something. Madame Preveza stopped talking and looked at him. He pointed towards Latimer and Marukakis, and for a moment her eyes rested dispassionately on them. Then she turned away, said a word to the waiter and resumed her conversation.

'She'll come in a minute,' said Marukakis.

Soon she left the fat man and went on making her tour of the room, nodding, smiling indulgently. At last she reached their table. Involuntarily, Latimer got to his feet. The eyes studied his face.

'You wished to speak with me, Messieurs?' Her voice was husky, a little harsh, and she spoke in strongly-accented French.

'We should be honoured if you would sit at our table for a moment,' said Marukakis.

'Of course.' She sat down beside him. Immediately, the waiter came up. She waved him away and looked at Latimer. 'I have not seen you before, Monsieur. Your friend I have seen, but not in my place.' She looked sideways at Marukakis. 'Are you going to write about me in the Paris newspapers, Monsieur? If so, you must see the rest of my entertainment – you and your friend.'

Marukakis smiled. 'No, Madame. We are trespassing on your hospitality to ask for some information.'

'Information?' A blank look had come into the dark eyes. 'I know nothing of any interest to anybody.'

'Your discretion is famous, Madame. This, however, concerns a man, now dead and buried, whom you knew over fifteen years ago.'

She laughed shortly and Latimer saw that her teeth were bad. She laughed again, uproariously, so that her body shook. It was an ugly sound that tore away her slumberous dignity, leaving her old. She coughed a little as the laughter died away. 'You pay the most delicate compliments, Monsieur,' she gasped. 'Fifteen years! You expect me to remember a man that long? Holy Mother of Christ, I think you shall buy me a drink after all.'

Latimer beckoned to the waiter. 'What will you drink, Madame?'

'Champagne. Not this filth. The waiter will know. Fifteen years!' She was still amused.

'We hardly dared to hope that you would remember,' said Marukakis a trifle coldly. 'But if a name means anything to you . . . it was Dimitrios – Dimitrios Makropoulos.'

She had been lighting a cigarette. Now she stopped still with the burning match in her fingers. Her eyes were on the end of the cigarette. For several seconds the only movement that Latimer saw in her face was the corners of her mouth turning slowly downward. It seemed to him that the noise about them had receded suddenly, that there was cotton wool in his ears. Then she slowly turned the match between her fingers and dropped it on to the plate in front of her. The eyes did not move. Then, very softly, she said: 'I don't like you here. Get out – both of you!'

'But . . .'

'Get out!' Still she did not raise her voice or move her head.

Marukakis looked across at Latimer, shrugged and stood up. Latimer followed suit. She glared up at them sullenly. 'Sit down,' she snapped. 'Do you think I want a scene here?'

They sat down. 'If you will explain, Madame,' said Marukakis acidly, 'how we can get out without standing up we should be grateful.'

The fingers of her right hand moved quickly and grasped the stem of a glass. For a moment Latimer thought that she was going to break it in the Greek's face. Then her fingers relaxed and she said something in Greek too rapid for Latimer to understand.

Marukakis shook his head. 'No, he is nothing to do with the police,' Latimer heard him reply. 'He is a writer of books and he seeks information.'

'Why?'

'He is curious. He saw the dead body of Dimitrios Makropoulos in Stambul a month or two ago, and he is curious about him.'

She turned to Latimer and gripped his sleeve urgently. 'He is dead? You are sure he is dead? You actually saw his body?'

He nodded. Her manner made him feel oddly like the doctor who descends the stairs to announce that all is over. 'He had been stabbed and thrown into the sea,' he added and cursed himself for putting it so clumsily. In her eyes was an emotion he could not quite identify. Perhaps, in her way, she had loved him. A slice of life! Tears should follow.

But there were no tears. She said: 'Had he any money on him?'

Slowly, uncomprehendingly, Latimer shook his head.

'*Merde!*' she said viciously. 'The son of a diseased camel owed me a thousand French francs. Now I shall never see it back. *Salop!* Get out, both of you, before I have you thrown out!

★

It was nearly half-past three before Latimer and Marukakis left *La Vièrge St Marie*.

The preceding two hours they had spent in Madame Preveza's private office, a be-flowered room filled with furniture: a walnut grand piano draped in a white silk shawl with a fringe and pen-painted birds in the corners of it, small tables loaded with bric-à-brac, many chairs, a browning palm tree in a bamboo stand, a chaise-longue and a large roll-top desk in Spanish oak. They had reached it, under her guidance, via the curtained door, a flight of stairs and a dimly lit corridor with numbered doors on either side of it and a smell that reminded Latimer of an expensive nursing home during visiting hours.

The invitation had been the very last thing that he had expected. It had come close on the heels of her final exhortation to them to 'get out'. She had become plaintive and apologized. A thousand francs was a thousand francs. Now she would never see it. Her eyes had filled with tears. To Latimer she had seemed fantastic. The money had been owing since 1923. She could not seriously have expected its return after fifteen years. Perhaps somewhere in her mind she had kept intact the romantic illusion that one day Dimitrios would walk in and scatter thousand franc notes like leaves about her. The fairy tale gesture! Latimer's news had shattered that illusion and when her first anger had gone she had felt herself in need of sympathy. Forgotten had been their request for information about Dimitrios. The bearers of the bad news must know how bad their news had been. She had been saying farewell to a legend. An audience had been necessary, an audience who would understand what a foolish, generous woman she was. Their drinks she had said, rubbing salt in the wound, were on the house.

They had seated themselves side by side on the chaise-longue while she had rummaged in the roll-top desk. From one of the innumerable pigeonholes she had produced a small dog-eared notebook. The pages of it had rustled through her fingers. Then:

'February fifteenth, 1923,' she had said suddenly. The notebook had shut with a snap and her eyes had moved upwards calling upon Heaven to testify to the accuracy of the date. 'That was when the money became due to me. A thousand francs and he promised faithfully that he would pay me. It was due to me and he had received it. Sooner than make a big scene – for I detest big scenes – I said that he could borrow it. And he said that he would repay me, that in a matter of weeks he would be getting plenty of money. And he did get that money, but he did not pay me my thousand francs. After all I had done for him, too!

'I picked that man up out of the gutter, Messieurs. That was in December. Dear Christ, it was cold. In the eastern provinces people were dying quicker than you could have machine-gunned them – and I have seen people machine-gunned. At that time I had no place like this, you understand. Of course, I was a girl then. Often I used to be asked to pose for photographs. There was one that was my favourite. I had on just a simple drape of white chiffon, caught in at the waist with a girdle, and a crown of small white flowers. In my right hand, which rested – so – upon a pretty white column, I held a single red rose. It was used for postcards, *pour les amoureux*, and the photographer coloured the rose and printed a very pretty poem at the bottom of the card.' The dark, moist lids had drooped over her eyes and she had recited softly:

Je veux que mon coeur vous serve d'oreiller,
Et à votre bonheur je saurai veiller.'

'Very pretty, don't you think?' The ghost of a smile had

tightened her lips. 'I burnt all my photographs several years ago. Sometimes I am sorry for that, but I think that I was right. It is not good to be reminded always of the past. That is why, Messieurs, I was angry tonight when you spoke of Dimitrios; for he is of the past. One must think of the present and of the future.

'But Dimitrios was not a man that one forgets easily. I have known many men, but I have been afraid of only two men in my life. One of them was the man I married and the other was Dimitrios. One deceives oneself you know. One thinks that one wants to be understood when one wants only to be half-understood. If a person really understands you, you fear him. My husband understood me because he loved me and I feared him because of that. But when he grew tired of loving me I could laugh at him and no longer fear him. But Dimitrios was different. Dimitrios understood me better than I understood myself, but he did not love me. I do not think he could love anyone. I thought that one day I should be able to laugh at him too, but that day never came. You could not laugh at Dimitrios. I found that out. When he had gone I hated him and told myself that it was because of the thousand francs he owed to me. I wrote it down in my book as proof. But I was lying to myself. He owed me more than a thousand francs. He had always cheated me over the money. It was because I feared him and could not understand him as he understood me that I hated him.

'I was living in a hotel then. A filthy place, full of scum. The *patron* was a dirty bully, but friendly with the police, and while one paid for one's room one was safe, even if one's papers were not in order.

'One afternoon I was resting when I heard the *patron*

shouting at someone in the next room. The walls were thin and I could hear everything. At first I paid no attention, for he was always shouting at someone, but after a while I began to listen because they were speaking in Greek and I understand Greek. The *patron* was threatening to call in the police if the room was not paid for. I could not hear what was said in reply for the other man spoke softly, but at last the *patron* went out and there was quiet. I was half-asleep when suddenly I heard the handle of my door being tried. The door was bolted. I watched the handle turn slowly as it was released again. Then there was a knock.

'I asked who was there but there was no answer. I thought that perhaps it was one of my friends and that he had not heard me so I went to the door and unbolted it. Outside was Dimitrios.

'He asked in Greek if he could come in. I asked him what he wanted and he said that he wanted to talk to me. I asked him how he knew that I spoke Greek, but he did not answer. I knew now that he must be the man in the next room. I had passed him once or twice on the stairs and he had always seemed very polite and nervous as he stood aside for me. But now he was not nervous. I said that I was resting and that he could come to see me later if he wished. But he smiled and pushed the door open and came in and leaned against the wall.

'I told him to get out, that I would call the *patron*, but he only smiled and stayed where he was. He asked me then whether I had heard what the *patron* had said and I replied that I had not heard. I had a pistol in the drawer of my table and I went to it, but he seemed to guess what I was thinking for he moved across the room as if by accident and leaned against the table as if he owned the place. Then he asked me to lend him some money.

'I was never a fool. I had a thousand leva pinned high up in the curtain but only a few coins in my bag. I said that I had no money. He seemed not to take any notice of that and began to tell me that he had not eaten anything since the day before, that he had no money and that he felt ill. But all the time he talked his eyes were moving, looking at the things in the room. I can see him now. His face was smooth and oval and pale and he had very brown, anxious eyes that made you think of a doctor's eyes when he is doing something to you that hurts. He frightened me. I told him again that I had no money, but that I had some bread if he wanted it. He said: "Give me the bread."

'I got the bread from the drawer and gave it to him. He ate it slowly, still leaning against the table. When he had finished he asked for a cigarette. I gave him one. Then he said that I needed a protector. I knew then what he was after. I said that I could manage my own affairs. He said that I was a fool and he could prove it. If I would do as he said he would get five thousand leva that day and give me half of it. I asked what he wanted me to do. He told me to write a note that he would dictate. It was addressed to a man whose name I had never heard and simply asked for five thousand leva. I thought he must be mad and to get rid of him I wrote the note and signed it "Irana". He said that he would meet me at a café that evening.

'I did not trouble to keep the appointment. The next morning he came again to my room. This time I would not let him in. He was very angry and said he had two thousand five hundred leva for me. Of course, I did not believe him, but he pushed a thousand leva note under the door and said that I should have the rest when I let him in. So I let him in. He gave me immediately another fifteen hundred leva. I asked him where he had got it and he said that he had delivered the note himself to the man who had given him the money immediately.

'I have always been discreet. I am not interested in the real names of my friends. Dimitrios had followed one of them to his home, had found out his real name and that he was an important man and then with my note in his hand had threatened to tell his wife and daughters of our friendship unless he paid.

'I was very angry. I said that for the sake of two thousand five hundred leva, I had lost one of my good friends. Dimitrios said that he could get me richer friends. He said, too, that he had given the money to me to show that he was serious and that he could have written the note himself and gone to my friend without telling me.

'I saw that this was true. I saw also that he might go to other friends unless I agreed with him. So Dimitrios became my protector and he *did* bring me richer friends. And he bought himself very smart clothes and sometimes went to the best cafés.

'But soon, someone I knew told me that he had become involved in politics and that he often went to certain cafés that the police watched. I told him that he was a fool, but he took no notice. He said that soon he would make a lot of money. And then he became suddenly angry and said that he would not stay behind for anyone, that he was tired of being poor. When I reminded him that it was because of me that he was not starving he turned upon me.

' "You!" he said. "Do you think that you make money for me? There are thousands like you. I chose you because, although you look soft and sentimental, you are cunning and can keep your head. When I came in that day, I guessed that you had money hidden in the curtain because your sort always has money in the curtain. It is an old trick. But it was at your bag that you kept looking so anxiously. I knew then that you were sensible. But you have no imagination. You do not understand money. You can buy anything you fancy, and in restaurants they look up to you. It is only those without imagination who stay poor. When you are rich people do not mind what you do. You have the power and that is what is important to a man!" And he went on to tell me about rich men he had seen in Smyrna, men who owned ships and grew figs and had great houses on the hills outside the town.

'Then, for a single moment, because when men become sentimental and tell me their dreams I despise them, I forgot my fear of Dimitrios. Sitting there in his smart clothes with his eyes on mine he appeared to me absurd. I laughed.

'He was always pale but now all the blood left his face and suddenly I was terrified. I thought he meant to kill me. He had a glass in his hand. Slowly he raised it, then smashed it on the edge of the table. Then he got up and with the broken half in his hand came towards me. I screamed. He stopped and dropped the glass on the floor. It was stupid, he said, to be angry with me. But I knew why he had stopped. He had remembered that I would be useless to him with my face cut about.

'After that I did not see him much. Often he left Sofia for several days at a time. He did not tell me where he went and I did not ask. But I knew that he had made important friends, for, once, when the police were making difficulties about his papers, he laughed and told me not to worry about the police. They would not dare to touch him, he said.

'But one morning he came to me in great agitation. He looked as if he had been travelling all night and had not shaved for several days. I had never seen him so nervous. He took me by the wrists and said that if anyone asked me I must say that he had been with me for the last three days. I had not seen him for over a week but I had to agree and he went to sleep in my room.

'Nobody asked me about him, but later that day I read in the newspaper that an attempt had been made on Stambulisky at Haskovo and I guessed where Dimitrios had been. I was frightened. An old friend of mine, whom I had known before Dimitrios, wanted to give me an apartment of my own. When Dimitrios had had his sleep and gone, I went to my friend and said that I would take this apartment.

'I was afraid when I had done it, but that night I met Dimitrios and told him. I had expected him to be angry but he was quite calm and said that it would be best for me. Yet I could not tell what he was thinking because he always looked the same, like a doctor when he is doing something to you that hurts. I took courage and reminded him that we had some business to settle. He agreed and said that he would meet me three days later to give me all the money that was due to me.'

She had paused then and looked from Latimer to Marukakis with a faint, taut smile on her lips. There had been something defensive in the smile. She had shrugged her shoulders slightly.

'You think it curious that I should trust Dimitrios. You

think that I was a fool. But because Dimitrios frightened me, I would trust him. To distrust him was to remind myself of that fear. All men can be dangerous; as tame animals in a circus can be dangerous when they remember too much. But Dimitrios was different. He had the appearance of being tame, but when you looked into his brown eyes you saw that he had none of the feelings that make ordinary men soft, that he was always dangerous. I trusted him because there was nothing else for me to do. But I also hated him.

'Three days later I waited for him in the café and he did not come. Several weeks after that I saw him and he said that he had been away but that if I would meet him on the following day, he would pay me the money he owed. The meeting place was a café in the Rue Perotska, a low place that I did not like.

'This time he came as he had promised. He said that he was in difficulties about money, that he had a great sum coming to him and that he would pay me within a few weeks.

'I wondered why he had kept the appointment merely to tell me that, but later I understood why. He had come to ask me a favour. He had to have certain letters received by someone he could trust. They were not his letters, but those of a friend of his, a Turk named Talat. If this friend could give the address of my apartment, Dimitrios himself would collect the letters when he paid me my money.

'I agreed. I could do nothing else. It meant that if Dimitrios had to collect these letters from me he would have to pay me the money. But I knew in my heart and he knew too that he could have collected the letters and not paid me a sou and I could have done nothing.

'We were sitting there drinking coffee – for Dimitrios was very mean in cafés – when the police came in to inspect papers. It was quite usual at that time, but it was not good to be found in that café because of its reputation. Dimitrios had his papers in order, but because he was a foreigner they took his name and mine because I was with him. When they had gone he was very angry, but I think he was angry, not because of their taking his name, but because they had taken my name as being with him. He was much put out and told me not to trouble about the letters as he would arrange for them with someone else. We left the café and that was the last time I saw him.'

She had had a Mandarine-Curaçao in front of her and now she had drunk it down thirstily. Latimer had cleared his throat.

'And the last you heard of him?'

Suspicion had flickered for an instant in her eyes. Latimer had said: 'Dimitrios is dead, Madame. Fifteen years have gone by. Times have changed in Sofia.'

Her queer, taut smile had hovered on her lips.

' "Dimitrios is dead, Madame." That sounds very curious to me. It is difficult to think of Dimitrios as dead. How did he look?'

'His hair was grey. He was wearing clothes bought in Greece and in France. Poor stuff.' Unconsciously he had echoed Colonel Haki's phrase.

'Then he did not become rich?'

'He did once become rich, in Paris, but he lost his money.'

She had laughed. 'That must have hurt him.' And then suspicion again: 'You know a lot about Dimitrios, Monsieur. If he is dead . . . I don't understand.'

'My friend is a writer,' Marukakis had put in. 'He is naturally interested in human nature.'

'What do you write?'

'Detective stories.'

She had shrugged. 'You do not need to know human nature for that. It is for love stories and romances that one must know human nature. *Romans policiers* are ugly. *Folle Farine* I think is a lovely story. Do you like it?'

'Very much.'

'I have read it seventeen times. It is the best of Ouida's books and I have read them all. One day I shall write my memoirs. I have seen a lot of human nature you know.' The smile had become a trifle arch and she had sighed and fingered a diamond brooch.

'But you wish to know more of Dimitrios. Very well. I heard of Dimitrios again a year later. One day I received a letter from him, from Adrianople. He gave a Poste Restante address. The letter asked me if I had received any letters for this Talat. If I had I was to write saying so, but to keep the letters. He said that I was to tell nobody that I had heard from him. He promised again to pay me the money he owed me. I had no letters addressed to Talat and wrote to tell him so. I also said that I needed the money because, now that he had gone away, I had lost all my friends. That was a lie, but I thought that by flattering him I would perhaps get the money. I should have known Dimitrios better. He did not even reply.

'A few weeks after that a man came to see me. A type of *fonctionnaire* he was, very severe and businesslike. His clothes looked expensive. He said that the police would probably be coming to question me about Dimitrios.

'I was frightened at that, but he said that I had nothing

to fear. Only I must be careful what I said to them. He told
me what to say; how I must describe Dimitrios so that the
police would be satisfied. I showed him the letter from
Adrianople and it seemed to amuse him. He said that I
could tell the police about the letter coming from Adrianople, but that I must say nothing about this name Talat.
He said that the letter was a dangerous thing to keep and
burnt it. That made me angry, but he gave me a thousand
leva note and asked me if I liked Dimitrios, if I was a friend.
I said that I hated him. Then he said that friendship was a
great thing and that he would give me five thousand leva
to say what he had told me to the police.'

She had shrugged. 'That is being serious, Messieurs.
Five thousand leva! When the police came I said what this
man had asked me to say and the following day an envelope
with five thousand leva in it arrived by post. There was
nothing else in the envelope, no letter. That was all right.
But listen! About two years later I saw this man in the
street. I went up to him, but the *salop* pretended that he
had not seen me before and called the police to me. Friendship is a great thing.'

She had picked up the book and put it back in its
pigeon-hole.

'If you will excuse me, Messieurs, it is time I returned
to my guests. I think I have talked too much. You see, I
know nothing about Dimitrios that is of any interest.'

'We have been most interested, Madame.'

She had smiled. 'If you are not in a hurry, Messieurs,
I can show you more interesting things than Dimitrios. I
have two most amusing girls who . . .'

'We are a little pressed for time, Madame. Another night

we would be delighted. Perhaps you would allow us to pay for our drinks.'

She had smiled. 'As you wish, Messieurs, but it has been most agreeable talking to you. No, no, please! I have a superstition about money being shown in my own private room. Please arrange it with the waiter at your table. You will excuse me if I don't come down with you? I have a little business to attend to. *Au'voir, Monsieur. Au'voir, Monsieur. A bientôt.*'

The dark, humid eyes had rested on them affectionately. Latimer had found himself feeling absurdly distressed at the leave-taking.

It had been a *gérant* who had responded to their request for a bill. He had had a brisk, cheerful manner.

'Eleven hundred leva, Messieurs.'

'What!'

'The price you arranged with Madame, Messieurs.'

'You know,' Marukakis remarked as they waited for their change, 'I think one does wrong to disapprove altogether of Dimitrios. He had his points.'

*

'Dimitrios was employed by Vazoff acting on behalf of the Eurasian Credit Trust to do work in connection with getting rid of Stambulisky. It would be interesting to know how they recruited him, but that is a thing we shall never know. However, they must have found him satisfactory because they employed him to do similar work in Adrianople. He probably used the name Talat there.'

'The Turkish police did not know that. They heard of him simply as "Dimitrios",' put in Latimer. 'What I cannot understand is why Vazoff – it obviously was Vazoff who visited La Preveza in 1924 – allowed her to tell the police that she had had that letter from Adrianople.'

'For only one reason, surely. Because Dimitrios was no longer in Adrianople.' Marukakis stifled a yawn. 'It's been a curious evening.'

They were standing outside Latimer's hotel. The night air was cold. 'I think I'll go in now,' he said.

'You'll be leaving Sofia?'

'For Belgrade. Yes.'

'Then you are still interested in Dimitrios?'

'Oh, yes.' Latimer hesitated. 'I can't tell you how grateful I am to you for your help. It has been a miserable waste of time for you.'

Marukakis laughed and then grinned apologetically. He said: 'I was laughing at myself for envying you your Dimitrios. If you find out any more about him in Belgrade I should like you to write to me. Would you do that?'

'Of course.'

But Latimer was not to reach Belgrade.

He thanked Marukakis again and they shook hands; then he went into the hotel. His room was on the second floor. Key in hand, he climbed the stairs. Along the heavily carpeted corridors his footsteps made no sound. He put the key in the lock, turned it and opened the door.

He had been expecting darkness and the lights in the room were switched on. That startled him a little. The thought flashed through his mind that perhaps he had mistaken the room, but an instant later he saw something which disposed of that notion. That something was chaos.

Strewn about the floor in utter confusion were the contents of his suitcases. Draped carelessly over a chair were the bedclothes. On the mattress, stripped of their bindings, were the few English books he had brought with him from Athens. The room looked as if a cageful of chimpanzees had been turned loose in it.

Dazed, Latimer took two steps forward into the room. Then a slight sound to the right of him made him turn his head. The next moment his heart jolted sickeningly.

The door leading to the bathroom was open. Standing just inside it, a disembowelled tube of toothpaste in one hand, a massive Lüger pistol held loosely in the other, and on his lips a sweet, sad smile, was Mr Peters.

7

Half a Million Francs

In only one of his books, *Murder's Arms*, had Latimer handled a situation in which one of the characters had been menaced by a murderer with a revolver. He had not enjoyed the task and if the incident had not been logical and necessary and had it not occurred in the last chapter but one (where a little of the more obvious sort of melodrama is sometimes permissible) he would have taken pains to avoid it. As it was, he had tried to go about the business intelligently. What, he had asked himself, would have been his own emotions in the circumstances? He had concluded that he would have been frightened out of his wits and completely tongue-tied.

Now, however, he was neither frightened out of his wits nor completely tongue-tied. It may have been that the circumstances were different. Mr Peters' attitude – he was holding his massive pistol as if it were a wet fish – could scarcely be described as menacing. Nor, as far as Latimer was aware, was Mr Peters a murderer. Also, he had met Mr Peters before and found him a bore. There was something quite illogically reassuring about that fact.

But if he were, as yet, neither frightened nor tongue-tied, he was very much bewildered. Accordingly, he failed to achieve the nonchalant 'Good evening', the cheerful

'Well, this is a surprise!' appropriate to the occasion. Instead, he emitted a single, stupid monosyllable.

He said: 'Oh.' And then, in a craven but quite involuntary attempt to ease the embarrassing situation: 'Something seems to have happened.'

Mr Peters took a firmer grasp of his pistol.

'Would you be so good,' he said gently, 'as to shut the door behind you? I think that if you stretched out your right arm you could do it without moving your feet.' The pistol was now levelled in an unmistakable fashion.

Latimer obeyed. Now, at last, he felt very frightened indeed, much more frightened than the character in the book had felt. He was afraid that he was going to be hurt; he could already feel the doctor probing for the bullet. He was afraid that Mr Peters was not used to the pistol, that he might fire accidentally. He was afraid of moving his hand too quickly lest the sudden movement should be misinterpreted. The door closed. He began to shake from head to foot and could not decide whether it was anger, fear or shock that made him do so. Suddenly he made up his mind to say something.

'What the hell does this mean?' he demanded harshly and then swore. It was not what he had intended to say and he was a man who very rarely swore. He was sure now that it was anger that was making him tremble. He glowered into Mr Peters' wet eyes.

The fat man lowered his pistol and sat down on the edge of the mattress.

'This is most awkward,' he said unhappily. 'I did not expect you back so soon. Your *maison close* must have proved disappointing. The inevitable Armenian girls, of course. Appealing enough for a while and then merely dull.

I often think that perhaps this great world of ours would be a better, finer place if . . .' He broke off. 'But we can talk about that another time.' Carefully he put the remains of the toothpaste tube on the bedside table. 'I had hoped to get things tidied a little before I left,' he added.

Latimer decided to play for time. 'Including the books, Mr Peters?'

'Ah, yes, the books!' He shook his head despondently. 'An act of vandalism. A book is a lovely thing, a garden stocked with beautiful flowers, a magic carpet on which to fly away to unknown climes. I am sorry. But it was necessary.'

'What was necessary? What are you talking about?'

Mr Peters smiled a sad, long-suffering smile. 'A little frankness, Mr Latimer, *please*. There could be only one reason why your room should be searched and you know it as well as I do. I can see your difficulty, of course. You are wondering exactly where I stand. If it is any consolation to you, however, I may say that my difficulty is in wondering exactly where *you* stand.'

This was fantastic. In his exasperation, Latimer forgot his fears. He took a deep breath.

'Now look here, Mr Peters, or whatever your name is, I am very tired and I want to go to bed. If I remember correctly, I travelled with you in a train from Athens several days ago. You were, I believe, going to Bucharest. I, on the other hand, got off here in Sofia. I have been out with a friend. I return to my hotel to find my room in a disgusting mess, my books destroyed, and you flourishing a pistol in my face. I conclude that you are either a sneak thief or a drunk. But for your pistol, of which I am, I confess, afraid, I should already have rung for assistance. But it seems to me on reflection that thieves do not ordinarily meet their victims in first-class sleeping cars, nor do they tear books to pieces. Again, you do not appear to be drunk. I begin, naturally, to wonder if, after all, you may not be mad. If you are, of course, I can do nothing but humour you and hope for the best. But if you are comparatively sane I must ask you once more for an explanation. I repeat, Mr Peters: what the hell does this mean?'

Mr Peters' tear-filled eyes were half-closed. 'Perfect,' he said raptly. 'Perfect! No, no, Mr Latimer, keep away from the bell-push, please. That is better. You know, for a moment I was almost convinced of your sincerity. Almost. But, of course, not quite. It really is not kind of you to try to deceive me. Not kind, not considerate and such a waste of time.'

Latimer took a step forward. 'Now listen to me . . .'

The Lüger jerked upwards. The smile left Mr Peters' mouth and his flaccid lips parted slightly. He looked adenoidal and very dangerous. Latimer stepped back quickly. The smile slowly returned.

'Come now, Mr Latimer. A little frankness, please. I have the best of intentions towards you. I did not seek this interview. But since you have returned so unexpectedly, since I could no longer meet you on a basis of, may I say, disinterested friendship, let us be frank with one another.' He leaned forward a little. 'Why are you so interested in Dimitrios?'

'Dimitrios!'

'Yes, dear Mr Latimer, Dimitrios. You have come from the Levant. Dimitrios came from there. In Athens you were very energetically seeking his record in the relief commission archives. Here in Sofia you have employed an agent to trace his police record. Why? Wait before you answer. I have no animosity towards you. I bear you no ill-will. Let that be clear. But, as it happens, I, too, am interested in Dimitrios and because of that I am interested in you. Now, Mr Latimer, tell me frankly where you stand. What – forgive the expression, please – is your game?'

Latimer was silent for a moment. He was trying to think quickly and not succeeding. He was confused. He had come to regard Dimitrios as his own property, a problem as academic as that of the authorship of an anonymous sixteenth-century lyric. And now, here was the odious Mr Peters, with his shabby appearance and his smiles and his Lüger pistol, claiming acquaintance with the problem as though he, Latimer, were the interloper. There was, of course, no reason why he should be surprised. Dimitrios must have been known to many persons. Yet he had felt instinctively that they must all have died with Dimitrios. Absurd, no doubt, but . . .

'Well, Mr Latimer.' The fat man's smile had lost none of its sweetness, but there was an edge to his husky voice that made Latimer think of a small boy pulling the legs off flies.

'I think,' he said slowly, 'that if I am going to answer questions, I ought to be allowed to ask some. In other words, Mr Peters, if you will tell me what *your* game is, I will tell you about mine. I have nothing at all to hide, but I have a curiosity to satisfy. And it really is no good your weighing your pistol so ominously. It is no longer an argument. It is of a large calibre and probably makes a considerable amount of noise when fired. Besides, you would gain nothing by shooting me. While I thought that you might fire it to protect yourself from arrest, it no doubt had its uses. Now, you might just as well put it away in your pocket.'

Mr Peters smiled on steadily. 'Very neatly and charmingly put, Mr Latimer. All the same, I think I shall keep my pistol for the moment.'

'As you please. Do you mind telling me what you hoped to find here – in the bindings of my books, or in the tube of toothpaste?'

'I was looking for an answer to my question, Mr Latimer. But all I found was this.' He held up a sheet of paper. It was the chronological table which Latimer had jotted down in Smyrna. As far as he remembered, he had left it folded in a book he had been reading. 'You see, Mr Latimer, I felt that if you hid papers between the leaves of books, you might also hide more interesting papers in the bindings.'

'It wasn't intended to be hidden.'

But Mr Peters took no notice. He held up the paper delicately between a finger and thumb – a schoolmaster about to consider a schoolboy essay. He shook his head.

'And is this all you know about Dimitrios, Mr Latimer?'

'No.'

'Ah!' He gazed pathetically at Latimer's tie. 'Now who, I wonder, is this Colonel Haki, who seems so well informed and so indiscreet? The name is Turkish. And poor Dimitrios was taken from us at Istanbul, was he not? And you have come from Istanbul, haven't you?'

Involuntarily, Latimer nodded and then could have kicked himself, for Mr Peters' smile broadened.

'Thank you, Mr Latimer. I can see that you are prepared to be helpful. Now let us see. You were in Istanbul, and so was Dimitrios, and so was Colonel Haki. There was a note here about a passport in the name of Talat. Another Turkish name. And there is Adrianople and the phrase "Kemal attempt". "Attempt" – ah, yes! Now, I wonder if you translated that word literally from the French "*attentat*". You won't tell me? Well, well. I think that perhaps we may take that for granted. You know it almost looks as if you have been reading a Turkish police dossier. Now, doesn't it, eh?'

Latimer had begun to feel rather foolish. He said: 'I don't think you're going to get very far that way. You're forgetting that for every question you ask you're going to have to answer one. For example, I should very much like to know whether you ever actually met Dimitrios?'

Mr Peters contemplated him for a moment without speaking. Then: 'I don't think that you are very sure of yourself, Mr Latimer,' he said slowly. 'I have an idea that I could tell you much more than you could tell me.' He dropped the Lüger into his overcoat pocket and got to his feet. 'I think I must be going,' he added.

This was not at all what Latimer expected or wanted, but he said 'Goodnight' calmly enough.

The fat man walked towards the door. But there he stopped. 'Istanbul,' Latimer heard him murmur thought-fully. 'Istanbul. Smyrna 1922, Athens the same year, Sofia 1923. Adrianople – no, because he comes from Turkey.' He turned round quickly. 'Now, I wonder . . .' He paused, and then seemed to make up his mind. 'I wonder if it would be very stupid of me to imagine that you might be thinking of going to Belgrade in the near future. Would it, Mr Latimer?'

Latimer was taken by surprise, and, even as he began to say very decidedly that it would be more than stupid of Mr

Peters to imagine any such thing, he knew by the other's triumphant smile that his surprise had been detected and interpreted.

'You will like Belgrade,' Mr Peters continued happily. 'Such a beautiful city. The views from the Terazija and the Kalemegdan! Magnificent! And you must certainly go out to Avala. But perhaps you know it better than I do. How I wish that I were going with you! Such beautiful girls! Broad-cheeked and graceful. For a young man like you they would be most amenable. Of course, such things do not interest me. I am a simple soul and getting old. I have only my memories left. But I do not disapprove of youth. I do not disapprove. One is only young once, and the Great One surely intended us to make what happiness we can. Life must go on, eh?'

Latimer pulled the bedclothes off the chair and sat down facing him. He was on the verge of losing his temper and his brain was beginning to work.

'Mr Peters,' he said, 'in Smyrna I had occasion to examine certain fifteen-year-old police records. I afterwards found out that those same records had been examined three months previously by someone else. I wonder if you would like to tell me if that someone else was you.'

But the fat man's watery eyes were staring into space. A slight frown gathered on his forehead. He said, as though he were listening to Latimer's voice for mistakes in intonation: 'Would you mind repeating that question?'

Latimer repeated the question.

There was another pause. Then Mr Peters shook his head decidedly. 'No, Mr Latimer, it was not I.'

'But you were yourself making inquiries about Dimitrios

in Athens, weren't you, Mr Peters? You were the person who came into the bureau while I was asking about Dimitrios, weren't you? You made a rather hurried exit, I seem to remember. Unfortunately I did not see it, but the official there commented on it. And it was design, not accident, that brought you to Sofia on the train by which I was travelling, wasn't it? You also took care to find out from me – very neatly, I admit – at which hotel I was staying, before I got off the train. That's right, isn't it?'

Mr Peters was smiling sunnily again. He nodded. 'Yes, Mr Latimer, all quite right. I know everything that you have done since you left the record bureau in Athens. I have already told you that I am interested in anyone who is interested in Dimitrios. Of course, you found out all about this man who had been before you in Smyrna?'

The last sentence was put in a little too casually. Latimer said: 'No, Mr Peters, I did not.'

'But surely you were interested?'

'Not very.'

The fat man sighed. 'I do not think that you are being frank with me. How much better if . . .'

'Listen!' Latimer interrupted rudely. 'I'm going to be frank. You are doing your level best to pump me. I'm not going to be pumped. Let that be clear. I made you an offer. You answer my questions and I'll answer yours. The only questions you've answered so far have been questions to which I had already guessed the answers. I still want to know why you are interested in this dead man Dimitrios. You said that you could tell me more than I could tell you. That may be so. But *I* have an idea, Mr Peters, that it is more important for you to have my answers than it is for me to have your answers. Breaking into hotel rooms and making this sort of mess isn't the sort of thing any man does in a spirit of idle inquiry. To be honest, I cannot for the life of me conceive of any reason for your interest in Dimitrios. It did occur to me that perhaps Dimitrios had kept some of that money he earned in Paris . . . You know about that, I expect?' And in response to a faint nod from Mr Peters: 'Yes, I thought you might. But, as I say, it did occur to me that Dimitrios might have hidden his treasure and that you were interested in finding out where. Unfortunately my own information disposes of that possibility. His belongings were on the mortuary table beside him, and there wasn't a penny piece there. Just a bundle of cheap clothes. And as for . . .'

But Mr Peters had stepped forward and was staring down at him with a peculiar expression on his face. Latimer allowed the sentence he had begun to trail off lamely into silence. 'What is the matter?' he added.

'Did I understand you to say,' said the fat man slowly, 'that you actually saw the body of Dimitrios in the mortuary?'

'Yes; what of it? Have I carelessly let slip another useful piece of information?'

But Mr Peters did not answer. He had produced one of his thin cheroots and was lighting it carefully. Suddenly he blew out a jet of smoke and started to waddle slowly up and down the room, his eyes screwed up as if he were in great pain. He began to talk.

'Mr Latimer, we must reach an understanding. We must stop this quarrelling.' He halted in his tracks and looked down at Latimer again. 'It is absolutely essential, Mr Latimer,' he said, 'that I know what you are after. No, no, please! Don't interrupt me. I admit that I probably need your answers more than you need mine. But I cannot give you mine at present. Yes, yes, I heard what you said. But I am talking seriously. Listen, please.

'You are interested in the history of Dimitrios. You are thinking of going to Belgrade to find out more about him. You cannot deny that. Now, both of us know that Dimitrios was in Belgrade in 1926. Also, I can tell you that he was never there after 1926. Why are you interested? You will not tell me. Very well. I will tell you something more. If you go to Belgrade you will not discover a single trace of Dimitrios. Furthermore, you may find yourself in trouble with the authorities if you pursue the matter. There is only one man who could and would, under certain circumstances, tell you what you want to know. He is a Pole, and he lives near Geneva.

'Now then! I will give you his name and I will give you a letter to him. I will do that for you. But first I must know why you want this information. I thought at first that you might perhaps be connected with the Turkish police – there are so many Englishmen in the Near Eastern police departments these days – but that possibility I no longer consider. Your passport describes you as a writer, but that is a very elastic term. Who are you, Mr Latimer, and what is your game?'

He paused expectantly. Latimer stared back at him with what he hoped was an inscrutable expression. Mr Peters, unabashed, went on:

'Naturally, when I ask what your game is, I use the phrase in a specific sense. Your game is, of course, to get money. But that is not the answer I need. Are you a rich man, Mr Latimer? No? Then what I have to say may be simplified. I am proposing an alliance, Mr Latimer, a pooling of resources. I am aware of certain facts which I cannot tell you about at the moment. You, on the other hand, possess an important piece of information. You may not know that it is important, but nevertheless it *is*. Now, my facts alone are not worth a great deal. Your piece of information is quite valueless without my facts. The two together, however, are worth at the very least – ' he stroked his chin ' – at the very least five thousand English pounds, a million French francs.' He smiled triumphantly. 'What do you say to that?'

'You will forgive me,' replied Latimer coldly, 'if I say that I cannot understand what you're talking about, won't you? Not that it makes any difference whether you do or don't. I am *tired*, Mr Peters, *very* tired. I want badly to go to bed.' He got to his feet and, pulling the bedclothes on to the bed, began to remake it. 'There is, I suppose, no reason why you should not know why I am interested in Dimitrios,' he went on as he dragged a sheet into position. 'The reason is certainly nothing to do with money. I write detective stories for a living. In Stambul I heard from a Colonel Haki, who is something to do with the police there, about a criminal named Dimitrios, who had been found dead in the Bosphorus. Partly for amusement – the sort of amusement that one derives from crossword puzzles – partly from a desire to try my hand at practical detection, I set out to trace the man's history. That is all. I don't expect you to understand it. You are probably wondering at the moment why I couldn't think of a more convincing story. I am sorry. If you don't like the truth, you can lump it.'

Mr Peters had listened in silence. Now he waddled to the window, pitched out his cheroot and faced Latimer across the bed.

'Detective stories! Now, that is most interesting to me, Mr Latimer. I am so fond of them. I wonder if you would tell me the names of some of your books.'

Latimer gave him several titles.

'And your publisher?'

'English, American, French, Swedish, Norwegian, Dutch or Hungarian?'

'Hungarian, please.'

Latimer told him.

Mr Peters nodded slowly. 'A good firm, I believe.' He seemed to reach a decision. 'Have you a pen and paper, Mr Latimer?'

Latimer nodded wearily towards the writing table. The other went to it and sat down. As he finished making the bed and began to collect his belongings from the floor, Latimer heard the hotel pen scratching over a piece of the hotel paper. Mr Peters was keeping his word.

At last he finished and the chair creaked as he got up. Latimer, who was replacing some shoe trees, straightened his back. Mr Peters had recovered his smile. Goodwill oozed from him like sweat.

'Here, Mr Latimer,' he announced, 'are three pieces of paper. On the first one is written the name of the man of whom I spoke to you. His name is Grodek – Wladyslaw Grodek. He lives just outside Geneva. The second is a letter to him. If you present that letter he will know that you are a friend of mine and that he can be frank with you. He is retired now, so I think I may safely tell you that he was at one time the most successful professional agent in Europe. More secret naval and military information has passed through his hands than through those of any other one man. It was always accurate, what is more. He dealt with quite a number of governments. His headquarters were in Brussels. To an author I should think he would be very interesting. You will like him, I think. He is a great lover of animals. A beautiful character *au fond*. Incidentally, it was he who employed Dimitrios in 1926.'

'I see. Thank you very much. What about the third piece of paper?'

Mr Peters hesitated. His smile became a little smug. 'I think you said that you were not rich.'

'No, I am not rich.'

'Half a million francs, two thousand five hundred English pounds, would be useful to you?'

'Undoubtedly.'

'Well, then, Mr Latimer, when you have tired of Geneva I want you to – how do you say? – to kill two birds with one stone.' He pulled Latimer's chronological table from his pocket. 'On this list of yours you have other dates besides 1926 still to be accounted for if you are to know what there is to know about Dimitrios. The place to account for them is Paris. That is the first thing. The second is that if you will come to Paris, if you will put yourself in touch with me there, if you will consider, then, the pooling of resources, the alliance that I have already proposed to you, I can definitely guarantee that in a very few days you will have at least two thousand five hundred English pounds to pay into your account – half a million French francs!'

'I do wish,' retorted Latimer irritably, 'that you would be a little more explicit. Half a million francs for doing what? Who is going to pay this money? You are far too mysterious, Mr Peters – far too mysterious to be true.'

Mr Peters' smile tightened. Here was a Christian, reviled

but unembittered, waiting steadfastly for the lions to be admitted into the arena.

'Mr Latimer,' he said gently, 'I know that you do not trust me. I know that. That is the reason why I have given you Grodek's address and that letter to him. I want to give you concrete evidence of my goodwill towards you, to prove that my word is to be trusted. And I want to show that I trust you, that I believe what you have told me. At the moment I cannot say more. But if you will believe in and trust me, if you will come to Paris, then here, on this piece of paper, is an address. When you arrive send a *pneumatique* to me. Do not call, for it is the address of a friend. If you will simply send a *pneumatique* giving me your address, I will be able to explain everything. It is perfectly simple.'

It was time, Latimer decided, to get rid of Mr Peters.

'Well,' he said, 'this is all very confusing. You seem to me to have jumped to a lot of conclusions. I had not definitely arranged to go to Belgrade. It is not certain that I shall have time to go to Geneva. As for going on to Paris, that is a thing which I could not possibly consider at the moment. I have a great deal of work to do, of course, and . . .'

Mr Peters buttoned up his overcoat. 'Of course.' And then, with a curious urgency in his tone: 'But if you *should* find time to come to Paris, do please send me that *pneumatique*. I have put you to so much trouble, I should like to make restitution in a practical way. Half a million francs is worth considering, eh? And I would guarantee it. But we must trust one another. That is most important.' He shook his head despondently. 'One goes through life like a flower with its face turned to the sun, ever seeking, ever hoping, wanting to trust others, but afraid to do so. How much better if we trusted one another, if we saw only the good things, the finer things in our fellow creatures! How much better if we were *frank* and *open*, if we went on our ways without the cloak of hypocrisy and lies that we wear now! Yes, Mr Latimer, hypocrisy and lies. None of us are guiltless. I am as guilty as others. It only causes trouble, and trouble is bad for business. Besides, life is so short. We are here on this globe for a short time only before the Great One recalls us.' He heaved a very noisy sigh. 'But you are a writer, Mr Latimer, and sensitive to these things. You could express them so much better than I could.' He held out his hand. 'Goodnight, Mr Latimer. I won't say "goodbye." '

Latimer took the hand. It was dry and very soft.

'Goodnight.'

At the door he half turned. 'Half a million francs, Mr Latimer, will buy a lot of good things. I do hope that we shall meet in Paris. Goodnight.'

'I hope so, too. Goodnight.'

The door closed and Mr Peters was gone, but to Latimer's overwrought imagination it seemed as if his smile, like the Cheshire cat's, remained behind him, floating in the air. He leaned against the door and surveyed for an instant the upturned suitcases. Outside it was beginning to get light. He looked at his watch. Five o'clock. The business of clearing up the room could wait. He undressed and got into bed.

For a while he lay there thinking, trying to rearrange his thoughts, to make adjustments, to form opinions. But his brain seemed drugged. It was as if he had come out of a theatre into a dark street with his mind full of images, fragments of passion clinging to a web of nerves. Mr Peters was really quite disgusting; though less disgusting perhaps than the absconding pimp, Dimitrios. But he only knew Dimitrios by hearsay. 'Like a doctor's eyes when he is doing something to you that hurts.' There was a world of horror there: Madame Preveza's own private world. What was Peters' game? That was the thing to know. He must think very carefully. There was so much to think about. So much. Half a million francs . . .

Within five minutes of his getting into bed he was asleep.

8

Grodek

It was eleven o'clock when Latimer, having been awake for about a quarter of an hour, finally opened his eyes. There, on the bedside table, were Mr Peters' three pieces of paper. They were an unpleasant reminder that he had some thinking to do and some decisions to make. But for their presence and the fact that in the morning light his room looked like a rag-picker's workshop, he might have dismissed his recollections of the visitation as being no more than part of the bad dreams which had troubled his sleep. He would have liked so to dismiss them. But Mr Peters, with his mystery, his absurd references to half a million francs, his threats and his hintings, was not so easily disposed of. He . . .

Latimer sat up in bed and reached for the three pieces of paper.

The first, as Peters had said, contained the Geneva address:

> *Wladyslaw Grodek,*
> *Villa Acacias,*
> *Chambésy.*
> *(At 7 km. from Geneva.)*

The writing was scratchy, florid and difficult to read. The figure seven was made with a stroke across the middle in the French way.

He turned hopefully to the letter. It consisted of only six lines and was written in a language and with an alphabet which he did not recognize, but which he concluded was probably Polish. It began, as far as he could see, without any preliminary 'Dear Grodek', and ended with an indecipherable initial. In the middle of the second line he made out his own name spelt with what looked like a 'Y' instead of an 'I'. He sighed. He could, of course, take the thing to a bureau and have it translated, but Mr Peters would no doubt have thought of that, and it was unlikely that the result would supply any sort of answer to the questions that he, Latimer, badly wanted answered: the questions of who and what was Mr Peters.

He supposed that the fact of Mr Peters' being on friendly terms with a retired professional spy should have been an important clue, but it was a clue that led in no particular direction. Taken in conjunction with the man's astonishing behaviour, it was, no doubt, suggestive. A person who searched rooms, brandished pistols, dangled promises of half a million franc fees for nameless services and then wrote instructions to Polish spies might reasonably be regarded with suspicion. But suspicion of what? He went over as much of their conversation as he could remember, and as he remembered more and more of it he became increasingly angry with himself. He really had behaved most stupidly. He had allowed himself to be intimidated by a pistol which its owner would not have dared to fire (although, of course, it was easier to think that way when both the pistol and its owner were absent), he had allowed himself to be drawn into a discussion with the man when he should have been capturing him for the police, and worst of all, not only had he been wearied into abandoning a strong negotiating position, but he had also allowed Mr Peters to depart, leaving behind him a note in Polish, two addresses and a cloud of unanswerable questions. He, Latimer, had not even remembered to ask how the man had got into the room. It was fantastic. He should have taken Mr Peters by the throat and forced him to explain himself – *forced* him! That, he reflected, was the worst of the academic mind. It always overlooked the possibilities of violence until violence was no longer useful.

He turned to the second address:

> *Mr Peters,*
>   *aux soins de Caillé,*
>   *3. Impasse des Huit Anges,*
>   *Paris 7.*

And that brought his thoughts back to their starting point. Why, in the name of all that was reasonable, should Mr Peters want him to go to Paris? What was this information that was worth so much money? Who was going to pay for it?

He tried to remember at exactly what point in their encounter Mr Peters had changed his tactics so abruptly. He had an idea that it had been when he had said something about having seen Dimitrios in the mortuary. But there could surely be nothing in that. Could it have been his reference to the 'treasure' of Dimitrios that had . . .

He snapped his fingers. Of course! What a fool not to think of it before! He had been ignoring an important fact. Dimitrios had not died a natural death. *Dimitrios had been murdered.*

Colonel Haki's doubts of the possibility of tracing the murderer and his own preoccupation with the past had caused him to lose sight of the fact or, at any rate, to see in it no more than a logical ending to an ugly story. He had failed to take into account the two consequent facts; that the murderer was still at large (and probably alive) and that there must have been a motive for murder.

A murderer and a motive. The motive would be monetary gain. What money? Naturally, the money that had been made out of the drug-peddling business in Paris, the money that had so unaccountably disappeared. Mr Peters' references to half a million francs did not seem quite as fantastic when you looked at the problem from that point of view. As for the murderer – why not Peters? It was not difficult to see him in the part. What was it he had said in the train? 'If the Great One wills that we shall do unpleasant things, depend upon it that He has a purpose even though that purpose is not always clear to us.' It was tantamount to a licence to murder. How odd if it had been his apology for the murder of Dimitrios! You could see his soft lips moving over the words as he pulled the trigger.

But at that Latimer frowned. No trigger had been pulled. Dimitrios had been stabbed. He began to reconstruct the picture in his mind, to see Peters stabbing someone. Yet the picture seemed wrong. It was difficult to see Peters wielding a stabbing knife. The difficulty made him begin to think again. There really was no reason at all even to suspect Peters of the murder. And even if there had been a reason, the fact of Peters' murdering Dimitrios for his money still did not explain the connection (if a connection existed) between that money and the half a million francs (if they existed). And, anyway, what was this mysterious piece of information he was supposed to possess? It was all very like being faced by an algebraic problem containing many unknown quantities and having only one biquadratic equation with which to solve it. If he *were* to solve it . . .

Now why should Peters be so anxious for him to go to Paris? Surely it would have been just as simple to have pooled their resources (whatever that might mean) in Sofia. Confound Mr Peters! Latimer got out of bed and turned on his bath. Sitting in the hot, slightly rusty water he reduced his predicament to its essentials.

He had a choice of two courses of action.

He could go back to Athens, work on his new book and put Dimitrios and Marukakis and Mr Peters and this Grodek out of his mind. Or, he could go to Geneva, see Grodek (if there were such a person) and postpone making any decision about Mr Peters' proposals.

The first course was obviously the sensible one. After all, the justification of his researches into the past life of Dimitrios had been that he was making an impersonal experiment in detection. The experiment must not be allowed to become an obsession. He had found out some interesting things about the man. Honour should be satisfied. And it was high time he got on with the book. He had his living to earn and no amount of information about Dimitrios and Mr Peters or anyone else would compensate for a lean bank balance six months hence. As for the half a million francs, that could not be taken seriously. Yes, he would return to Athens at once.

On the other hand, there was the disturbing reflection that, but for Peters' intervention, he would by now have been on his way to Belgrade to unearth, if he could, more information about Dimitrios. After all, all that had happened was that a mysterious person named Peters had suggested unearthing it in Switzerland instead of in Yugoslavia. The fact that Mr Peters had, in making the suggestion, created an additional problem should have nothing to do with the original proposition. Besides, he was inclined to doubt his ability to put Dimitrios and Mr Peters out of his mind. Was honour indeed satisfied? Not by any means. That stuff about impersonal experiments in detection was nonsense and always had been nonsense. What real detecting had he done? None. His interest in Dimitrios had already become an obsession. 'Obsession' was an ugly word. It conjured up visions of bright, stupid eyes and proofs that the world was flat. Yet this business of Dimitrios did fascinate him and in an unaccountable way. For instance, would he be able to get on with his work knowing that there might be a man named Grodek in existence who could tell him things he was curious to know? And if the answer to that were 'no', then would it not be a waste of time to go back to Athens? Of course it would! Again, would his bank balance really be lean six months hence if he were a few weeks late with his new book? It would not.

He got out of the bath and began to dry himself.

There was the matter of Mr Peters to be cleared up, too. He could not reasonably be expected to leave these things as they were and hurry off to write a detective story. It was too much to ask of any man. Besides, here was *real* murder: not neat, tidy book-murder with corpse and clues and suspects and hangman, but murder over which a chief of police shrugged his shoulders, wiped his hands and consigned the stinking victim to a coffin. Yes, that was it. It was real. Dimitrios was or had been real. Here were no strutting paper figures, but tangible evocative men and women, as real as Proudhon, Montesquieu and Rosa Luxemburg. The worlds of escape, the fantasies you created for your own comfort were well enough if you could live within them. But split the membrane that divided you from the real world and the fantasies perished. You were free and alive, but in a world of frustration.

Aloud Latimer murmured: 'Comfortable, very comfortable! You want to go to Geneva. You don't want to work. You're feeling lazy and your curiosity has been aroused. In any case, the detective story-writer has no business with reality except in so far as it concerns the technicalities of such things as ballistics, medicine, the laws of evidence and police procedure. Let that be quite clear. Now then! No more of this nonsense.'

He shaved, dressed, collected his belongings, packed and went downstairs to enquire about the trains to Athens. The reception clerk brought him a timetable and found the Athens page.

Latimer stared at it in silence for a moment. Then:

'Supposing,' he said slowly, 'that I wanted to go to Geneva from here.'

★

On his second evening in Geneva, Latimer received a letter bearing the Chambésy postmark. It was from Wladyslaw Grodek and was in answer to a letter Latimer had sent enclosing Mr Peters' note.

Herr Grodek wrote briefly and in French:

Eric Ambler

> Villa Acacias,
> Chambésy.
>
> Friday.

My dear Mr Latimer,

I should be pleased if you could come to the Villa Acacias for luncheon tomorrow. Unless I hear that you cannot come, my chauffeur will call at your hotel at eleven-thirty.

Please accept the expression of my most distinguished sentiments.

Grodek.

The chauffeur arrived punctually, saluted, ushered Latimer ceremoniously into a huge chocolate-coloured *coupé de ville*, and drove off through the rain as if he were escaping from the scene of a crime.

Idly, Latimer surveyed the interior of the car. Everything about it from the inlaid wood panelling and ivory fittings to the too-comfortable upholstery suggested money, a great deal of money. Money, he reflected, that, if Peters were to be believed, had been made out of espionage. Unreasonably he found it odd that there should be no evidence in the car of the sinister origin of its purchase price. He wondered what Herr Grodek would look like. He might possibly have a pointed white beard. Peters had said that he was a Polish national, a great lover of animals and a beautiful character *au fond*. Did that mean that superficially he was an ugly character? As for his alleged love of animals, that meant nothing. Great animal lovers were sometimes pathetic in their hatred of humanity. Would a professional spy, uninspired by any patriotic motives, hate the world he worked in? A stupid question.

For a time they travelled along the road which ran by the northerly shore of the lake, but at Pregny they turned to the left and began to climb a long hill. About a kilometre farther on, the car swung off into a narrow lane through a pine forest. They stopped before a pair of iron gates which the chauffeur got out to open. Then they drove on up a steep drive with a right-angle turn in the middle to stop at last before a large, ugly chalet.

The trees in front of it had been cleared and, through the drifting mist of snow turned rain, Latimer could see, on the slope below, a small village with its white, wooden-steepled church. Beyond and below the village was the lake, grey and lifeless without the sun. A steamer churned its way towards Geneva. To Latimer, who had seen the lake in the summer time, it was a desolate scene; desolate in the special way that a theatre is desolate when the dust sheets are on the stalls, the curtain is up and the stage, in the pallid glare of a single gas-filled lamp, has lost its magic.

The chauffeur opened the door and he got out and walked towards the door of the house. As he did so it was opened by a stout, cheerful-looking woman who looked as though she might be the housekeeper. He went in.

He found himself in a small lobby no more than six feet wide. On one wall was a row of clothes pegs draped care-lessly with hats and coats, a woman's and a man's, a climbing rope and an odd ski-stick. Against the opposite wall were stacked three pairs of well-greased skis.

The housekeeper took his coat and hat and he walked through the lobby into a large room.

It was built rather like an inn with stairs leading to a gallery which ran along two sides of the room, and a vast cowled fireplace. A wood fire roared in the grate and the pinewood floor was covered with thick rugs. It was very warm and clean.

With a smiling assurance that Herr Grodek would be down immediately, the housekeeper withdrew. There were armchairs in front of the fire and Latimer walked towards them. As he did so there was a quick rustle and a Siamese cat leaped on to the back of the nearest chair and stared at him with hostile blue eyes. It was joined by another. Latimer moved towards them and they drew back arching their backs. Giving them a wide berth, Latimer made his way to the fire. The cats watched him narrowly. The logs shifted restlessly in the grate. There was a moment's silence; then Herr Grodek came down the stairs.

The first thing that drew Latimer's attention to the fact was that the cats lifted their heads suddenly, stared over his shoulder and then jumped lightly to the floor. He looked round. The man had reached the foot of the stairs. Now he turned and walked towards Latimer with his hand outstretched and words of apology on his lips.

He was a tall, broad-shouldered man of about sixty with thinning grey hair still tinged with the original straw colour which had matched the fair, clean-shaven cheeks and blue-grey eyes. His face was pear-shaped, tapering from a broad forehead, past a small tight mouth to a chin which receded almost into the neck. You might have put him down as an Englishman or a Dane of more than average intelligence; a retired consulting engineer, perhaps. In his slippers and his thick baggy tweeds and with his vigorous, decisive movements he looked like a man enjoying the well-earned fruits of a blameless and worthy career.

He said: 'Excuse me, please, Monsieur. I did not hear the car arrive.'

His French, though curiously accented, was very ready, and Latimer found the fact incongruous. The small mouth would have been more at home with English.

'It is very kind of you to receive me so hospitably, Monsieur Grodek. I don't know what Peters said in his letter, because . . .'

'Because,' interrupted the tall man heartily, 'you very wisely have never troubled to learn Polish. I can sympathize with you. It is a horrible tongue. You have introduced yourself to Anton and Simone here.' He indicated the cats. 'I am convinced that they resent the fact that I do not speak Siamese. Do you like cats? Anton and Simone have critical intelligence, I am sure of it. They are not like ordinary cats, are you, *mes enfants?*' He seized one of them and held it up for Latimer's inspection. '*Ah, Simone cherie, comme tu es mignonne! Comme tu es bête!*' He released it so that it stood on the palms of his hands. '*Allez vite! Va promener avec ton vrai amant, ton cher Anton!*' The cat jumped to the floor and stalked indignantly away. Grodek dusted his hands lightly together. 'Beautiful, aren't they! And so human. They become ill-tempered when the weather is bad. I wish so much that we could have had a fine day for your visit, Monsieur. When the sun is shining the view from here is very pretty.'

Latimer said that he had guessed from what he had seen that it would be. He was puzzled. Both his host and his reception were totally unlike those he had expected. Grodek might look like a retired consulting engineer, but he had a quality which seemed to render the simile absurd. It was a quality that derived somehow from the contrast between his appearance and his quick, neat gestures, the urgency of his small lips. You could picture him without effort in the role of lover; which was a thing, Latimer reflected, that you could say of few men of sixty and few of under sixty. He wondered about the woman whose belongings he had seen in the entrance lobby. He added lamely: 'It must be agreeable here in the summer.'

Grodek nodded. He had opened a cupboard by the fireplace. 'Agreeable enough. What will you drink? English whisky?'

'Thank you.'

'Good. I, too, prefer it as an aperitif.'

He began to splash whisky into two tumblers. 'In the summer I work outside. That is very good for me but not good for my work, I think. Do you find that you can work out of doors?'

'No, I don't. The flies . . .'

'Exactly! The flies. I am writing a book, you know.'

'Indeed. Your memoirs?'

Grodek looked up from the bottle of soda water he was opening and Latimer saw a glint of amusement in his eyes as he shook his head. 'No, Monsieur. A life of St Francis. I confidently expect to be dead before it is finished.'

'It must be a very exhaustive study.'

'Oh yes.' He handed Latimer a drink. 'You see, the advantage of St Francis from my point of view is that he has been written about so extensively that I need not go to sources for my material. There is no original research for me to do. The work therefore serves its purpose in permitting me to live here in almost absolute idleness with an easy conscience. At the first signs of boredom, of spiritual malaise, I dip into my library of standard works about St Francis and compose another thousand words of my book. When I have convinced myself of the usefulness of the work I am doing, I stop. I may say that I quote extensively from Sabatier. His books are quite the most long-winded on the subject and help to fill the pages very nicely. For pleasure, I read the German monthly magazines.' He raised his glass. '*A votre santé.*'

'*A la vôtre.*' Latimer was beginning to wonder if his host were, after all, no more than an affected ass. He drank a little of his whisky. 'I wonder,' he said, 'if Peters mentioned the purpose of my visit to you in the letter I brought with me from Sofia.'

'No, Monsieur, he did not. But I received a letter from him yesterday which did mention it.' He was putting down his glass and he gave Latimer a sidelong look as he added: 'It interested me very much.' And then: 'Have you known Peters long?'

There was an unmistakable hesitation at the name. Latimer guessed that the other's lips had been framing a word of a different shape.

'I have met him once or twice. Once in a train, once in my hotel. And you, Monsieur? You must know him very well.'

Grodek raised his eyebrows. 'And what makes you so sure of that, Monsieur?'

Latimer smiled easily because he felt uneasy. He had, he felt, committed some sort of indiscretion. 'If he had not known you very well he would surely not have given me an introduction to you or asked you to give me information of so confidential a character.' He felt pleased with that speech.

Grodek regarded him thoughtfully and Latimer found himself wondering how on earth he could have been as foolish as to liken the man to a retired consulting engineer.

For no reason that he could fathom, he wished suddenly that he had Mr Peters' Lüger in his hand. It was not that there was anything menacing in the other's attitude. It was just that . . .

'Monsieur,' said Herr Grodek, 'I wonder what your attitude would be if I were to ask an impertinent question; if I were, for instance, to ask you to tell me seriously if a literary interest in human frailty were your only reason for approaching me.'

Latimer felt himself redden. 'I can assure you . . .' he began.

'I am quite certain that you can,' Grodek interrupted smoothly. 'But – forgive me – what are your assurances worth?'

'I can only give you my word, Monsieur, to treat any information you may give me as confidential,' retorted Latimer stiffly.

The other sighed. 'I don't think I have made myself quite clear,' he said carefully. 'The information itself is nothing. What happened in Belgrade in 1926 is of little importance now. It is my own position of which I am thinking. To be frank, our friend Peters has been a little indiscreet in sending you to me. He admits it, but craves my indulgence and asks me as a favour – he recalls that I am under a slight obligation to him – to give you the information you need about Dimitrios Talat. He explains that you are a writer and that your interest is merely that of a writer. Very well! There is one thing, however, which I find inexplicable.' He paused, picked up his glass and drained it. 'As a student of human behaviour, Monsieur,' he went on, 'you must have noticed that most persons have behind their actions one stimulus which tends to dominate all others. With some of us it is vanity, with others the gratification of the senses, with still others the desire for money, and so on. Er – Peters happens to be one of those with the money stimulus very highly developed. Without being unkind to him, I think I may tell you that he has the miser's love of money for its own sake. Do not misunderstand me, please. I do not say that he will act only under that money stimulus. What I mean is that I cannot from my knowledge of Peters imagine him going to the trouble of sending you here to me and writing to me in the way he has written, in the interests of the English detective story. You see my point? I am a little suspicious, Monsieur. I still have enemies in this world. Supposing, therefore, that you will tell me just what your relations with our friend Peters are. Would you like to do that?'

'I should be delighted to do so. Unfortunately I cannot do so. And for a very simple reason. I don't know what those relations are myself.'

Grodek's eyes hardened. 'I was not joking, Monsieur.'

'Nor was I. I have been investigating the history of this man Dimitrios. While doing so I have met Peters. For some reason that I do not know of, he, too, is interested in Dimitrios. He overheard me making inquiries in the relief commission archives in Athens. He then followed me to Sofia and approached me there – behind a pistol, I may add – for an explanation of my interest in this man, who, by the way, was murdered some weeks ago before I ever heard of him. He followed this up with an offer. He said that if I would meet him in Paris and collaborate with him in some scheme he had in mind we should each profit to the extent of half a million francs. He said that I possessed a piece of information which, though valueless by itself, would, when used in conjunction with information in his possession, be of great value. I did not believe him and refused to have anything to do with his scheme. Accordingly, as an inducement to me and as evidence of his goodwill, he gave me the note to you. I had told him, you see, that my interest was that of a writer and admitted that I was about to go to Belgrade to collect more information there if I could. He told me that you were the only person who could supply it.'

Grodek's eyebrows went up. 'I don't want to seem too inquisitive, Monsieur, but I should like to know how you knew that Dimitrios Talat was in Belgrade in 1926.'

'I was told by a Turkish official with whom I became friendly in Istanbul. He described the man's history to me; his history, that is, as far as it was known in Istanbul.'

'I see. And what, may I ask, is this so valuable piece of information in your possession?'

'I don't know.'

Grodek frowned. 'Come now, Monsieur. You ask for my confidences. The least you can do is to give me yours.'

'I am telling you the truth. I don't know. I talked fairly freely to Peters. Then, at one point in the conversation, he became excited.'

'At what point?'

'I was explaining, I think, how I knew that Dimitrios had no money when he died. It was after that he started talking about this half a million francs.'

'And how *did* you know?'

'Because when I saw the body everything taken from it was on the mortuary table. Everything, that is, except his *carte d'identité* which had been removed from the lining of

his coat and forwarded to the French authorities. There
was no money. Not a penny.'

For several seconds Grodek stared at him. Then he
walked over to the cupboard where the drinks were kept.
'Another drink, Monsieur?'

He poured the drinks out in silence, handed Latimer his
and raised his glass solemnly. 'A toast, Monsieur. To the
English detective story!'

Amused, Latimer raised his glass to his lips. His host
had done the same. Suddenly, however, he choked and,
dragging a handkerchief from his pocket, set his glass down
again. To his surprise, Latimer saw that the man was
laughing.

'Forgive me, Monsieur,' he gasped. 'A thought crossed
my mind that made me laugh. It was – ' he hesitated a
fraction of a second ' – it was the thought of our friend
Peters confronting you with a pistol. He is quite terrified of
firearms.'

'He seemed to keep his fears to himself quite successfully.' Latimer spoke a trifle irritably. He had a suspicion
that there was another joke somewhere, the point of which
he had missed.

'A clever man, Peters.' Grodek chuckled and patted
Latimer on the shoulder. He seemed suddenly in excellent
spirits. 'My dear chap, please don't say that I have offended
you. Look, we will have luncheon now. I hope you will like
it. Are you hungry? Greta is really a splendid cook and
there is nothing Swiss about my wines. Afterwards, I will
tell you about Dimitrios and the trouble he caused me, and
Belgrade and 1926. Does that please you?'

'It's very good of you to put yourself out like this.'

He thought that Grodek was about to laugh again, but

the Pole seemed to change his mind. He became instead very solemn. 'It is a pleasure, Monsieur. Peters is a very good friend of mine. Besides, I like you personally, and we have so few visitors here.' He hesitated. 'May I be permitted as a friend to give you a word of advice, Monsieur?'

'Please do.'

'Then, if I were in your place, Monsieur, I should be inclined to take our friend Peters at his word and go to Paris.'

Latimer was perplexed. 'I don't know . . .' he began slowly.

But the housekeeper, Greta, had come into the room.

'Luncheon!' exclaimed Grodek with satisfaction.

Later, when he had an opportunity of asking Grodek to explain his 'word of advice', Latimer forgot to do so. By that time he had other things to think about.

9

Belgrade, 1926

Men have learned to distrust their imaginations. It is, there-fore, strange to them when they chance to discover that a world conceived in the imagination, outside experience, does in fact exist. The afternoon which Latimer spent at the Villa Acacias, listening to Wladyslaw Grodek, he recalls as, in that sense, one of the strangest of his life. In a letter (written in French) to the Greek, Marukakis, which he began that evening, while the whole thing was still fresh in his mind, and finished on the following day, the Sunday, he placed it on record.

Geneva.

Saturday.

My dear Marukakis,

I remember that I promised to write to you to let you know if I discovered anything more about Dimitrios. I wonder if you will be as surprised as I am that I have actually done so. Discovered something, I mean; for I intended to write to you in any case to thank you again for the help you gave me in Sofia.

When I left you there, I was bound, you may remember, for Belgrade. Why, then, am I writing from Geneva?

I was afraid that you would ask that question.

My dear fellow, I wish that I knew the answer. I know

part of it. The man, the professional spy, who employed Dimitrios in Belgrade in 1926, lives just outside Geneva. I saw him today and talked with him about Dimitrios. I can even explain how I got in touch with him. I was introduced. But just why I was introduced and just what the man who introduced us hopes to get out of it I cannot imagine. I shall, I hope, discover those things eventually. Meanwhile, let me say that if you find this mystery irritating, I find it no less so. Let me tell you about Dimitrios.

Did you ever believe in the existence of the 'master' spy? Until today I most certainly did not. Now I do. The reason for this is that I have spent the greater part of today talking to one. I cannot tell you his name, so I shall call him, in the best spy-story tradition, 'G'.

G. was a 'master' spy (he has retired now) in the same sense that the printer my publisher uses is a 'master' printer. He was an employer of spy labour. His work was mainly (though not entirely) administrative in character.

Now I know that a lot of nonsense is talked and written about spies and espionage, but let me try to put the question to you as G. put it to me.

He began by quoting Napoleon as saying that in war the basic element of all successful strategy was surprise.

G. is, I should say, a confirmed Napoleon-quoter. No doubt Napoleon did say that, or something like it. I am quite sure he wasn't the first military leader to do so. Alexander, Caesar, Genghis Khan and Frederick of Prussia all had the same idea. In 1918 Foch thought of it, too. But to return to G.

G. says that 'the experiences of the 1914–18 conflict' showed that in a future war (that sounds so beautifully distant, doesn't it?) the mobility and striking power of modern armies and navies and the existence of air forces would render the element of surprise more important than ever; so important, in fact, that it was possible that the people who got in with a surprise attack first might win the war. It was more than ever necessary to guard against surprise, to guard against it, moreover, *before* the war had started.

Now, there are roughly twenty-seven independent states in Europe. Each has an army and an air force and most have some sort of navy as well. For its own security, each of those armies, air forces and navies must know what each corresponding force in each of the other twenty-six countries is doing – what its strength is, what its efficiency is, what secret preparation it is making. That means spies – armies of them.

In 1926 G. was employed by Italy, and in the spring of that year he set up house in Belgrade.

Relations between Yugoslavia and Italy were strained at the time. The Italian seizure of Fiume was still as fresh in Yugoslav minds as the bombardment of Corfu; there were rumours, too (not unfounded as it was learned later in the year) that Mussolini contemplated occupying Albania.

Italy, on her side, was suspicious of Yugoslavia. Fiume was held under Yugoslav guns. A Yugoslav Albania alongside the Straits of Otranto was an unthinkable proposition. An independent Albania was tolerable only as long as it was under a predominantly Italian influence. It might be desirable to make certain of things. But the Yugoslavs might put up a fight. Reports from Italian agents in Belgrade indicated that in the event of war Yugoslavia intended to protect her seaboard by bottling herself up in the Adriatic with minefields laid just north of the Straits of Otranto.

I don't know much about these things, but apparently one does not have to lay a couple of hundred miles worth of mines to make a two-hundred-miles wide corridor of sea impassable. One just lays one or two small fields without letting one's enemy know just where. It is necessary, then, for them to find out the positions of those minefields.

That, then, was G.'s job in Belgrade. Italian agents found out about the minefields. G., the expert spy, was commissioned to do the real work of discovering where they were to be laid, without – a most important point this – without letting the Yugoslavs find out that he had done so. If they did find out, of course, they would promptly change the positions.

In that last part of his task G. failed. The reason for his failure was Dimitrios.

It has always seemed to me that a spy's job must be an extraordinarily difficult one. What I mean is this: if I were sent to Belgrade by the British Government with orders to get hold of the details of a secret mine-laying project for the Straits of Otranto, I should not even know where to start. Supposing I knew, as G. knew, that the details were recorded by means of markings on a navigational chart of the Straits. Very well. How many copies of the chart are kept? I would not know. Where are they kept? I would not know. I might reasonably suppose that at least one copy would be kept somewhere in the Ministry of Marine, but the Ministry of Marine is a large place. Moreover, the chart will almost certainly be under lock and key. And even if, as seems unlikely, I were able to find in which room it is kept and how to get to it, how should I set about obtaining a copy of it without letting the Yugoslavs know that I had done so?

When I tell you that within a month of his arrival in Belgrade, G. had not only found out where a copy of the chart was kept, but had also made up his mind how he was going to copy that copy *without the Yugoslavs knowing*, you will see that he is entitled to describe himself as competent.

How did he do it? What ingenious manoeuvre, what subtle trick made it possible? I shall try to break the news gently.

Posing as a German, the representative of an optical instrument-maker in Dresden, he struck up an acquaintance with a clerk in the Submarine Defence Department (which dealt with submarine nets, booms, mine-laying and mine-sweeping) of the Ministry of Marine!

Pitiful, wasn't it! The amazing thing is that he himself regards it as a very astute move. His sense of humour is quite paralysed. When I asked him if he ever read spy stories, he said that he did not, as they always seemed to him very naïve. But there is worse to come.

He struck up this acquaintance by going to the Ministry and asking the doorkeeper to direct him to the Department of Supply, a perfectly normal request for an outsider to make. Having got past the doorkeeper, he stopped someone in a corridor, said that he had been directed to the Submarine Defence Department and had got lost and asked to be redirected. Having got to the S.D. Department, he marched in and asked if it was the Department of Supply. They said that it was not, and out he went. He was in there not more than a minute, but in that time he had cast a quick eye over the personnel of the department, or, at all events, those of them he could see. He marked down three. That evening he waited outside the Ministry until the first of them came out. This man he followed home. Having found out his name and as much as he could about him, he repeated the process on succeeding evenings with the other two. Then he made his choice. It fell on a man named Bulić.

Now, G.'s actual methods may have lacked subtlety, but there was considerable subtlety in the way he employed them. He himself is quite oblivious of any distinction here. He is not the first successful man to misunderstand the reasons for his own success.

G.'s first piece of subtlety lay in his choice of Bulić as a tool.

Bulić was a disagreeable, conceited man of between forty and fifty, older than most of his fellow clerks and disliked by them. His wife was ten years younger than he, dissatisfied and pretty. He suffered from catarrh. He was in the habit of going to a café for a drink when he left the Ministry for the day, and it was in this café that G. made his acquaintance by the simple process of asking him for a match, offering him a cigar and, finally, buying him a drink.

You may imagine that a clerk in a government department dealing with highly confidential matters would naturally tend to be suspicious of café acquaintances who tried to pump him about his work. G. was ready to deal with those suspicions long before they entered Bulić's head.

The acquaintance ripened. G. would be in the café every evening when Bulić entered. They would carry on a desultory conversation. G., as a stranger to Belgrade, would ask Bulić's advice about this and that. He would pay for Bulić's drinks. He let Bulić condescend to him. Sometimes they would play a game of chess. Bulić would win. At other times they would play four-pack *bezique* with other frequenters of the café. Then, one evening, G. told Bulić a story.

He had been told by a mutual acquaintance, he said, that he, Bulić, held an important post in the Ministry of Marine.

For Bulić the 'mutual acquaintance' could have been one of several men with whom they played cards and exchanged opinions and who were vaguely aware that he worked in the Ministry. He frowned and opened his mouth. He was probably about to enter a mock-modest qualification of the adjective 'important', but G. swept on. As chief salesman for a highly respectable firm of optical instrument makers, he was deputed to obtain an order due to be placed by the Ministry of Marine for binoculars. He had submitted his quotation and had hopes of securing the order but, as Bulić would know, there was nothing like a friend at court in these affairs. If, therefore, the good and influential Bulić would bring pressure to bear to see that the Dresden company secured the order, Bulić would be in pocket to the tune of twenty thousand dinar.

Consider that proposition from Bulić's point of view. Here was he, an insignificant clerk, being flattered by the representative of a great German company and promised twenty thousand dinar, as much as he ordinarily earned in six months, for doing precisely nothing. If the quotation were already submitted, there was nothing to be done there. It would stand its chance with the other quotations. If the Dresden company secured the order he would be twenty thousand dinar in pocket without having compromised himself in any way. If they lost it *he* would lose nothing except the respect of this stupid and misinformed German.

G. admits that Bulić did make a half-hearted effort to be honest. He mumbled something about his not being sure that his influence could help. This, G. chose to treat as an attempt to increase the bribe. Bulić protested that no such thought had been in his mind. He was lost. Within five minutes he had agreed.

In the days that followed, Bulić and G. became close friends. G. ran no risk. Bulić could not know that no quotation had been submitted by the Dresden company as all quotations received by the Department of Supply were confidential until the order was placed. If he were inquisitive enough to make inquiries, he would find, as G. had found by previous reference to the *Official Gazette*, that quotations for binoculars had actually been asked for by the Department of Supply.

G. now got to work.

Bulić, remember, had to play the part assigned to him by G., the part of influential official. G., furthermore, began to make himself very amiable by entertaining Bulić and the pretty but stupid Madame Bulić at expensive restaurants and nightclubs. The pair responded like thirsty plants to rain. Could Bulić be cautious when, having had the best part of a bottle of sweet champagne, he found himself involved in an argument about Italy's overwhelming naval strength and her threat to Yugoslavia's seaboard? It was unlikely. He was a little drunk. His wife was present. For the first time in his dreary life, his judgement was being treated with the deference due to it. Besides, he had his part to play. It would not do to seem to be ignorant of what was going

on behind the scenes. He began to brag. He himself had
seen the very plans that in operation would immobilize
Italy's fleet in the Adriatic. Naturally, he had to be discreet, but . . .

By the end of that evening G. knew that Bulić had
access to a copy of the chart. He had also made up his
mind that Bulić was going to get that copy for him.

He made his plans carefully. Then he looked round
for a suitable man to carry them out. He needed a go-
between. He found Dimitrios.

Just how G. came to hear of Dimitrios is not clear.
I fancy that he was anxious not to compromise any of
his old associates. One can conceive that his reticence
might be understandable. Anyway, Dimitrios was
recommended to him. I asked in what business the rec-
ommender was engaged. I hoped, I admit, to be able to
find some link with the Eurasian Credit Trust episode.
But G. became vague. It was so very long ago. But he
remembered the verbal testimonial which accompanied
the recommendation.

Dimitrios Talat was a Greek-speaking Turk with an
'effective' passport and a reputation for being 'useful'
and at the same time discreet. He was also said to have
had experience in 'financial work of a confidential
nature'.

If one did not happen to know just what he was
useful for and the nature of the financial work he had
done, one might have supposed that the man under discussion was some sort of accountant. But there is, it
seems, a jargon in these affairs. G. understood it and
decided that Dimitrios was the man for the job in hand.
He wrote to Dimitrios – he gave me the address as

though it were a sort of American Express *poste restante* – care of the Eurasian Credit Trust in Bucharest!

Dimitrios arrived in Belgrade five days later and presented himself at G.'s house just off the Knez Miletina.

G. remembers the occasion very well. Dimitrios, he says, was a man of medium height who might have been almost any age between thirty-five and fifty – he was actually thirty-seven. He was smartly dressed and . . . But I had better quote G.'s own words:

'He was chic in an expensive way, and his hair was becoming grey at the sides of his head. He had a sleek, satisfied, confident air and something about the eyes that I recognized immediately. The man was a pimp. I can always recognize it. Do not ask me how. I have a woman's instinct for these things.'

So there you have it. Dimitrios had prospered. Had there been any more Madame Prevezas'? We shall never know. At all events, G. detected the pimp in Dimitrios and was not displeased. A pimp, he reasoned, could be relied upon not to fool about with women to the detriment of the business in hand. Also Dimitrios was of pleasing address. I think that I had better quote G. again:

'He could wear his clothes gracefully. Also he looked intelligent. I was pleased by this because I did not care to employ riff-raff from the gutters. Sometimes it was necessary but I never liked it. They did not always understand my curious temperament.'

G., you see, was fussy.

Dimitrios had not wasted his time. He could now speak both German and French with reasonable accuracy. He said:

'I came as soon as I received your letter. I was busy

in Bucharest, but I was glad to get your letter as I had heard of you.'

G. explained carefully and with circumspection (it did not do to give too much away to a prospective employee) what he wanted done. Dimitrios listened unemotionally. When G. had finished, he asked how much he was to be paid.

'Thirty thousand dinar,' said G.

'Fifty thousand,' said Dimitrios, 'and I would prefer to have it in Swiss francs.'

They compromised on forty thousand to be paid in Swiss francs. Dimitrios smiled and shrugged his agreement.

It was the man's eyes when he smiled, says G., that first made him distrust his new employee.

I found that odd. Could it be that there was honour among scoundrels, that G., being the man he was and knowing (up to a point) the sort of man Dimitrios was, would yet need a smile to awaken distrust? Incredible. But there was no doubt that he remembered those eyes very vividly. Preveza remembered them, too, didn't she? 'Brown, anxious eyes that made you think of a doctor's eyes when he is doing something to you that hurts.' That was it, wasn't it? My theory is that it was not until Dimitrios smiled that G. realized the quality of the man whose services he had bought. 'He had the appearance of being tame, but when you looked into his brown eyes you saw that he had none of the feelings that make ordinary men soft, that he was always dangerous.' Preveza again. Did G. sense the same thing? He may not have explained it to himself in that way – he is not the sort of man to set much store by feelings – but I think he may have wondered if he had made a mistake in employing Dimitrios. Their two minds were not so very dissimilar and that sort of wolf prefers to hunt alone. At all events, G. decided to keep a wary eye on Dimitrios.

Meanwhile, Bulić was finding life more pleasant than it had ever been before. He was being entertained at rich places. His wife, warmed by unfamiliar luxury, no longer looked at him with contempt and distaste in her eyes. With the money they saved on the meals provided by the stupid German she could drink her favourite cognac, and when she drank she became friendly and agreeable. In a week's time, moreover, he might become the possessor of twenty thousand dinar. There was a chance. He felt very well, he said one night, and added that cheap food was bad for his catarrh. That was the nearest he came to forgetting to play his part.

The order for the binoculars was given to a Czech firm. The *Official Gazette*, in which the fact was announced, was published at noon. At one minute past noon, G. had a copy and was on his way to an engraver on whose bench lay a half-finished copper die. By six o'clock he was waiting opposite the entrance to the Ministry. Soon after six, Bulić appeared. He had seen the *Official Gazette*. A copy was under his arm. His dejection was visible from where G. stood. G. began to follow him.

Ordinarily, Bulić would have crossed the road before many minutes had passed, to get to his café. Tonight he hesitated and then walked straight on. He was not anxious to meet the man from Dresden.

G. turned down a side street and hailed a taxi. Within two minutes his taxi had made a detour and was approaching Bulić. Suddenly, he signalled to the driver to stop, bounded out on to the pavement and embraced Bulić delightedly. Before the bewildered clerk could protest, he was bundled into the taxi and G. was pouring congratulations and thanks into his ear and pressing a cheque for twenty thousand dinar into his hand.

'But I thought you'd lost the order,' mumbles Bulić at last.

G. laughs as if at a huge joke. 'Lost it!' And then he 'understands'. 'Of course! I forgot to tell you. The quotation was submitted through a Czech subsidiary of ours. Look, does this explain it?' He thrusts one of the newly-printed cards into Bulić's hand. 'I don't use this card often. Most people know that these Czechs are owned by our company in Dresden.' He brushes the matter aside. 'But we must have a drink immediately. Driver!'

That night they celebrated. His first bewilderment over, Bulić took full advantage of the situation. He became drunk. He began to brag of the potency of his influence in the Ministry until even G., who had every reason for satisfaction, was hard put to it to remain civil.

But towards the end of the evening, he drew Bulić aside. Estimates, he said, had been invited for range-finders. Could he, Bulić, assist? Of course he could. And now Bulić became cunning. Now that the value of his co-operation had been established, he had a right to expect something on account.

G. had not anticipated this, but, secretly amused, he agreed at once. Bulić received another cheque; this time it was for ten thousand dinar. The understanding was that he should be paid a further ten thousand when the order was placed with G.'s 'employers'.

Bulić was now wealthier than ever before. He had

thirty thousand dinar. Two evenings later, in the supper room of a fashionable hotel, G. introduced him to a Freiherr von Kiessling. The Freiherr von Kiessling's other name was, needless to say, Dimitrios.

'You would have thought,' says G., 'that he had been living in such places all his life. For all I know, he may have been doing so. His manner was perfect. When I introduced Bulić as an important official in the Ministry of Marine, he condescended magnificently. With Madame Bulić he was superb. He might have been greeting a princess. But I saw the way his fingers moved across the palm of her hand as he bent to kiss the back of it.'

Dimitrios had displayed himself in the supper room before G. had affected to claim acquaintance with him in order to give G. time to prepare the ground. The 'Freiherr', G. told the Bulićs after he had drawn their attention to Dimitrios, was a very important man. Something of a mystery, perhaps, but a very important factor in international big business. He was enormously rich and was believed to control as many as twenty-seven companies. He might be a useful man to know.

The Bulićs were enchanted to be presented to him. When the 'Freiherr' agreed to drink a glass of champagne at their table, they felt themselves honoured indeed. In their halting German they strove to make themselves agreeable. This, Bulić must have felt, was what he had been waiting for all his life: at last he was in touch with the people who counted, the real people, the people who made men and broke them, the people who might make him. Perhaps he saw himself a director of one of the 'Freiherr's' companies, with a fine house and others dependent on him, loyal servants who would respect him as a man as well as a master. When, the next morning, he went to his stool in the Ministry, there must have been joy in his heart, joy made all the sweeter by the faint misgivings, the slight prickings of conscience which could so easily be stilled. After all, G. had received his money's worth. He, Bulić, had nothing to lose. Besides, you never knew what might come of it all. Men had taken stranger paths to fortune.

The 'Freiherr' had been good enough to say that he would have supper with Herr G. and his two charming friends two evenings later.

I questioned G. about this. Would it not have been better to have struck while the iron was hot. Two days gave the Bulićs time to think. 'Precisely,' was G.'s reply; 'time to think of the good things to come, to prepare themselves for the feast, to dream.' He became preternaturally solemn at the thought and then, grinning, suddenly quoted Goethe at me. '*Ach! warum, ihr Götter, ist unendlich, alles, alles, endlich unser Glück nur?*' G., you see, lays claim to a sense of humour.

That supper was the critical moment for him. Dimitrios got to work on Madame. It was such a pleasure to meet such pleasant people as Madame – and of course, her husband. She – and her husband, naturally – must certainly come and stay with him in Bavaria next month. He preferred it to his Paris house and Cannes was sometimes chilly in the spring. Madame would enjoy Bavaria, and so, no doubt, would her husband. That was, if he could tear himself away from the Ministry.

Crude, simple stuff, no doubt, but the Bulićs were crude, simple people. Madame lapped it up with her sweet champagne while Bulić became sulky. Then the great moment arrived.

The flower girl stopped by the table with her tray of orchids. Dimitrios turned round and, selecting the largest and most expensive bloom, handed it with a little flourish to Madame Bulić with a request that she accept it as a token of his esteem. Madame would accept it. Dimitrios drew out his wallet to pay. The next moment a thick wad of thousand dinar notes fell from his breast pocket on to the table.

With a word of apology Dimitrios put the money back in his pocket. G., taking his cue, remarked that it was rather a lot of money to carry in one's pocket and asked if the 'Freiherr' always carried as much. No, he did not. He had won the money at Alessandro's earlier in the evening and had forgotten to leave it upstairs in his room. Did Madame know Alessandro's? She did not. Both the Bulićs were silent as the 'Freiherr' talked on: they had never seen so much money before. In the 'Freiherr's' opinion Alessandro's was the most reliable gambling place in Belgrade. It was your own luck not the croupier's skill that mattered at Alessandro's. Personally he was having a run of luck that evening – this with velvety eyes on Madame – and had won a little more than usual. He hesitated at that point. And then: 'As you have never been in the place, I should be delighted if you would accompany me as my guests later.'

Of course, they went, and, of course, they were expected and preparations had been made. Dimitrios had arranged everything. No roulette – it is difficult to cheat a man at roulette – but there was *trente et quarante*. The minimum stake was two hundred and fifty dinar.

They had drinks and watched the play for a time. Then G. decided that he would play a little. They watched him win twice. Then the 'Freiherr' asked madame if she would like to play. She looked at her husband. He said, apologetically, that he had very little money with him. But Dimitrios was ready for that. No trouble at all, Herr Bulić! He personally was well known to Alessandro. Any friend of his could be accommodated. If he should happen to lose a few dinar, Alessandro would take a cheque or a note.

The farce went on. Alessandro was summoned and introduced. The situation was explained to him. He raised protesting hands. Any friend of the 'Freiherr' need not even ask such a thing. Besides, he had not yet played. Time to talk of such things if he had a little bad luck.

G. thinks that if Dimitrios had allowed the two to talk to one another for even a moment, they would not have played. Two hundred and fifty dinar was the minimum stake, and not even the possession of thirty thousand could overcome their consciousness of the value, in terms of food and rent, of two hundred and fifty. But Dimitrios did not give them a chance to exchange misgivings. Instead, as they were waiting at the table behind G.'s chair, he murmured to Bulić that if he, Bulić, had time, he, the 'Freiherr', would like to talk business with him over luncheon one day that week.

It was beautifully timed. It could, I feel, have meant only one thing to Bulić: 'My dear Bulić, there really is no need for you to concern yourself over a paltry few hundred dinar. I am interested in you, and that means that your fortune is made. Please do not disappoint me by showing yourself less important than you seem now.'

Madame Bulić began to play.

Her first two hundred and fifty she lost on *couleur*.

The second won on *inverse*. Then, Dimitrios, advising greater caution, suggested that she play *à cheval*. There was a *refait* and then a second *refait*. Ultimately she lost again.

At the end of an hour the five thousand dinar's worth of chips she had been given had gone. Dimitrios, sympathising with her for her 'bad luck', pushed across some five hundred dinar chips from a pile in front of him and begged that she would play with them 'for luck'.

The tortured Bulić may have had the idea that these were a gift, for he made only the faintest sound of protest. That they had not been a gift he was presently to discover. Madame Bulić, thoroughly miserable now and becoming a little untidy, played on. She won a little; she lost more. At half-past two Bulić signed a promissory note to Alessandro for twelve thousand dinar. G. bought them a drink.

It is easy to picture the scene between the Bulićs when at last they were alone – the recriminations, the tears, the interminable arguments – only too easy. Yet, bad as things were, the gloom was not unrelieved; for Bulić was to lunch the following day with the 'Freiherr'. And they were to talk business.

They did talk business. Dimitrios had been told to be encouraging. No doubt he was. Hints of big deals afoot, of opportunities for making fabulous sums for those who were in the know, talk of castles in Bavaria – it would all be there. Bulić had only to listen and let his heart beat faster. What did twelve thousand dinar matter? You had to think in millions.

All the same, it was Dimitrios who raised the subject of his guest's debt to Alessandro. He supposed that

Bulić would be going along that very night to settle it. He personally would be playing again. One could not, after all, win so much without giving Alessandro a chance to lose some more. Supposing that they went along together – just the two of them. Women were bad gamblers.

When they met that night Bulić had nearly thirty-five thousand dinar in his pocket. He must have added his savings to G.'s thirty thousand. When Dimitrios reported to G. – in the early hours of the following morning – he said that Bulić had, in spite of Alessandro's protests, insisted on redeeming his promissory note before he started to play. 'I pay my debts,' he told Dimitrios proudly. The balance of the money he spent, with a flourish, on five hundred dinar chips. Tonight he was going to make a killing. He refused a drink. He meant to keep a cool head.

G. grinned at this and perhaps he was wise to do so. Pity is sometimes too uncomfortable; and I do find Bulić pitiable. You may say that he was a weak fool. So he was. But providence is never quite as calculating as were G. and Dimitrios. It may bludgeon away at a man, but it never feels between his ribs with a knife. Bulić had no chance. They understood him and used their understanding with skill. With the cards as neatly stacked against me as they were against him, I should perhaps be no less weak, no less foolish. It is a comfort to believe that the occasion is unlikely to arise.

Inevitably he lost. He began to play with just over forty chips. It took him two hours of winning and losing to get rid of them. Then, quite calmly, he took another twenty on credit. He said that his luck must change. The poor wretch did not even suspect that he might be being cheated. Why should he suspect? The 'Freiherr' was losing even more than he was. He doubled his stakes and survived for forty minutes. He borrowed again and lost again. He had lost thirty-eight thousand dinar more than he had in the world when, white and sweating, he decided to stop.

After that it was plain sailing for Dimitrios. The following night Bulić returned. They let him win thirty thousand back. The third night he lost another fourteen thousand. On the fourth night, when he was about twenty-five thousand in debt, Alessandro asked for his money. Bulić promised to redeem his notes within a week. The first person to whom he went for help was G.

G. was sympathetic. Twenty-five thousand was a lot of money, wasn't it? Of course, any money he used in connection with orders received was his employers', and he was not empowered to do what he liked with it. But he himself could spare two hundred and fifty for a few days if it were any help. He would have liked to do more, but . . . Bulić took the two hundred and fifty.

With it G. gave him a word of advice. The 'Freiherr' was the man to get him out of his difficulty. He never lent money – with him it was a question of principle, he believed – but he had a reputation for helping his friends by putting them in the way of earning quite substantial sums. Why not have a talk with him?

The 'talk' between Bulić and Dimitrios took place after a dinner for which Bulić paid and in the 'Freiherr's' hotel sitting-room. G. was out of sight in the adjoining bedroom.

When Bulić at last got to the point, he asked about Alessandro. Would he insist on his money? What would happen if he were not paid?

Dimitrios affected surprise. There was no question, he hoped, of Alessandro's not being paid. After all, it was on his personal recommendation that Alessandro had given credit in the first place. He would not like there to be any unpleasantness. What sort of unpleasantness? Well, Alessandro held the promissory notes and could take the matter to the police. He hoped sincerely that that would not happen.

Bulić was hoping so, too. Now, he had everything to lose, including his post at the Ministry. It might even come out that he had taken money from G. That might even mean prison. Would they believe that he had done nothing in return for those thirty thousand dinar? It was madness to expect them to do so. His only chance was to get the money from the 'Freiherr' – somehow.

To his pleas for a loan Dimitrios shook his head. No. That would simply make matters worse, for then he would owe the money to a friend instead of to an enemy; besides, it was a matter of principle with him. At the same time, he wanted to help. There was just one way, but would Herr Bulić feel disposed to take it? That was the question. He scarcely liked to mention the matter, but, since Herr Bulić pressed him, he knew of certain persons who were interested in obtaining some information from the Ministry of Marine that could not be obtained through the usual channels. They could probably be persuaded to pay as much as fifty thousand dinar for this information if they could rely upon its being accurate.

G. said that he attributed quite a lot of the success of his plan (he deems it successful in the same way that a surgeon deems an operation successful when the patient leaves the operating theatre alive) to his careful use of figures. Every sum from the original twenty thousand dinar to the amounts of the successive debts to Alessandro (who was an Italian agent) and the final amount offered by Dimitrios was carefully calculated with an eye to its psychological value. That final fifty thousand, for example. Its appeal to Bulić was two-fold. It would pay off his debt and still leave him with nearly as much as he had had before he met the 'Freiherr'. To the incentive of fear they added that of greed.

But Bulić did not give in immediately. When he heard exactly what the information was, he became frightened and angry. The anger was dealt with very efficiently by Dimitrios. If Bulić had begun to entertain doubts about the *bona fides* of the 'Freiherr' those doubts were now made certainties; for when he shouted 'dirty spy', the 'Freiherr's' easy charm deserted him. Bulić was kicked in the abdomen and then, as he bent forward retching, in the face. Gasping for breath and with pain and bleeding from the mouth, he was flung into a chair while Dimitrios explained coldly that the only risk he ran was in not doing as he was told.

His instructions were simple. Bulić was to get a copy of the chart and bring it to the hotel when he left the Ministry the following evening. An hour later the chart would be returned to him to replace in the morning. That was all. He would be paid when he brought the chart. He was warned of the consequences to himself if he should decide to go to the authorities with his story, reminded of the fifty thousand that awaited him and dismissed.

He duly returned the following night with the chart folded in four under his coat. Dimitrios took the chart into G. and returned to keep watch on Bulić while it was photographed and the negative developed. Apparently Bulić had nothing to say. When G. had finished he took the money and the chart from Dimitrios and went without a word.

G. says that in the bedroom at that moment, when he heard the door close behind Bulić and as he held the negative up to the light, he was feeling very pleased with himself. Expenses had been low; there had been no wasted effort; there had been no tiresome delays; everybody, even Bulić, had done well out of the business. It only remained to hope that Bulić would restore the chart safely. There was really no reason why he should not do so. A very satisfactory affair from every point of view.

And then Dimitrios came into the room.

It was at that moment that G. realized that he had made one mistake.

'My wages,' said Dimitrios, and held out his hand.

G. met his employee's eyes and nodded. He needed a gun and he had not got one. 'We'll go to my house now,' he said and started towards the door.

Dimitrios shook his head deliberately. 'My wages are in your pocket.'

'Not your wages. Only mine.'

Dimitrios produced a revolver. A smile played about his lips. 'What I want is in your pocket, *mein Herr*. Put your hands behind your head.'

G. obeyed. Dimitrios walked towards him. G., looking steadily into those brown anxious eyes, saw that he was in danger. Two feet in front of him Dimitrios stopped. 'Please be careful, *mein Herr*.'

The smile disappeared. Dimitrios stepped forward suddenly and, jamming his revolver into G.'s stomach, snatched the negative from G.'s pocket with his free hand. Then, as suddenly, he stood back. 'You may go,' he said.

G. went. Dimitrios, in turn, had made *his* mistake.

All that night men, hastily recruited from the criminal cafés, scoured Belgrade for Dimitrios. But Dimitrios had disappeared. G. never saw him again.

What happened to the negative? Let me give you G.'s own words:

'When the morning came and my men had failed to find him, I knew what I must do. I felt very bitter. After all my careful work it was most disappointing. But there was nothing else for it. I had known for a week that Dimitrios had got in touch with a French agent. The negative would be in that agent's hands by now. I really had no choice. A friend of mine in the German Embassy was able to oblige me. The Germans were anxious to please Belgrade at the time. What could be more natural than that they should pass on an item of information interesting to the Yugoslav government?'

'Do you mean,' I said, 'that you deliberately arranged for the Yugoslav authorities to be informed of the removal of the chart and of the fact that it had been photographed?'

'Unfortunately, it was the only thing I could do. You see, I had to render the chart worthless. It was really very foolish of Dimitrios to let me go, but he was inexperienced. He probably thought that I should blackmail Bulić into bringing the chart out again. But I realized that I should not be paid much for bringing in information already in the possession of the French. Besides, my reputation would have suffered. I was very bitter about the whole affair. The only amusing aspect of it was that the French had paid over to Dimitrios half the agreed price for the chart before they discovered that the information on it had been rendered obsolete by my little *démarche*.'

'What about Bulić?'

G. pulled a face. 'Yes, I was sorry about that. I always have felt a certain responsibility towards those who work for me. He was arrested almost at once. There was no doubt as to which of the Ministry copies had been used. They were kept rolled in metal cylinders. Bulić had folded this one to bring it out of the Ministry. It was the only one with creases in it. His fingerprints did the rest. Very wisely he told the authorities all he knew about Dimitrios. As a result they sent him to prison for life instead of shooting him. I quite expected him to implicate me, but he did not. I was a little surprised. After all it was I who introduced him to Dimitrios. I wondered at the time whether it was because he was unwilling to face an additional charge of accepting bribes or because he felt grateful to me for lending him that two hundred and fifty dinar. Probably he did not connect me with the business of the chart at all. In any case, I was pleased. I still had work to do in Belgrade, and being wanted by the police, even under another name, might have complicated my life. I have never been able to bring myself to wear disguises.'

I asked him one more question. Here is his answer:

'Oh, yes, I obtained the new charts as soon as they had been made. In quite a different way, of course. With so much of my money invested in the enterprise I could not return empty-handed. It is always the same: for one reason or another there are always these delays, these wastages of effort and money. You may say that I was careless in my handling of Dimitrios. That would be unjust. It was a small error of judgment on my part, that is all. I counted on his being like all the other fools in the world, on his being too greedy; I thought he would wait until he had from me the forty thousand dinar due to him before he tried to take the photograph as well. He took me by surprise. That error of judgement cost me a lot of money.'

'It cost Bulić his liberty.' I am afraid I said it a trifle grimly, for he frowned.

'My dear Monsieur Latimer,' he retorted stiffly, 'Bulić was a traitor and he was rewarded according to his desserts. One cannot sentimentalize over him. In war there are always casualties. Bulić was very lucky. I should certainly have used him again, and he might ultimately have been shot. As it was, he went to prison. For all I know he is still in prison. I do not wish to seem callous, but I must say that he is better off there. His liberty? Rubbish! He had none to lose. As for his wife, I have no doubt that she has done better for herself. She always gave me the impression of wanting to do so. I do not blame her. He was an objectionable man. I seem to remember that he tended to dribble as he ate. What is more, he was a nuisance. You would have thought, would you not, that on leaving Dimitrios that evening he would have gone there and then to Alessandro to pay his debt? He did not do so. When he was arrested late the following day he still had the fifty thousand dinar in his pocket. More waste. It is at times like those, my friend, that one needs one's sense of humour.'

Well, my dear Marukakis, that is all. It is, I think, more than enough. For me, wandering among the ghosts of old lies, there is comfort in the thought that you might write to me and tell me that all this was worth finding out. You might. For myself, I begin to wonder. It is such a poor story, isn't it? There is no hero, no heroine; there are only knaves and fools. Or do I mean only fools?

But it really is too early in the afternoon to pose such questions. Besides, I have packing to do. In a few days I shall send you a postcard with my name and new address on it in the hope that you will have time to write. In any case, we shall, I hope, meet again very soon. *Croyez en mes meilleurs souvenirs.*

Charles Latimer.

10

The Eight Angels

It was on a slate-grey November day that Latimer arrived in Paris.

As his taxi crossed the bridge to the Ile de la Cité, he saw for a moment a panorama of low, black clouds moving quickly in the chill, dusty wind. The long façade of the houses on the Quai de Corse were still and secretive. It was as if each window concealed a watcher. There seemed to be few people about. Paris, in that late autumn afternoon, had the macabre formality of a steel engraving.

It depressed him, and as he climbed the stairs of his hotel on the Quai Voltaire he wished fervently that he had gone back to Athens.

His room was cold. It was too early for an aperitif. He had been able to eat enough of his meal on the train to render an early dinner unnecessary. He decided to inspect the outside of number three, Impasse des Huit Anges. With some difficulty he found the Impasse tucked away in a side street off the Rue de Rennes.

It was a wide, cobbled passage shaped like an L and flanked at the entrance by a pair of tall iron gates. They were fastened back against the walls that supported them with heavy staples, and had evidently not been shut for years. A row of spiked railings separated one side of the Impasse from the blank side wall of the adjoining block of houses. Another blank cement wall, unguarded by railings

but protected by the words 'DEFENCE D'AFFICHER, LOI DU
10 AVRIL 1929' in weatherbeaten black paint, faced it.

There were only three houses in the Impasse. They were
grouped out of sight of the road, in the foot of the L, and
looked out through the narrow gap between the building
on which bill-posting was forbidden and the back of a hotel
over which drainpipes writhed like snakes, on to yet
another sightless expanse of cement. Life in the Impasse
des Huit Anges would, Latimer thought, be rather like a
rehearsal for Eternity. That others before him had found it
so was suggested by the fact that, of the three houses, two
were shuttered and obviously quite empty, while the third,
number three, was occupied on the fourth and top floors
only.

Feeling as if he were trespassing, Latimer walked slowly
across the irregular cobbles to the entrance of number
three.

The door was open and he could see along a tiled corridor to a small, dank yard at the back. The concierge's
room, to the right of the door, was empty and showed no
signs of having been used recently. Beside it, on the wall,
was nailed a dusty board with four brass name slots
screwed to it. Three of the slots were empty. In the fourth
was a grimy piece of paper with the name 'CAILLE' clumsily
printed on it in violet ink.

There was nothing to be learned from this but the fact,
which Latimer had not doubted, that Mr Peters' accommodation address existed. He turned and walked back to
the street. In the Rue de Rennes he found a post office
where he bought a *pneumatique* letter-card, wrote in it his
name and that of his hotel, addressed it to Mr Peters and
dropped it down the chute. He also sent a postcard to

Marukakis. What happened now depended to a great extent on Mr Peters. But there was something he could and should do: that was to find out what, if anything, the Paris newspapers had had to say about the breaking up in December 1931 of a drug-peddling gang.

At nine o'clock the following morning, being without word from Peters, he decided to spend the morning with newspaper files.

The paper he finally selected for detailed reading had made a number of references to the case. The first was dated 29th November 1931. It was headed: 'DRUG TRAFFICKERS ARRESTED,' and went on:

A man and a woman engaged in the distribution of drugs to addicts were arrested yesterday in the Alésia quarter. They are said to be members of a notorious foreign gang. The police expect to make further arrests within a few days.

That was all. It read curiously, Latimer thought. Those three bald sentences looked as if they had been lifted out of a longer report. The absence of names, too, was odd. Police censorship, perhaps.

The next reference appeared on 4th December under the heading: 'DRUG GANG, THREE MORE ARRESTS.'

Three members of a criminal drug-distributing organiz- ation were arrested late last night in a café near the Porte d'Orleans. *Agents* entering the café to make the arrests were compelled to fire on one of the men who was armed and who made a desperate attempt to escape. He was slightly wounded. The other two, one of whom was a foreigner, did not resist.

This brings the number of drug gang arrests to five,

for it is believed that the three men arrested last night belonged to the same gang as the man and woman arrested a week ago in the Alésia quarter.

The police state that still more arrests are likely to be made, as the Bureau Général des Stupéfiants has in its possession evidence implicating the actual organizers of the gang.

Monsieur Auguste Lafon, director of the Bureau, said:

'We have known of this gang for some time and have conducted painstaking investigations into their activities. We could have made arrests but we held our hands. It was the leaders, the big criminals whom we wanted. Without leaders, with their sources of supply cut off, the army of drug pedlars that infests Paris will be powerless to carry on their nefarious trade. We intend to smash this gang and others like it.'

Then, on 11th December the newspaper reported:

DRUG GANG SMASHED
NEW ARRESTS
'Now we have them all,' says Lafon.
THE COUNCIL OF SEVEN

Six men and one woman are now under arrest as a result of the attack launched by Monsieur Lafon, director of the Bureau Général des Stupéfiants, on a notorious gang of foreign drug traffickers operating in Paris and Marseilles.

The attack began with the arrest two weeks ago of a woman and her male accomplice in the Alésia quarter. It reached its climax yesterday with the arrest in Marseilles of two men believed to be the remaining members of the gang's 'Council of Seven', which was responsible for the organization of this criminal enterprise.

At the request of the police we have hitherto remained silent as to the names of those arrested as it was desired not to put the others on their guard. Now that restriction has been lifted.

The woman, Lydia Prokofievna, is a Russian who is believed to have come to France from Turkey with a Nansen passport in 1924. She is known in criminal circles as 'The Grand Duchess'. The man arrested with her was a Dutchman named Manus Visser who, through his association with Prokofievna, was sometimes referred to as 'Monsieur le Duc'.

The names of the other five under arrest are: Luis Galindo, a naturalized Frenchman of Mexican origin, who now lies in hospital with a bullet wound in the thigh; Jean-Baptiste Lenôtre, a Frenchman from Bordeaux, and Jacob Werner, a Belgian, who were arrested with Galindo; Pierre Lamare or 'Jo-jo', a Niçois, and Frederik Petersen, a Dane, who were arrested in Marseilles.

In a statement to the press last night, Monsieur Lafon said: 'Now we have them all. The gang is smashed. We have cut off the head and with it the brains. The body will now die a speedy death. It is finished.'

Lamare and Petersen are to be questioned by the examining magistrate today. It is expected that there will be a mass-trial of the prisoners.

See the special article, SECRETS OF THE DRUG GANGS, *on page 3.*

In England, Latimer reflected, Monsieur Lafon would have found himself in serious trouble. It hardly seemed worthwhile trying the accused after he and the press between them had already pronounced the verdict. But then, the accused was always guilty in a French trial. To give him a trial at all was, practically speaking, merely to ask him whether he had anything to say before he was sentenced.

He turned to the special article on page three.

The author, who called himself '*Veilleur*', revealed that the stuff known as morphine was an opium derivative with the formula $C_{17}H_{19}O_3N$ and that its usual medical form was morphine hydrochloride, that heroin (diacetylmorphine), another opium derived alkaloid, was preferred to morphine by addicts because it acted more speedily and powerfully and was easier to take, that cocaine was made from the leaves of the coco bush and served up in the form of cocaine hydrochloride (formula $C_{17}H_{21}O_4N$, HCl) and that the effects of all three drugs were approximately the same, namely: that they were aphrodisiac, that they produced states of mental and physical exhilaration in the early stages and that eventually the addict suffered physical and moral degeneration and mental tortures of the most appalling kind. The traffic in these drugs, declared '*Veilleur*', was carried on on a gigantic scale and it was possible for anyone to obtain them in Paris and Marseilles. There were illicit factories in every country in Europe. World production of these drugs exceeded legitimate medical consumption many times over. There were millions of addicts in Western Europe. Drug smuggling was a vast well-organized business. There followed a list of recent seizures of illicit drugs: sixteen kilos of heroin found in each of six cases of machinery consigned from Amsterdam to Paris, twenty-five kilos of cocaine found between the false sides of a drum of oil consigned from New York to Cherbourg, ten kilos of morphine found in the false bottom of a cabin trunk landed at Marseilles, two hundred kilos of heroin found in an illicit factory in a garage near Lyons. The gangs that peddled these drugs were controlled by rich and outwardly respectable men. The police were bribed by these vermin. There were bars and dancings in Paris where the drugs were distributed under the very eyes of the police who were laughed at by the pedlars. *'Veilleur'* choked with indignation. Had he been writing three years later he would certainly have implicated Stavisky and half the Chamber of Deputies. But for once, he went on, the police had taken action. It was to be hoped that they would do so again. Meanwhile, however, there were thousands of Frenchmen – yes, *and* Frenchwomen! – suffering the tortures of the damned through this diabolical traffic which was sapping the virility of the nation. All of which suggested that, although *'Veilleur's'* heart was in the right place, he knew none of the secrets of the drug gangs.

With the arrest of the 'Council of Seven', interest in the case seemed to wane. The fact that 'The Grand Duchess' had been transferred to Nice to stand trial there for a fraud committed three years previously may have been responsible for this. The trial of the men was dealt with briefly. All were sentenced: Galindo, Lenôtre and Werner to fines of five thousand francs and three months' imprisonment, Lamare, Petersen and Visser to fines of two thousand francs and one month's imprisonment.

Latimer was amazed by the lightness of the sentences. *'Veilleur'*, who bobbed up again to comment on the affair, was outraged but not amazed. But for the existence of a set of obsolete and wholly ridiculous laws, he thundered, the whole six would have been imprisoned for life. And which of them was the leader of the gang? Ah! Did the police suppose that these alley rats had financed an organization which, on the evidence given in court, had in one month taken delivery of and distributed heroin and morphine to the value of two and a half million francs? It was absurd. The police . . .

It was the nearest the newspaper got to the fact that the police had failed to find Dimitrios. That was not surprising. The police were not going to tell the press that the arrests were made possible only by a dossier obligingly supplied by some anonymous well-wisher whom they suspected of being the leader of the gang. All the same, it was irritating to find that he knew more than the newspaper he had relied upon to clarify the affair for him.

He was about to shut the file in disgust when his attention was caught by an illustration. It was a smudgy reproduction of a photograph of three of the prisoners being led from the court by detectives to whom they were handcuffed. All three had turned their faces away from the camera but the fact of their being handcuffed had prevented them from concealing themselves effectively.

Latimer left the newspaper office in better spirits than those in which he had entered it.

At his hotel a message awaited him. Unless he sent a *pneumatique* making other arrangements, Mr Peters would call upon him at six o'clock that evening.

*

Mr Peters arrived soon after half-past five. He greeted Latimer effusively.

'My *dear* Mr Latimer! I cannot tell you how pleased I

am to see you. Our last meeting took place under such inauspicious circumstances that I hardly dared hope . . . But let us talk of pleasanter things. Welcome to Paris! Have you had a good journey? You are looking well. Tell me, what did you think of Grodek? He wrote telling me how charming and sympathetic you were. A good fellow, isn't he? Those cats of his! He worships them.'

'He was very helpful. Do, please, sit down.'

'I knew he would be.'

For Latimer, Mr Peters' sweet smile was like the greeting of an old and detested acquaintance. 'He was also mysterious. He urged me to come to Paris to see you.'

'Did he?' Mr Peters did not seem pleased. His smile faded a little. 'And what else did he say, Mr Latimer?'

'He said that you were a clever man. He seemed to find something I said about you amusing.'

Mr Peters sat down carefully on the bed. His smile had quite gone. 'And what was it you said?'

'He insisted upon knowing what business I had with you. I told him all I could. As I knew nothing,' went on Latimer spitefully, 'I felt that I could safely confide in him. If you do not like that, I am sorry. You must remember that I am still in complete ignorance concerning this precious scheme of yours.'

'Grodek did not tell you?'

'No. Could he have done so?'

The smile once more tightened his soft lips. It was as if some obscene plant had turned its face to the sun. 'Yes, Mr Latimer, he could have done so. What you have told me explains the flippant tone of his letter to me. I am glad you satisfied his curiosity. The rich are so often covetous of others' goods in this world of ours. Grodek is a dear friend of mine, but it is just as well that he knows that we stand in no need of assistance. He might otherwise be tempted by the prospect of gain.'

Latimer regarded him thoughtfully for a moment. Then: 'Have you got your pistol with you, Mr Peters?'

The fat man looked horrified. 'Dear me no, Mr Latimer. Why should I bring such a thing on a friendly visit to you?'

'Good,' said Latimer curtly. He backed towards the door and turned the key in the lock. The key he put in his pocket. 'Now then,' he went on grimly, 'I don't want to seem a bad host, but there are limits to my patience. I have come a long way to see you and I still don't know why. I want to know why.'

'And so you shall.'

'I've heard that before,' answered Latimer rudely. 'Now before you start beating about the bush again there are one or two things *you* should know. I am not a violent man, Mr Peters. To be honest with you, I dread violence. But there are times when the most peace-loving among us must use it. This may be one of them. I am younger than you and, I should say, in better condition. If you persist in being mysterious I shall attack you. That is the first thing.

'The second is that I know who you are. Your name is not Peters but Petersen, Frederik Petersen. You were a member of the drug-peddling gang organized by Dimitrios and you were arrested in December 1931, fined two thousand francs and sentenced to one month's imprisonment.'

Mr Peters' smile was tortured. 'Did Grodek tell you this?' He asked the question gently and sorrowfully. The word 'Grodek' might have been another way of saying 'Judas'.

'No. I saw a picture of you this morning in a newspaper file.'

'A newspaper. Ah, yes! I could not believe that my friend Grodek . . .'

'You don't deny it?'

'Oh, no. It is the truth.'

'Well then, Mr Petersen . . .'

'Peters, Mr Latimer. I decided to change the name.'

'All right then – Peters. We come to my third point. When I was in Istanbul I heard some interesting things about the end of that gang. It was said that Dimitrios betrayed the lot of you by sending to the police, anonymously, a dossier convicting the seven of you. Is that true?'

'Dimitrios behaved very badly to us all,' said Mr Peters huskily.

'It was also said that Dimitrios had become an addict himself. Is that true?'

'Unhappily, it is. Otherwise I do not think he would have betrayed us. We were making so much money for him.'

'I was also told there was talk of vengeance, that you all threatened to kill Dimitrios as soon as you were free.'

'*I* did not threaten,' Mr Peters corrected him. 'Some of the others did so. Galindo, for example, was always a hothead.'

'I see. You did not threaten: you preferred to act.'

'I don't understand you, Mr Latimer.' And he looked as if he really did not understand.

'No? Let me put it to you this way. Dimitrios was murdered near Istanbul roughly two months ago. Very shortly after the time when the murder could have taken place, you were in Athens. That is not very far from Istanbul, is it?

Dimitrios, it is said, died a poor man. Now is that likely? As you have just pointed out, his gang made a lot of money for him in 1931. From what I have heard of him, he was not the man to lose money he had made. Do you know what is in my mind, Mr Peters? I am wondering whether it would not be reasonable to suppose that you killed Dimitrios for his money. What have you to say to that?'

Mr Peters did not answer for a moment but contemplated Latimer unhappily in the manner of a good shepherd about to admonish an erring lamb.

Then he said: 'Mr Latimer, I think that you are very indiscreet.'

'Do you?'

'And also very fortunate. Just suppose that I had, as you suggest, killed Dimitrios. Think what I would be forced to do. I would be forced to kill you also, now wouldn't I?' He put his hand in his breast pocket. It emerged holding the Lüger pistol. 'You see, I lied to you just now. I admit it. I was so curious to know what you were going to do if you thought I was unarmed. Besides, it seemed so impolite to come here carrying a pistol. The fact that I did not bring the pistol with me because of you would be a difficult one to prove. So I lied. Do you understand my feelings a little? I am so anxious to have your confidence.'

'All of which is as skilful a reply to an accusation of murder as one could wish for.'

Mr Peters put away his pistol wearily. 'Mr Latimer, this is not a detective story. There is no *need* to be so stupid. Even if you cannot be discreet, at least use your imagination. Is it likely that Dimitrios would make a will in my favour? No. Then how do you suppose that I could kill him for his money? People in these days do not keep their wealth in treasure chests. Come now, Mr Latimer, let us please be sensible. Let us eat dinner together and then talk business. I suggest that after dinner we drink coffee in my apartment – it is a little more comfortable than this room – though if you would prefer to go to a café I shall understand. You probably disapprove of me. I really cannot blame you. But at least let us cultivate the illusion of friendship.'

For a moment Latimer felt himself warming to Mr Peters. True, the last part of his appeal had been accompanied by an almost visible accretion of self-pity, but he had not smiled. Besides, the man had already made him feel a fool: it would be too much if he made him feel a prig as well. At the same time . . .

'I am as hungry as you,' he said, 'and I can see no reason why I should prefer a café to your apartment. At the same time, Mr Peters, anxious though I am to be friendly, I feel that I should warn you now that unless I have, this evening, a satisfactory explanation of your asking me to meet you here in Paris, I shall – half a million francs or no half a million francs – leave by the first available train. Is that clear?'

Mr Peters' smile returned. 'It could not be clearer, Mr Latimer. And may I say how much I appreciate your frankness?' The smile became rancid. 'How much better if we could always be so frank, if we could always open our hearts to our fellow men without fear, fear of being misunderstood, misinterpreted! How much easier this life of ours would be! But we are so blind, so very blind. If the Great One chooses that we should do things of which the world may disapprove, let us not be ashamed of those things. For we are, after all, merely doing his Will and how can we understand His purposes? How?'

'I don't know.'

'Ah! None of us knows, Mr Latimer. None of us knows – until he reaches the Other Side.'

'Quite so. Where shall we dine? There is a Danish place near here, isn't there?'

Mr Peters struggled into his overcoat. 'No, Mr Latimer, as you are doubtless well aware, there is not.' He sighed unhappily. 'It is unkind of you to make fun of me. And in any case I prefer French cooking.'

Mr Peters' capacity for making him feel a fool was, Latimer reflected as they descended the stairs, remarkable.

★

At Mr Peters' suggestion and expense they ate in a cheap restaurant in the Rue Jacob. Afterwards they went to the Impasse des Huit Anges.

'What about Caillé?' said Latimer as they climbed the dusty stairs.

'He is away. At the moment I am in sole possession.'

'I see.'

Mr Peters, who was breathing heavily by the time they had reached the second landing, paused for a moment. 'You have concluded, I suppose, that I am Caillé.'

'Yes.'

Mr Peters began to climb again. The stairs creaked under his weight. Latimer, following two or three stairs behind, was reminded of a circus elephant picking its way unwillingly up a pyramid of coloured blocks to perform a balancing trick. They reached the fourth floor. Mr Peters stopped and, standing panting before a battered door, hauled out a bunch of keys. A moment later he pushed open the door, pressed a switch and waved Latimer in.

The room ran from front to back of the house and was divided into two by a curtain to the left of the door. The half beyond the curtain was of a different shape from that which contained the door as it included the space between the end of the landing, the rear wall and the next house. The space formed an alcove. At each end of the room was a tall French window.

But if it was, architecturally speaking, the sort of room that one would expect to find in a French house of that type and age, it was in every other respect fantastic.

The first thing that Latimer saw was the dividing curtain. It was of imitation cloth of gold. The walls and ceiling were distempered an angry blue and bespattered with gold five-pointed stars. Scattered all over the floor, so that not a square inch of it showed, were cheap Moroccan rugs. They overlapped a good deal so that in places there were humps of three and even four thicknesses of rug. There were three huge divans piled high with cushions, some tooled leather ottoman seats and a Moroccan table with a brass tray upon it. In one corner stood an enormous brass gong. The light came from fretted oak lanterns. In the centre of it all stood a small chromium-plated electric radiator. There was a choking smell of upholstery dust.

'Home!' said Mr Peters. 'Take your things off, Mr Latimer. Would you like to see the rest of the place?'

'Very much.'

'Outwardly, just another uncomfortable French house,' commented Mr Peters as he toiled up the stairs again. 'Actually an oasis in a desert of discomfort. This is my bedroom.'

Latimer had another glimpse of French Morocco. This time it was adorned by a pair of crumpled flannel pyjamas.

'And the toilet.'

Latimer looked at the toilet and learned that his host had a spare set of false teeth.

'Now,' said Mr Peters, 'I will show you something curious.'

He led the way out on to the landing. Facing them was a large clothes cupboard. He opened the door and struck a match. Along the back of the cupboard was a row of metal clothes pegs. Grasping the centre one, he turned it like a latch and pulled. The back of the cupboard swung towards them and Latimer felt the night air on his face and heard the noises of the city.

'There is a narrow iron platform running along the outside wall to the next house,' explained Mr Peters. 'There is another cupboard there like this one. You can see nothing because there are only blank walls facing us. Equally, no one could see us should we choose to leave that way. It was Dimitrios who had this done.'

'Dimitrios!'

'Dimitrios owned all three of these houses. They were kept empty for reasons of privacy. Sometimes, they were used as stores. These two floors were used for meetings. Morally, no doubt, the houses still belong to Dimitrios. Fortunately for me, he took the precaution of buying them in my name. I also conducted the negotiations. The police never found out about them. I was able, therefore, to move in when I came out of prison. In case Dimitrios should ever wonder what had happened to his property, *I* took the precaution of buying them from myself in the name of Caillé. Do you like Algerian coffee?'

'Yes.'

'It takes a little longer to prepare than French, but I prefer it. Shall we go downstairs again?'

They went downstairs. Having seen Latimer uncomfortably ensconced amid a sea of cushions, Mr Peters disappeared into the alcove.

Latimer got rid of some of the cushions and looked about him. It was odd to feel that the house had once belonged to Dimitrios. Yet the evidence around him of the tenancy of the preposterous Mr Peters was a good deal odder. There was a small (fretted) shelf above his head. On it were paperbound books. There was *Pearls of Everyday Wisdom*. That was the one he had been reading in the train from Athens. There was, besides, Plato's Symposium, in French and uncut, an anthology called *Poèmes Erotiques*, which had no author's name on it and *had* been cut, Aesop's *Fables* in English, Mrs Humphry Ward's *Robert Elsmere* in French, a German Gazetteer, and several books by Dr Frank Crane in a language which Latimer took to be Danish.

Mr Peters came back carrying a Moroccan tray on which were a curious looking coffee percolator, a spirit lamp, two cups and a Moroccan cigarette box. The spirit lamp he lit and put under the percolator. The cigarettes he placed beside Latimer on the divan. Then he reached up above Latimer's head, brought down one of the Danish books and flicked over one or two of the pages. A small photograph fluttered to the floor. He picked it up and handed it to Latimer.

'Do you recognize him, Mr Latimer?'

It was a faded head and shoulders photograph of a middle-aged man with . . .

Latimer looked up. 'It's Dimitrios!' he exclaimed. 'Where did you get it?'

Mr Peters took the photograph from Latimer's fingers. 'You recognize it? Good.' He sat down on one of the ottoman seats and adjusted the spirit lamp. Then he looked up. If it had been possible for Mr Peters' wet, lustreless eyes to gleam, Latimer would have said that they were gleaming with pleasure.

'Help yourself to cigarettes, Mr Latimer,' he said. 'I am going to tell you a story.'

11
Paris, 1928–1931

'Often, when the day's work is done,' said Mr Peters reminiscently, 'I sit by the fire, like this, and wonder if my life has been as successful as it might have been. True, I have made money – a little property, some *rentes*, a few shares here and there – but it is not of money that I think. Money is not everything. What have I done with my life in this world of ours? I think sometimes that it would have been better if I had married and brought up a family, but I have always been too restless, too interested in this world of ours as a whole. Perhaps it is that I have never known what I have wanted of life. So many of us poor human creatures are like that. We go on year after year, ever seeking, ever hoping – for what? We do not know. Money? Only when we have little. I sometimes think that he who has only a crust is happier than many millionaires. For the man with a crust knows what he wants – two crusts. His life is not complicated by possessions. I only know that there *is* something that I want above all else. Yet, how shall I know what it is? I have –' he waved a hand towards the bookshelf '– sought consolation in philosophy and the arts. Plato, H. G. Wells; yes, I have read widely. These things comfort, yet they do not satisfy.' He smiled bravely, the victim of an almost unbearable *Weltschmerz*. 'We must all just wait until the Great One summons us.'

Waiting for him to go on, Latimer wondered if he had

ever before disliked anyone quite as much as he now disliked Mr Peters. It was incredible that he should believe in this tawdry nonsense of his. Yet believe in it he obviously did. It was that belief which made the man so loathsome. If he had his tongue in his cheek he would have been a good joke. As it was he was anything but a joke. His mind was divided too neatly. With one half he could peddle drugs and buy *rentes* and read *Poèmes Erotiques,* while with the other he could excrete a warm, sickly fluid to conceal his obscene soul. You could do nothing but dislike him.

Then, Latimer turned to watch the subject of these reflections carefully, almost lovingly, adjusting the coffee percolator, and thought how difficult it was to dislike a man when he was making coffee for you. The stubby fingers gave the lid a gentle, congratulatory pat and Mr Peters straightened his back and turned again with a sigh of satisfaction.

'Yes, Mr Latimer, most of us go through life without knowing what we want of it. But Dimitrios, you know, was not like that. Dimitrios knew exactly what he wanted. He wanted money and he wanted power. Just those two things; as much of them as he could get. The curious thing is that I helped him to get them.

'It was in 1928 that I first set eyes on Dimitrios. It was here in Paris. I was, at the time, the part-owner, with a man named Giraud, of a *boîte* in the rue Blanche. We called it *Le Kasbah Parisien* and it was a very jolly and cosy place with divans and amber lights and rugs. I had met Giraud in Marrakesh and we decided that everything should be just like a place we knew there. Everything was Moroccan; everything, that is, except the band for dancing which was South American.

'We opened it in 1926 which was a good year in Paris. The Americans and English, but especially the Americans, had money to spend on champagne and the French used to come, too. Most Frenchmen are sentimental about Morocco unless they have done their military service there. And the *Kasbah was* Morocco. We had Arab and Senegalese waiters and the champagne actually came from Meknes. It was a little sweet for the Americans, but very nice all the same and quite cheap.

'With a *boîte*, you know, it takes time to build up a clientèle and you have to have luck. It is curious how everyone will suddenly begin to go to one particular place in the quarter for no other reason than that everyone else is going there. There are other ways of filling one's place, of course. The tourist guides will bring people to you but the guides have to be paid and the profit is reduced. Another way is to let your place be one where special sorts of people may meet. But it takes time to be known for one's type of clientèle and the police are not always friendly even though one does not break the law. It is best and cheapest to have luck. And Giraud and I had luck in due course. Naturally we had to work for it. But it came. We had a good *chasseur*, the tango was *chic* because of Valentino, and our South Americans soon learned to play well so that people came to dance. When more people came we had to put out more tables so that the floor was smaller, but it did not make any difference. People still came to dance. We used to stay open until five o'clock in the morning and people would come on from other places to ours.

'For two years we made money and then, as is the way with such places, the clientèle began to change in character. We had more French and fewer Americans, more *maquereaux* and fewer gentlemen, more *poules* and fewer chic ladies. We still made a profit but it was not as great and we had to do more for it. I began to think that it was time to move on.

'It was Giraud who brought Dimitrios to *Le Kasbah*.

'As I said, I had met Giraud when I was in Marrakesh. He was a half-caste, his mother being an Arab and his father a French soldier. He was born in Algiers and had a French passport.

'Mostly you would not have known that he had Arab blood. It was only when you saw him with Arabs that you knew. He never really liked Arabs. I never really liked him. It was not that he did not trust me – that was no more than hurtful to me – but that I could not trust him. If I had had enough money to open *Le Kasbah* by myself I would not have taken him as a partner. He would try to trick me over the accounts and though he never succeeded I did not like it. I cannot stand dishonesty. By the spring of 1928 I was very weary of Giraud.

'I do not know exactly how he met Dimitrios. I think that it was at some *boîte* higher up the rue Blanche; for we did not open until eleven o'clock and Giraud liked to dance at other places beforehand. But, one evening, he brought Dimitrios into *Le Kasbah* and then took me aside. He remarked that profits had been getting smaller and said that we could make some money for ourselves if we did business with this friend of his, Dimitrios Makropoulos.

'The first time I saw Dimitrios I was not impressed by him. He was, I thought, just such a type of *maquereau* as I had seen before. His clothes fitted tightly and he had greying hair and polished fingernails and he looked at women in a way that those who came to *Le Kasbah* would not like. But I went over to his table with Giraud and we shook hands. Then he pointed to the chair beside him and told me to sit down. One would have thought that I was a waiter instead of the *patron*.'

He turned his watery eyes to Latimer. 'You may think, Mr Latimer, that, for one who was not impressed, I remember the occasion very clearly. That is true. I do remember it clearly. You understand, I did not then know Dimitrios as I came to know him later. He made his impression without seeming to do so. At the time he irritated me. Without sitting down, I asked him what he wanted.

'For a moment he looked at me. He had very soft, brown eyes, you know. Then he said: "I want champagne, my friend. Have you any objection? I can pay for it, you know. Are you going to be polite to me or shall I take my business proposals to more intelligent people?"

'I am an even-tempered man. I do not like trouble. I often think how much pleasanter a place this world of ours would be if people were polite and softly spoken with one another. But there are times when it is difficult. I told Dimitrios that nothing would induce me to be polite to him and that he could go when he pleased.

'But for Giraud he would have gone and I should not be sitting here talking to you. Giraud sat down at the table with him, apologizing for me. Dimitrios was watching me while Giraud was speaking, and I could see that he was wondering about me.

'I was now quite sure that I did not want to do business of any kind with this Dimitrios, but because of Giraud I agreed to listen, and we sat down together while Dimitrios told us what his proposal was. He talked very convincingly, and at last I agreed to do what he wanted. We had been in association with Dimitrios for several months, when one day . . .'

'Just a moment,' interrupted Latimer; 'what was this association? Was this the beginning of the drug-peddling?'

Mr Peters hesitated and frowned. 'No, Mr Latimer, it was not.' He hesitated again and then broke suddenly into French. 'I will tell you what our business together was if you insist, but it is so difficult to explain these things to a person who does not understand the milieu, who is not sympathetic. It involves matters so much outside your experience.'

Latimer's 'Indeed?' was a trifle acid.

'You see, Mr Latimer, I have read one of your books. It terrified me. There was about it an atmosphere of intolerance, of prejudice, of ferocious moral rectitude that I found quite unnerving.'

'I see.'

'I am not one of those persons,' pursued Mr Peters, 'who object to the idea of capital punishment. You, I gather, are. The practical side of execution by hanging shocks you. Yet, shuddering with horror at your own barbarity, you proceeded to hunt this unfortunate murderer of yours with a kind of compassionate glee that was quite repellent to me. Your attitude reminded me of that of a sentimental young man as he follows his rich aunt's coffin to the graveside: his eyes are filled with tears, but his heart is leaping for joy. The Spaniard, you know, finds the objections of the English-speaking peoples to bullfighting very odd. What the simple fellow does not realize is that he has neglected to show that it is a moral and legal necessity for him to torture the horses and the bull and that he dislikes doing it. Please do not misunderstand me, Mr Latimer. I do not fear your moral censure, but I resent, mildly yet quite definitely, your being shocked.'

'As you have not yet told me what I am expected to be shocked at,' Latimer pointed out irritably, 'it is a little difficult for me to answer you.'

'Yes, yes, of course. But, forgive me, does not your interest in Dimitrios arise largely from the fact that you are shocked by him?'

Latimer thought for a moment. 'I think that that may be true. But it is just because I am shocked by him that I am trying to understand, to explain him. I do not believe in the inhuman, professional devil that one reads about in crime stories; and yet everything that I have heard about Dimitrios suggests that he consistently acted with quite revolting inhumanity – not just once or twice, but consistently.'

'Are the desires for money and power inhuman? With money and power a vain man can do so much to give himself pleasure. His vanity was one of the first things that I noticed about Dimitrios. It was that quiet, profound vanity that makes the man who has it so much more dangerous than ordinary people with their peacock antics. Come now, Mr Latimer, be reasonable! The difference between Dimitrios and the more respectable type of successful businessman is only a difference of method – legal method or illegal method. Both are in their respective ways equally ruthless.'

'Rubbish!'

'No doubt. It is interesting, though, is it not, to note that I am now attempting to defend Dimitrios against attack from the forces of moral rectitude. He would not, I feel sure, be at all grateful to me for doing so. Dimitrios was, for all his apparent *savoir faire*, hopelessly uneducated. The words "moral rectitude" would mean nothing to him. Ah! The coffee is ready.'

He poured it out in silence, raised his own cup to his nose and sampled the aroma. Then he put the cup down.

'Dimitrios,' he said, 'was connected at the time with what I believe you call the white slave traffic. It is such an interesting phrase to me. "Traffic" – a word full of horrible significance. "White slave" – consider the implications of the adjective. Does anyone talk nowadays about the *coloured* slave traffic? I think not. Yet the majority of the women involved are coloured. I fail to see why the consequences of the traffic should be any more disagreeable to a white girl from a Bucharest slum than to a negro girl from Dakar or a Chinese girl from Harbin. The League of Nations Committee is unprejudiced enough to appreciate that aspect of the question. They are intelligent enough, too, to mistrust the word "slave". They refer to the "traffic in women".

'I have never liked the business. It is impossible to treat human beings as one would treat ordinary inanimate merchandise. There is always trouble. There is always the possibility, too, that in an isolated case the adjective "white" might have a religious instead of a merely racial application. From my experience, I should say that the possibility is remote, but there it is. I may be illogical and sentimental, but I should not care to be associated with anything like that. Besides, the overhead expenses of a trafficker in what is considered a fair way of business are enormous. There are always false birth, marriage and death certificates to be obtained and travelling expenses and bribes to pay, quite apart from the cost of maintaining several identities. You have no idea of the cost of forged documents, Mr Latimer. There used to be three recognized sources of supply: one in Zürich, one in Amsterdam and one in Brussels. All neutrals! Odd, isn't it? You used to be able to get a false-real Danish passport – that is, a real Danish passport treated chemically to remove the original entries and photograph and then filled in with new ones – for, let me see, about two thousand francs at the present rate of exchange. A real-false – manufactured from start to finish by the agent – would have cost you a little less, say fifteen hundred. Nowadays you would have to pay twice as much. Most of the business is done here in Paris now. It is the refugees, of course. The point is that a trafficker needs plenty of capital. If he is known there are always plenty of people willing to provide it, but they expect fantastic dividends. It is better to have one's own capital.

'Dimitrios had his own capital, but he also had access to capital which was not his own. He represented certain very rich men. He was never at a loss for money. When he came to Giraud and me he was in a different sort of difficulty. Owing to League of Nations activities the laws in quite a number of countries had been altered and tightened up in such a way that it was sometimes very difficult indeed to get women from one place to another. All very praiseworthy, but a great nuisance to men like Dimitrios. It was not that it made it impossible for them to do their business. It didn't. But it made things more complicated and expensive for them.

'Before Dimitrios came to us he had had a very simple technique. He knew people in Alexandria who would advise him about their requirements. Then he would go to, say, Poland, recruit the women, take them to France on their own passports and then ship them from Marseilles. That was all. It was enough to say that the girls were going to fulfil a theatrical engagement. When the regulations were tightened up, however, it was no longer as simple. The night he came to *Le Kasbah* he told us that he had just encountered his first trouble. He had recruited twelve women from a Madame in Vilna, but the Poles would not let him bring them out without guarantees as to their destination and the respectability of their future employment. Respectability! But that was the law.

'Naturally, Dimitrios had told the Polish authorities that he would provide the guarantees. It would have been fatal for him not to have done so, for then he would have been suspect. Somehow he had to obtain the guarantees. That was where Giraud and I came in. We were to say that we were employing the girls as cabaret dancers and deal with any inquiries that might be made by the Polish Consular authorities. As long as they stayed in Paris for a week or so, we were perfectly safe. If inquiries were made after that we knew nothing. They had completed their engagement and gone. Where they had gone to was no business of ours.

'That was the way Dimitrios put it to us. He said that for our part of the affair he would pay us five thousand francs. It was money easily earned, but I was doubtful, and it was Giraud who finally persuaded me to agree. But I told Dimitrios that my agreement only applied to this particular case and that I could not consider myself committed to helping him again. Giraud grumbled, but agreed to accept the condition.

'A month later Dimitrios came to see us again, paid us the balance of the five thousand francs and said that he had another job for us. I objected, but, as Giraud immediately pointed out, we had had no trouble on the first occasion and my objection was not very firm. The money was useful. It paid the South Americans for a week.

'I believe now that Dimitrios lied to us about that first five thousand francs. I do not think that we earned it. I think he gave it to us simply to gain our confidence. It was like him to do a thing like that. Another man might try to trick you into serving his ends, but Dimitrios bought you. Yet he bought you cheaply. He set one's common sense fighting against one's instinctive suspicions of him.

'I have said that we earned that first five thousand francs without trouble. The second caused us a lot of trouble. The Polish authorities made some *chi-chi*, and we had the police visiting us and asking questions. Worse, we had to have these women in *Le Kasbah* to prove that we were employing them. They could not dance a step and were a great inconvenience to us, as we had to be amiable to them in case one should go to the police and tell the truth. They drank champagne all the time, and if Dimitrios had not agreed to pay for it we should have lost money.

'He was, of course, very apologetic and said that there had been a mistake. He paid us ten thousand francs for our trouble and promised that if we would continue to help him there would be no more Polish girls and no more *chi-chi*. After some argument we agreed, and for several months we were paid our ten thousand francs. We had during that time only occasional visits from the police, and there was no unpleasantness. But at last we had trouble again. This time it was because of the Italian authorities. Both Giraud and I were questioned by the examining magistrate for the district and kept for a day at the Commissariat. The day after that I quarrelled with Giraud.

'I say that I quarrelled. It would be more correct to say that our quarrel became open. I have told you that I did not like Giraud. He was crude and stupid and, as I have said, he sometimes tried to cheat me. He was suspicious, too; suspicious in a loud, stupid way like an animal, and he encouraged the wrong sort of clientèle. His friends were detestable: *maquereaux*, all of them. He used to call people "*mon gar*". He would have been better as the *patron* of a bistro. For all I know he may be one now, but I think it more likely that he is in a prison. He often became violent when he was angry and sometimes injured people badly.

'That day after our unpleasantness with the police I said that we should have no more to do with this business of the women. That made him angry. He said that we should be fools to give up ten thousand francs a month because of a few police and that I was too nervous for his taste. I understood his point of view. He had had much to do with the police both in Marrakesh and Algiers, and he had a contempt for them. As long as he could keep out of prison and make money he was satisfied. I have never thought that way. I do not like the police to be interested in me, even though they cannot arrest me. Giraud was right. I was nervous. But although I understood his point of view I could not agree with it, and I said so. I also said that, if he wished, he could buy my share in *Le Kasbah Parisien* for the amount of money I had originally invested.

'It was a sacrifice on my part, you know, but I was tired of Giraud and wanted to be rid of him. I did get rid of him. He agreed immediately. That night we saw Dimitrios and explained the situation to him. Giraud was delighted with his bargain and enjoyed himself very much cracking clumsy jokes at my expense. Dimitrios smiled at these jokes, but when Giraud left us alone for a moment, he asked me to leave soon after he did and meet him at a café as he had something to say to me.

'I very nearly did not go. On the whole, I think that it was as well that I did go. I profited by my association with Dimitrios. There are, I think, very few associates of Dimitrios who could say as much, but I was lucky. Besides, I think that he had a respect for my intelligence. Generally he could bluff me, but not always.

'He was waiting in the café for me, and I sat down beside him and asked him what he wanted. I was never polite to him.

'He said: "I think you are wise to leave Giraud. The business with the women has become too dangerous. It was always difficult. Now I have finished with it."

'I asked him if he proposed to tell Giraud that and he smiled.

' "Not yet," he said. "Not until you have your money from him."

'I said suspiciously that he was very kind, but he shook his head impatiently. "Giraud is a fool," he said. "If you had not been there with him, I should have made other arrangements about the women. Now, I am offering you a chance to work with me. I should be a fool if I made you angry with me to begin with by costing you your invest-ment in *Le Kasbah*."

'Then he asked me if I knew anything about the heroin business. I did know a little about it. He then told me that he had sufficient capital to buy twenty kilogrammes a month and finance its distribution in Paris and asked me if I were interested in working for him.

'Now, twenty kilogrammes of heroin is a serious thing,

Mr Latimer. It is worth a lot of money. I asked him how he proposed to distribute so much. He said that, for the moment, that would be his affair. What he wanted me to do was to negotiate the purchases abroad and find ways of bringing it into the country. If I agreed to his proposal I was to begin by going to Bulgaria as his representative, dealing with suppliers there of whom he already knew and arranging for the transport of the stuff to Paris. He offered me 10 per cent of the value of every kilo I supplied him with.

'I said that I would think it over, but my mind was already made up. With the price of heroin as it was then, I knew that I would make nearly twenty thousand francs a month. I also knew that he was going to make a great deal more than that for himself. Even if, with my commission and expenses, he had to pay in effect fifteen thousand francs a kilo for the stuff, it would be good business for him. Selling heroin by the gramme in Paris, one can get nearly one hundred thousand francs a kilo for it. With the commissions to the actual pedlars and others, he would make not less than thirty thousand francs on each kilo. That meant over half a million francs a month for him. Capital is a wonderful thing if one knows just what to do with it and does not mind a little risk.

'In the September of 1928 I went to Bulgaria for Dimitrios with instructions from him to get the first twenty kilos to him by November. He had already begun to make arrangements with agents and pedlars. The sooner I could get the stuff the better.

'Dimitrios had given me the name of a man in Sofia who would put me in touch with the suppliers. This man did so. He also arranged for the credits with which I was to make the purchases. He—'

Latimer had an idea. He said suddenly: 'What was this man's name?'

Mr Peters frowned at the interruption. 'I do not think that you ought to ask me that, Mr Latimer.'

'Was it Vazoff?'

Mr Peters' eyes watered at him. 'Yes, it was.'

'And were the credits arranged through the Eurasian Credit Trust?'

'You evidently know a great deal more than I had thought.' Mr Peters was obviously not pleased by the fact. 'May I ask . . .?'

'I was guessing. But you need not have worried about compromising Vazoff. He died three years ago.'

'I am aware of it. Did you guess that Vazoff was dead? And how much more guessing have you done, Mr Latimer?'

'That is all. Please continue.'

'Frankness . . .' began Mr Peters, and then stopped and drank his coffee. 'We will return to the subject,' he said at last. 'Yes, Mr Latimer, I admit that you are right. Through Vazoff, I purchased the supplies Dimitrios needed and paid for them with drafts on Eurasian Credit Trust of Sofia. There was no difficulty about that. My real task was to transport the stuff to France. I decided to send it by rail to Salonika and ship it from there to Marseilles.'

'As heroin?'

'Obviously not. But I must confess it was difficult to know how to disguise it. The only goods which come into France from Bulgaria regularly, and which would not, therefore, be subject to special examination by the French

Customs, were things like grain and tobacco and attar of roses. Dimitrios was pressing for delivery and I was at my wits' end.' He paused dramatically.

'Well, how *did* you smuggle it?'

'In a coffin, Mr Latimer. The French, I reflected, are a race with a great respect for the solemnity of death. Have you ever attended a French funeral? *Pompe funèbre*, you know. It is most impressive. No customs official, I felt certain, would care to play the ghoul. I purchased the coffin in Sofia. It was a beautiful thing with very fine carving on it. I also purchased a suit of mourning clothes and accompanied the coffin myself. I am a man who responds very readily to emotion and really I was most moved by the marks of simple respect for my grief shown by the stevedores who handled the coffin at the dock. Not even my own personal luggage was examined at Customs.

'I had warned Dimitrios, and a hearse was waiting for me and the coffin. I was pleased by my success, but Dimitrios, when I saw him, shrugged. I could not, he said very reasonably, arrive in France with a coffin every month. I think he thought the whole affair a little unbusinesslike. He was right, of course. He had, however, a suggestion. There was an Italian shipping line which ran one cargo steamer a month from Varna to Genoa. The stuff could be shipped to Genoa in small cases and manifested as special tobacco consigned to France. That would prevent the Italian Customs examining it. There was a man in Nice who could arrange for the transport of the stuff from Genoa by bribing the warehouse people to release it from bond, and then smuggling it through by road. I wished to know how that would affect my financial interest in the supplies. He said that I should lose nothing as there was other work for me to do.

'It was curious how we all accepted his leadership almost without question. Yes, he had the money, but there was more than that to it. He dominated us because he knew precisely what he wanted and precisely how to get it with the least possible trouble and at the lowest possible cost. He knew how to find the people to work for him, too, and, when he had found them, he knew how to handle them.

'There were seven of us who took our instructions directly from Dimitrios, and not one was the sort of person to take instructions easily. For instance, Visser, the Dutchman, had sold German machine-guns to the Chinese, spied for the Japanese and served a term of imprisonment for killing a coolie in Batavia. He was not an easy man to handle. It was he who made the arrangements with the clubs and bars through which we reached the addicts.

'You see, the system of distribution was very carefully organized. Both Lenôtre and Galindo had for several years been peddling drugs which they bought from a man in the employ of a big French wholesale drug manufacturer. That sort of thing used to be quite easy before the 1931 regulations. Both those men knew well those who needed the stuff and where to find them. Before Dimitrios came on the scene they had been dealing mostly in morphine and cocaine and always they had been handicapped by limited supplies. When Dimitrios offered them unlimited supplies of heroin they were quite ready to abandon the wholesale chemist and sell their clients heroin.

'But that was only one part of the business. Drug addicts, you know, are always very eager to get other people to take drugs too. Consequently, your circle of consumers is ever-widening. It is most important, as you may imagine, to see that when you are approached by new customers they are not representatives of the *Brigade des Stupéfiants* or other similar undesirables. That was where Visser's work came in. The would-be buyer would come to, say, Lenôtre in the first place on the recommendation of a regular customer known to Lenôtre. But, on being asked for drugs, Lenôtre would pretend to be astonished. Drugs? He knew nothing of such things. Personally, he never used them. But, if one did use them, he had heard that the place to go to was the So-and-So Bar. At the So-and-So Bar, which would be on Visser's list, the prospective customer would receive much the same sort of answer. Drugs? No. Nothing of that kind at the So-and-So Bar, but if it should be possible to call in again the following night, there might possibly be someone who could help. The following night, the Grand Duchess would be there.

'She was a curious woman. She had been brought into the business by Visser and was, I think, the only one of us Dimitrios had not found for himself. She was very clever. Her capacity for weighing up complete strangers was extra-ordinary. She could, I think, tell the most cleverly disguised detective just by looking at him across a room. It was her business to examine the person who wanted to buy and decide whether he or she should be supplied or not and how much was to be charged. She was very valuable to us.

'The other man was the Belgian, Werner. It was he who dealt with the small pedlars. He had been a chemist at one time and he used, I believe, to dilute the heroin. Dimitrios never mentioned that part of the business.

'Some dilution very soon became necessary. Within six months of our beginning, I had had to increase the monthly heroin supply to fifty kilos. And I had other work to do. Lenôtre and Galindo had reported in the early stages that, if they were to get all the business they knew of, they would have to have morphine and cocaine to sell as well as heroin. Morphine addicts did not always like heroin, and cocaine addicts would sometimes refuse it if they could get cocaine elsewhere. I had then to arrange for supplies of morphine and cocaine. The morphine problem was a simple one as it could be supplied at the same time and by the same people as the heroin, but the cocaine was a different matter. For that, it was necessary to go to Germany. I had plenty to do.

'We had our troubles, of course. They usually came to my part of the business. By the time we had been operating for a year, I had made several alternative arrangements for bringing in our supplies. In addition to the Genoa route for heroin and morphine which Lamare handled, I had come to terms with a sleeping car attendant on the Orient Express. He used to take the stuff aboard at Sofia and deliver it when the train was shunted into the siding in Paris. It was not a very safe route and I had to take elaborate precautions to protect myself in case of trouble, but it was rapid. Cocaine used to come in in cases of machinery from Germany. We had also begun to receive consignments of heroin from an Istanbul factory. These were brought by a cargo boat which left them floating outside the port of Marseilles in anchored containers for Lamare to collect at night.

'There was one week of disaster. In the last week of the June of 1929, fifteen kilos of heroin were seized on the Orient Express, and the police arrested six of my men including the sleeping car attendant. That would have been bad enough, but during the same week Lamare had to abandon a consignment of forty kilos of heroin and morphine near Sospel. He himself escaped but we were in a serious difficulty, for the loss of those fifty-five kilos meant that we were left with only eight kilos to meet commitments for over fifty. None was due on the Istanbul boat for several days. We were in despair. Lenôtre and Galindo and Werner had a terrible time. Two of Galindo's clientèle committed suicide, and in one of the bars there was a *fracas* in which Werner had his head cut.

'I did the best I could. I went to Sofia myself and brought back ten kilos in a trunk, but that was not enough. Dimitrios did not, I must say, blame me. It would have been unfair to have done so. But he was angry. He decided that, in future, reserve stocks must be held. It was soon after that week that he bought these houses. Until then we had always met him in a room over a café near the Porte d'Orleans. Now he said that these houses should be our headquarters. We never knew where he lived and could never get in touch with him until he chose to telephone one or other of us. We were to discover later that this ignorance of his address put us at a disastrous disadvantage. But other things happened before we made that discovery.

'The task of creating stocks was left to me. It was by no means easy. If we were both to create stocks and to maintain existing supplies we had to increase the size of the consignments. That meant that there was a greater risk of seizure. It also meant that we had to find more new methods of bringing the stuff in. Things were complicated, too, by the Bulgarian Government's closing down the factory at Radomir from which we drew the bulk of our supplies. It soon opened again in a different part of the

country, but inevitably there were delays. We were forced
to rely more and more upon Istanbul.

'It was a trying time. In two months we lost by seizure
no less than ninety kilos of heroin, twenty of morphine and
five of cocaine. But, in spite of ups and downs, the stock
increased steadily. By the end of 1930, we had, beneath the
floorboards of those houses next door, two hundred and
fifty kilos of heroin, two hundred odd kilos of morphine,
ninety kilos of cocaine and a small quantity of prepared
Turkish opium.'

Mr Peters poured out the remainder of the coffee and
extinguished the spirit lamp. Then he took a cigarette,
wetted the end of it with his tongue and lit it.

'Have you ever known a drug addict, Mr Latimer?' he
asked suddenly.

'I don't think so.'

'Ah, you don't *think* so. You do not know for certain.
Yes, it is possible for a drug taker to conceal his little weak-
ness for quite a time. But he – especially *she* – cannot
conceal it indefinitely, you know. The process is always
roughly the same. It begins as an experiment. Half a
gramme, perhaps, is taken through the nostrils. It may
make you feel sick the first time, but you will try again and
the next time it will be as it should be. A delicious sen-
sation, warm, brilliant. Time stands still, but the mind
moves at a tremendous pace and, it seems to you, with
incredible efficiency. You were stupid; you become highly
intelligent. You were unhappy; you become carefree. What
you do not like you forget; and what you do like you experience with an intensity of pleasure undreamed of. Three
hours of paradise. And afterwards it is not too bad; not
nearly as bad as it was when you had too much champagne.

You want to be quiet; you feel a little ill at ease, that is all. Soon you are yourself again. Nothing has happened to you except that you have enjoyed yourself amazingly. If you do not wish to take the drug again, you tell yourself you need not do so. As an intelligent person you are superior to the stuff. Then, therefore, there is no logical reason why you should not enjoy yourself again, is there? Of course there isn't! And so you do. But this time it is a little disappointing. Your half a gramme was not quite enough. Disappointment must be dealt with. You must wander in paradise just once more before you decide not to take the stuff again. A trifle more; nearly a gramme perhaps. Paradise again and still you don't feel any the worse for it. And since you don't feel any the worse for it, why not continue? Everybody knows that the stuff does ultimately have a bad effect on you, but the moment you detect any bad effects *you* will stop. Only fools become addicts. One and a half grammes. It really is something to look forward to in life. Only three months ago everything was so dreary, but now . . . Two grammes. Naturally, as you are taking a little more it is only reasonable to expect to feel a little ill and depressed afterwards. It's four months now. You must stop soon. Two and a half grammes. Your nose and throat get so dry these days. Other people seem to get on your nerves, too. Perhaps it is because you are sleeping so badly. They make too much noise. They talk so loudly. And what are they saying? Yes, *what*? Things about *you*, vicious lies. You can see it in their faces. Three grammes. And there are other things to be considered, other dangers. You have to be careful. Food tastes horrible. You cannot remember things that you have to do; important things. Even if you should happen to remember them, there are so many other things to worry you apart from this beastliness of having to live. For instance, your nose keeps running: that is, it is not really running but you think it must be, so you have to keep touching it to make sure. Another thing: there is always a fly annoying you. This terrible fly will *never* leave you alone and in peace. It is on your face, on your hand, on your neck. You must pull yourself together. Three and a half grammes. You see the idea, Mr Latimer?'

'You don't seem to approve of drug-taking.'

'Approve!' Mr Peters stared, aghast. 'It is terrible, *terrible*! Lives are ruined. They lose the power to work yet they must find money to pay for their special stuff. Under such circumstances people become desperate and may even do something criminal to get it. I see what is in your mind, Mr Latimer. You feel that it is strange that I should have been connected with, that I should have made money out of, a thing of which I disapprove so sternly. But consider. If *I* had not made the money, someone else would have done so. Not one of those unfortunate creatures would have been any better off and I should have lost money.'

'What about this ever-increasing clientèle of yours? You cannot pretend that all of those your organization supplied were habitual drug-takers before you went to work.'

'Of course they were not. But that side of the business was nothing to do with *me*. That was Lenôtre and Galindo. And I may tell you that Lenôtre and Galindo and Werner, too, were themselves addicts. They used cocaine. It is harder on the constitution but, whereas one can become a dangerous heroin addict in a few months, one can spend several years killing oneself with cocaine.'

'What did Dimitrios take?'

'Heroin. It was a great surprise to us the first time we noticed it. We would meet him in this room as a rule at about six o'clock in the evening. It was on one of those evenings in the spring of 1931 when we had our surprise!

'Dimitrios arrived late. That in itself was unusual, but we took little notice of it. As a rule, at these meetings, he would sit very quietly with his eyes half-closed, looking a little troubled as though he had a headache, so that even when one became used to him one constantly wished to ask if all was well with him. Watching him sometimes I used to be amazed at myself for allowing myself to be led by him. Then I would see his face change as he turned to meet some objection from Visser – it was always Visser who objected – and I would understand. Visser was a violent man, and quick and cunning as well, but he seemed a child beside Dimitrios. Once when Dimitrios had been making a fool of him, Visser pulled out a pistol. He was white with rage. I could see his finger squeezing the trigger. If I had been Dimitrios, I would have prayed. But Dimitrios only smiled in the insolent way he had and, turning his back on Visser, began to talk to me about some business matter. Dimitrios was always quiet like that, even when he was angry.

'That was why we were so surprised that evening. He came in late and he stood inside the door looking at us for nearly a minute. Then he walked over to his place and sat down. Visser had been saying something about the *patron* of a café who had been making trouble and now he went on. There was nothing remarkable about what he was saying. I think he was telling Galindo that he must stop using the café as it was unsafe.

'Suddenly, Dimitrios leaned across the table, shouted "*Imbecile!*" and spat in Visser's face.

'Visser was as surprised as the rest of us. He opened his mouth to speak, but Dimitrios did not give him time to say anything. Before we could grasp what was happening, he was accusing Visser of the most fantastic things. The words poured out and he spat again like a guttersnipe.

'Visser went white and got to his feet with his hand in the pocket where he kept his pistol, but Lenôtre, who was beside him, got up, too, and whispered something to him which made Visser take his hand from his pocket. Lenôtre was used to people who had been taking drugs and he and Galindo and Werner had recognized the signs as soon as Dimitrios had entered the room. But Dimitrios had seen Lenôtre whisper and turned to him. From Lenôtre he came to the rest of us. We were fools, he told us, if we thought that he did not know that we were plotting against him. He called us a lot of very unpleasant names in French and Greek. Then he began to boast that he was cleverer than the rest of us together, that but for him we should be starving, that he alone was responsible for our success (which was true, although we did not like to be told it) and that he could do with us as he wished. He went on for half an hour, abusing us and boasting alternately. None of us said a word. Then, as suddenly as he had started, he stopped, stood up and walked out of the room.

'I suppose that we should have been prepared for treachery after that. Heroin addicts have a reputation for it. Yet we were not prepared. I think it may have been that we were so conscious of the amount of money he was making. I only know that, when he had gone, Lenôtre and Galindo laughed and asked Werner if the boss were paying for the stuff he used. Even Visser grinned. A joke was made of it, you see.

'Next time we saw Dimitrios he was quite normal and no reference was made to his outburst. But as the months went by, although we had no more outbursts, he became bad-tempered and little difficulties would make him angry. His appearance was changing, too. He looked thin and ill and his eyes were dull. He did not always come to the meetings.

'Then, we had our second warning.

'Early in September, he announced suddenly that he proposed to reduce the consignments for the next three months and use our stock. This startled us, and there were many objections. I was one of the objectors. I had had a great deal of trouble building up the stock and did not want to see it distributed without reason. The others reminded him of the trouble they had had when supplies ran out before. But Dimitrios would not listen. He had been warned, he said, that there was to be a new drive by the police. Not only, he said, would so large a stock compromise us seriously if it were discovered, but its seizure would be a serious financial loss. He, too, was sorry to see it go, but it was best to play for safety.

'I do not think that the notion that he might be liquidating his assets before he got out occurred to any of us, and you may say that for people of experience we were very trusting. You would be right to say that. With the exception of Visser we seemed always to be on the defensive in our dealings with Dimitrios. Even Lydia, who understood so much about people, was defeated by him. As for Visser, he was too paralysed by his own conceit to believe that anyone, even a drug addict, could betray him. Besides, why should we suspect him? We were making money, but he was making more, much more. What logical reason was there for suspecting him? Who could possibly have foreseen that he would behave like a madman?'

He shrugged. 'You know the rest. He turned informer. We were all arrested. I was in Marseilles with Lamare when we were caught. The police were quite clever. They watched us for a week before they took us. They hoped, I think, to catch us with some of the stuff. Luckily, we noticed them the day before we were due to take delivery of a big consignment from Istanbul. Lenôtre and Galindo and Werner were not so lucky. They had some of the stuff in their pockets. The police tried, of course, to make me tell them about Dimitrios and showed me the dossier he had sent them. They might as well have asked me for the moon. Visser, I found out later, knew more than the rest of us, but he did not tell the police what it was. He had other ideas. He told the police that Dimitrios had had an apartment in the seventeenth arrondissement. That was a lie. Visser wanted to get a lighter sentence than the rest of us. He did not. He died not long ago, poor fellow.' Mr Peters heaved a sigh and produced one of his cheroots.

Latimer touched his second cup of coffee. It was quite cold. He took a cigarette and accepted a light from his host's match.

'Well?' he said when he saw that the cheroot was alight. 'What then? I am still waiting to hear how I am to earn a half a million francs.'

Mr Peters smiled as if he were presiding at a Sunday School treat and Latimer had asked for a second currant bun. 'That, Mr Latimer, is part of another story.'

'What story?'

'The story of what happened to Dimitrios after he disappeared from view.'

'Well, what *did* happen to him?' Latimer demanded testily.

Without replying, Mr Peters picked up the photograph that lay on the table and handed it to him again.

Latimer looked at it and frowned. 'Yes, I've seen this. It's Dimitrios all right. What about it?'

Mr Peters smiled very sweetly and gently. 'That, Mr Latimer, is a photograph of Manus Visser.'

'What on earth do you mean?'

'I told you that Visser had other ideas about using the knowledge he had been clever enough to acquire about Dimitrios. What you saw on the mortuary table in Istanbul, Mr Latimer, was Visser after he had tried to put those ideas into practice.'

'But it was Dimitrios. I saw . . .'

'You saw the body of Visser, Mr Latimer, after Dimitrios had killed him. Dimitrios himself, I am glad to say, is alive and in good health.'

12

Monsieur C. K.

Latimer stared. His jaw had dropped and he knew that he looked ridiculous and that there was nothing to be done about the fact. Dimitrios was alive. It did not even occur to him to question the statement seriously. He knew instinctively that it was true. It was as if a doctor had warned him that he was suffering from a dangerous disease, the symptoms of which he had been only vaguely aware. He was surprised beyond words, resentful, curious and a little frightened, while his mind began to work feverishly to meet and deal with a new and strange set of conditions. He shut his mouth, then opened it again to say, feebly: 'I can't believe it.'

Mr Peters was clearly gratified by the effect of his announcement.

'I scarcely hoped,' he said, 'that you would have had no suspicions of the truth. Grodek, of course, understood. He had been puzzled by certain questions I asked him some time ago. When you came he was even more curious. That was why he wanted to know so much. But as soon as you told him that you had seen the body in Istanbul, he understood. He saw at once that the one thing that rendered you unique from my point of view was the fact of your having seen the face of the man buried as Dimitrios. It was obvious. Not to you, perhaps. I suppose that when one sees a perfect stranger on a mortuary slab and a policeman tells one that his name is Dimitrios Makropoulos, one assumes, if one has your respect for the police, that one has the truth of the matter. I *knew* that it was not Dimitrios you saw. But . . . I could not prove it. You, on the other hand, can. *You* can identify Manus Visser.' He paused significantly and then, as Latimer made no comment, added: 'How did they identify him as Dimitrios?'

'There was a French *carte d'identité*, issued in Lyons a year ago to Dimitrios Makropoulos, sewn inside the lining of his coat.' Latimer spoke mechanically. He was thinking of Grodek's toast to the English detective story and of Grodek's inability to stop himself laughing at his own joke. Heavens! What a fool the man must have thought him!

'A French *carte d'identité*!' echoed Mr Peters. 'That I find amusing. Very amusing.'

'It had been pronounced genuine by the French authorities and it had a photograph in it.'

Mr Peters smiled tolerantly. 'I could get you a dozen genuine French *cartes d'identité*, Mr Latimer, each in the name of Dimitrios Makropoulos and each with a different photograph. Look!' He drew a green *permis de séjour* from his pocket, opened it and, with his fingers over the space taken up by the identifying particulars, displayed the photograph in it. 'Does that look very much like me, Mr Latimer?'

Latimer shook his head.

'And yet,' declared Mr Peters, 'it *is* a genuine photograph of me taken three years ago. I made no effort to deceive. It is simply that I am not *photogénique*, that is all. Very few men are. The camera is a consistent liar. Dimitrios could have used photographs of anyone with the same type of face as Visser. That photograph I showed you a few moments ago is of someone like Visser.'

'If Dimitrios is still alive, where is he?'

'Here in Paris.' Mrs Peters leaned forward and patted Latimer's knee. 'You have been very reasonable, Mr Latimer,' he said kindly. 'I shall tell you everything.'

'It's very good of you,' said Latimer bitterly.

'No! No! You have a *right* to know,' said Mr Peters warmly. He pursed his lips with the air of one who knows justice when he sees it. 'I shall tell you everything,' he said again and relit his cheroot.

'As you may imagine,' he went on, 'we were all very angry with Dimitrios. Some of us threatened revenge. But, Mr Latimer, I have never been one to beat my head against a wall. Dimitrios had disappeared and there was no way of finding him. The indignities of prison life a memory, I purged my heart of malice and went abroad to regain my sense of proportion. I became a wanderer, Mr Latimer. A little business here, a little business there, travel and medi- tation – that was my life. I could afford to sit, when I wished, in a café and see this world of ours go by and try to understand my fellow men. How little true under- standing there is! As I go through this life of ours, Mr Latimer, I sometimes wonder if perhaps it is not all a dream and if one day we shall not wake up to find that we have only been asleep like children in a cradle rocked by the Great One. That will be a great day. I have, I know, done things of which I have been ashamed, but the Great One will understand. That is how I think of the Great One: as someone who understands that it is sometimes necessary, for business reasons, to do unpleasant things; someone who understands not as a judge in a courtroom,' he added a trifle vindictively, 'but as a *friend.*'

He wiped the corners of his mouth. 'You will think, Mr Latimer, that I am something of a mystic. Perhaps I am. I do not believe in coincidence. If the Great One wills that one shall meet a person, then one meets him. There is nothing strange about it. That was why, when I met Visser, I was not surprised. It was a little under two years ago that I met him, and in Rome.

'I had not, of course, seen him for five years. Poor fellow! He had had a bad time. A few months after his release from prison he was pressed for money and forged a cheque. They sent him back to prison for three years and then, when he came out, deported him. He was almost penniless and he could not work in France where he knew useful people. I could not blame him for feeling bitter.

'He asked me to lend him money. We had met in a café and he told me that he had to go to Zürich to buy a new passport, but that he had no money. His Dutch passport was useless because it was in his real name. I would have liked to have helped him; for, although I had never liked him very much, I felt sorry for him. But I hesitated. So often one's generous instincts run away with one. I should have been wiser to have said at once that I had no money to lend, but as I hesitated he knew that I had money. It was a foolish mistake on my part I thought at the time. It is only since that I have learned that my generous instinct was working for my own good.

'He became very pressing and swore that he would pay me back. This life of ours is so difficult sometimes, is it not? A person swears that he will repay money and you know that he is sincere. Yet you know also that he may tomorrow tell himself with equal sincerity that your money is his by right of need, that you can afford to lose so insignificant a sum and that you must in any case pay for your magnanimity. And then he grows to dislike you and you have lost a friend as well as your money. I decided to refuse Visser.

'At my refusal he became angry and accused me of not trusting him to pay a debt of honour, which was a foolish way for him to talk. Then he pleaded with me. He could prove, he said, that he would be able to repay the money and began to tell me some interesting things.

'I have said that Visser had known a little more about Dimitrios than the rest of us. That was true. He had taken a lot of trouble finding it out. It was just after that evening when he had pulled out a pistol to threaten Dimitrios and Dimitrios had turned his back upon him. Nobody had treated him like that before and he wished to know more about the man who had humiliated him: that, at least, is what I believe. He himself said that he had suspected that Dimitrios would betray us, but that, I knew, was nonsense. Whatever his reason, however, he decided to follow Dimitrios when he left the Impasse.

'The first night that he tried he was unsuccessful. There was a large closed car waiting at the entrance to the Impasse and Dimitrios was driven off in it before Visser could find a taxi in which to follow. The second night he had a hired car ready. He did not come to the meeting, but waited for Dimitrios in the Rue de Rennes. When the closed car appeared, Visser drove off after it. Dimitrios stopped outside a big apartment house in the Avenue de Wagram and went inside while the big car drove away. Visser noted the address and about a week later, at a time when he knew that Dimitrios would be here in this room, he called at the apartment house and asked for Monsieur Makropoulos. Naturally, the concièrge knew of no one of that name, but Visser gave him money and described Dimitrios and found that he had an apartment there in the name of Rougemont.

'Now Visser, for all his conceit, was no fool. He knew that Dimitrios would have foreseen that he might be followed and guessed that the Rougemont apartment was not his only place. Accordingly he set himself to watch Monsieur Rougemont's comings and goings. It was not long before he discovered that there was another way out of the apartment house at the rear and that Dimitrios used to leave that way.

'One night when Dimitrios left by the back entrance Visser followed him. He did not have far to go. He found that Dimitrios lived in a big house just off the Avenue Hoche. It belonged, he found, to a titled and very *chic* woman. I shall call her Madame la Comtesse. Later Visser saw Dimitrios leave with her for the opera. Dimitrios was *en grande tenue* and they had a large Hispano to take them there.

'At that point Visser lost interest. He knew where Dimitrios lived. No doubt he felt that he had in some way obtained his revenge by discovering that much. He must, too, have been tired of waiting about in the streets. His curiosity was satisfied. What he had discovered was, after all, very much what he might have expected to discover. Dimitrios was a man with a large income. He was spending it in the same way as other men with large incomes.

'They told me that, when Visser was arrested in Paris, he said very little about Dimitrios. Yet he must have had

ugly thoughts, for he was by nature a violent man and very
conceited. It would have been useless, in any case, for him
to have tried to have Dimitrios arrested, for he could only
have sent them to the apartment in the Avenue de Wagram
and the house of Madame la Comtesse off the Avenue
Hoche, and he knew that Dimitrios would have gone away.
He had, as I said, other ideas about his knowledge.

'I think that, to begin with, he had intended to kill Dimitrios when he found him, but as he began to get short of
money his hatred of Dimitrios became more reasonable.
He probably remembered the Hispano and the luxury of
the house of Madame la Comtesse. She would perhaps be
worried to hear that her friend made his money by selling
heroin and Dimitrios might be ready to pay good money
to save her that worry. But it was easier to think about
Dimitrios and his money than it was to find them. For
several months after he was released from prison early in
1932, Visser looked for Dimitrios. The apartment in the
Avenue de Wagram was no longer occupied. The house of
Madame la Comtesse was shut up and the concièrge said
that she was in Biarritz. Visser went to Biarritz and found
that she was staying with friends. Dimitrios was not with
her. Visser returned to Paris. Then he had what I think was
quite a good idea. He himself was pleased with it. Unfortunately for him, it came a little too late. He remembered one
day that Dimitrios had been a drug addict, and it occurred
to him that Dimitrios might have done what many other
wealthy addicts do when their addiction reaches an
advanced stage. He might have entered a clinic to be cured.

'There are five private clinics near Paris which specialize
in such cures. On the pretext of making enquiries as to
terms on behalf of an imaginary brother, Visser went to

each one in turn, saying that he had been recommended by friends of Monsieur Rougemont. At the fourth his idea was proved to be good. The doctor in charge asked after the health of Monsieur Rougemont.

'I think that Visser derived a certain vulgar satisfaction from the thought of Dimitrios being cured of a heroin addiction. The cure is terrible, you know. The doctors go on giving the patient drugs, but gradually reduce the quantity. For him the torture is almost unbearable. He yawns and sweats and shivers for days, but he does not sleep and he cannot eat. He longs for death and babbles of suicide, but he has not the strength left to commit it. He shrieks and screams for his drug and it is withheld. He . . . But I must not bore you with horrors, Mr Latimer. The cure lasts three months and costs five thousand francs a week. When it is over the patient may forget the torture and start taking drugs again. Or he may be wiser and forget paradise. Dimitrios, it seems, was wise.

'He had left the clinic four months before Visser visited it, and so Visser had to think of another good idea. He *did* think of it, but it involved going to Biarritz again and he had no money. He forged a cheque, cashed it and set off again. He reasoned that as Dimitrios and Madame la Comtesse had been friends, she would probably know his present whereabouts. But he could not simply go to her and ask for his address. Even if he could have invented a pretext for doing so, he did not know under what name Dimitrios was known to her. There were difficulties, you see. But he found a way to overcome them. For several days he watched the villa where she was staying. Then, when he had found out enough about it, he broke into her room one afternoon, when the house was empty except for two drowsy servants, and looked through her baggage. He was looking for letters.

'Dimitrios had never liked written records in our business, and he never corresponded with any of us. But Visser had remembered that on one occasion Dimitrios had scribbled an address for Werner on a piece of paper. I remembered the occasion myself. The writing had been curious: quite uneducated, with clumsy, badly formed letters and many flourishes. It was this writing that Visser was looking for. He found it. There were nine letters in the writing. All were from an expensive hotel in Rome. I beg your pardon, Mr Latimer. You said something?'

'I can tell you what he was doing in Rome. He was organizing the assassination of a Yugoslav politician.'

Mr Peters did not seem impressed. 'Very likely,' he said indifferently. 'He would not be where he is today without that special organizing ability of his. Where was I? Ah, yes! The letters.

'All were from Rome and all were signed with initials which I shall tell you were "C. K.". The letters themselves were not what Visser had expected. They were very formal and stilted and brief. Most of them said no more than that the writer was in good health, that business was interesting and that he hoped to see his dear friend soon. No *tu-toi*, you know. But in one he said that he had met a relation by marriage of the Italian Royal family and in another that he had been presented to a Rumanian diplomat with a title. He was very pleased with these encounters, it seems. It was all very *snob*, and Visser felt that Dimitrios would certainly wish to buy his friendship. He noted the name of the hotel and, leaving everything as he found it, went back to Paris en route for Rome. He arrived in Paris the following morning. The police were waiting for him. He was not, I should think, a very clever forger.

'But you may imagine the poor fellow's feelings. During the three interminable years that followed he thought of nothing but Dimitrios; of how near he had been to him and how far he was now. He seemed, for some strange reason, to regard Dimitrios as the one responsible for his being in prison again. The idea served to feed his hatred of him and strengthen his resolve to make him pay. He was, I think, a little mad. As soon as he was free he got a little money in Holland and went to Rome. He was over three years behind Dimitrios, but he was determined to catch up with him. He went to the hotel and, posing as a Dutch private detective, asked to be permitted to see the records of those who had stayed there three years before. The *affiches* had, of course, gone to the police, but they had the bills for the period in question and he had the initials. He was able to discover the name which Dimitrios had used. Dimitrios had also left a forwarding address. It was a Poste Restante in Paris.

'Visser was now in a new difficulty. He knew the name, but that was useless unless he could get into France to trace the owner of it. It was no use his writing his demands for money. Dimitrios would not go on calling for letters for three years. And yet he could not enter France without being turned at the frontier or risking another term of imprisonment. He had somehow to get a new name and a new passport, and he had no money with which to do so.

'I lent him three thousand francs, and I will confess to you, Mr Latimer, that I felt myself to be truly stupid. Yet I was sorry for him. He was not the Visser I had known in Paris. Prison had broken him. Once his passions had been in his eyes, but now they were in his mouth and cheeks.

One felt he was getting old. I gave him the money out of pity and to get rid of him. I did not believe his story. I never expected to hear from him again. You may, therefore, imagine my astonishment when, a year ago, I received here a letter from him enclosing a *mandat* for the three thousand francs.

'The letter was very short. It said: "I have found him as I said I would. Here, with my profound thanks, is the money you lent me. It is worth three thousand francs to surprise you." That was all. He did not sign it. He gave no address. The *mandat* had been bought in Nice and posted there.

'That letter made me think, Mr Latimer. Visser had recovered his conceit. He could afford to indulge it to the extent of three thousand francs. That meant that he had a great deal more money. Conceited persons dream of such gestures, but they very rarely make them. Dimitrios must have paid, and since he was not a fool he must have had a very good reason for paying.

'I was idle at the time, Mr Latimer; idle and a little restless. I had my books, it is true, but one wearies of books, the ideas, the affectations of other men. It might be interesting, I thought, to find Dimitrios for myself and share in Visser's good fortune. It was not greed that prompted me, Mr Latimer; I should not like you to think that. I was *interested*. Besides, I felt that Dimitrios owed me something for the discomforts and indignities I had experienced because of him. For two days I played with the idea. Then, on the third day, I made up my mind. I set out for Rome.

'As you may imagine, Mr Latimer, I had a difficult time and many disappointments. I had the initials, which Visser, in his eagerness to convince me, had revealed, but the only thing I knew about the hotel was that it was expensive. There are, unfortunately, a great many expensive hotels in Rome. I began to investigate them one after the other, but when, at the fifth hotel, they refused, for some reason, to let me see the bills for 1932, I abandoned the attempt. Instead, I went to an Italian friend of mine in one of the Ministries. He was able to use his influence on my behalf and, after a lot of *chi-chi* and expense, I was permitted to inspect the Ministry of Interior archives for 1932. I found out the name Dimitrios was using, and I also found out what Visser had not found out – that Dimitrios had taken the course, which I myself took in 1932, of purchasing the citizenship of a certain South American republic which is sympathetic in such matters if one's pocketbook is fat enough. Dimitrios and I had become fellow citizens.

'I must confess, Mr Latimer, that I went back to Paris with hope in my heart. I was to be bitterly disappointed. Our consul was not helpful. He said that he had never heard of Señor C. K. and that even if I were Señor C. K.'s dearest and oldest friend he could not tell me where he was. He was offensive, which was unpleasant, but also I could tell that he was lying when he said that he had no knowledge of Dimitrios. That was tantalizing. And yet another disappointment awaited me. The house of Madame la Comtesse off the Avenue Hoche had been empty for two years.

'You would think, would you not, that it would be easy to find out where a chic and wealthy woman was? It was most difficult. The *Bottin* gave nothing. Apparently she had no house in Paris. I was, I will confess, about to abandon the search when I found a way out of my difficulty. I

reflected that a fashionable woman like Madame la Comtesse would be certain to have gone somewhere for the
winter sports season that was just over. Accordingly, I commissioned Hachettes to purchase for me a copy of every
French, Swiss, German and Italian winter sports and social
magazine which had been published during the previous
three months.

'It was a desperate idea, but it yielded results. You have
no idea how many such magazines there are, Mr Latimer.
It took me a little over a week to go through them all carefully, and I can assure you that by the middle of that week
I was very nearly a social-democrat. By the end of it,
however, I had recovered my sense of humour. If repetition
makes nonsense of words it makes even more fantastic nonsense of smiling faces, even if their owners are rich.
Besides, I had found what I wanted. In one of the German
magazines for February there was a small paragraph which
said that Madame la Comtesse was at St Anton for the
winter sports. In a French magazine there was a *couturier's*
picture of her in skating clothes. I went to St Anton. There
are not many hotels there, and I soon found that Monsieur
C. K. had been in St Anton at the same time. He had given
an address in Cannes.

'At Cannes I found that Monsieur C. K. had a villa on
the Estoril, but that he himself was abroad on business at
the moment. I was not discontented. Dimitrios would
return to his villa sooner or later. Meanwhile I set myself
to discover something about Monsieur C. K.

'I have always said, Mr Latimer, that the art of being
successful in this life of ours is the art of knowing the
people who will be useful to one. I have in my time met
and done business with many important people – people,

you know, who are informed of what goes on and why –
and I have always taken care to be helpful to them. It has
paid me. A man, for example, who is interested in selling
field guns to the Greek Government will be glad to know
the personal expectations in the affair of the responsible
Greek official. This official in his turn will be glad to know
that his expectations are clearly understood without he
himself having had to submit to the indignity and risk of
stating them directly. By performing that delicate exchange
of courtesies, I secure the gratitude of both parties. I am
then in a position to ask favours in return.

'So, where Visser might have had to prowl about in the
darkness in search of his information, I was able to get mine
from a friend. It proved easier than I had expected to do
so, for I found that, in certain circles, Dimitrios, with the
name of Monsieur C. K., had become quite important. In
fact, when I learned just how important he had become, I
was pleasantly surprised. I began to realize that Visser must
be living on the money he got from Dimitrios. Yet what
did Visser know? Only that Dimitrios had dealt illegally in
drugs; a fact that it would be difficult for him to prove. He
knew nothing about the dealings in women. I did. There
must, I reasoned, be other things, too, which Dimitrios
would prefer not to be generally known. If, before I
approached Dimitrios, I could find out some of those
things, my financial position would be very strong indeed.
I decided to see some more of my friends.

'Two of them were able to help me. Grodek was one. A
Rumanian friend of mine was another. You know of
Grodek's acquaintance with Dimitrios when he called
himself Talat. The Rumanian friend told me that in 1925
Dimitrios had had questionable financial dealings with

Codreanu, the lamented leader of the Rumanian Iron Guard, and that he was known to, but not wanted by, the Bulgarian police.

'Now there was nothing criminal about any of those affairs. Indeed, Grodek's information depressed me somewhat. It was unlikely that the Yugoslav Government would apply for extradition after so many years; while, as for the French, they might hold that, as Dimitrios had rendered some sort of service to the Republic in 1926, he was entitled to a little tolerance in the matter of dealings in drugs and women. I decided to see what I could find out in Greece. A week after I arrived in Athens and while I was still trying unsuccessfully to trace in the official records a reference to my particular Dimitrios, I read in an Athens' paper of the discovery, by the Istanbul police, of the body of a Greek from Smyrna with the name of Dimitrios Makropoulos.'

He raised his eyes to Latimer's. 'Do you begin to see, Mr Latimer, why I found your interest in Dimitrios a little difficult to explain?' And then, as Latimer nodded: 'I, too, of course, inspected the Relief Commission dossier, but I followed you to Sofia instead of going to Smyrna. I wonder if you would care to tell me now what you found out from the police records there?'

'Dimitrios was suspected of murdering a moneylender named Sholem in Smyrna in 1922. He escaped to Greece. Two years later, he was involved in an attempt to assassinate Kemal. He escaped again, but the Turks used the murder as a pretext for issuing a warrant for his arrest.'

'A murder in Smyrna! That makes it even clearer.' Mr Peters smiled. 'A wonderful man, Dimitrios, don't you think? So economical.'

'What do you mean?'

'Let me finish my story and you will see. As soon as I read that newspaper paragraph, I sent a telegram to a friend in Paris asking him to let me know the whereabouts of Monsieur C. K. He replied two days later, saying that Monsieur C. K. had just returned to Cannes after an Aegean cruise with a party of friends in a Greek diesel yacht which he had chartered two months previously.

'Do you see now what had happened Mr Latimer? You tell me that the *carte d'identité* was a year old when they found it on the body. That means that it was obtained a few weeks before Visser sent me that three thousand francs. You see, from the moment Visser found Dimitrios, he was doomed. Dimitrios must have made up his mind at once to kill him. You can see why. Visser was dangerous. He was such a conceited fellow. He might have blurted out indiscretions at any time when he had been drinking and wanted to boast. He would have to be killed.

'Yet, see how clever Dimitrios was! He could have killed Visser at once, no doubt. But he did not do so. His economical mind had evolved a better plan. If it were necessary to kill Visser, could he not dispose of the body in some advantageous way? Why not use it to safeguard himself against the consequences of that old indiscretion in Smyrna? It was unlikely that there would be consequences, but here was his chance to make certain of the fact. The body of the villain, Dimitrios Makropoulos, would be delivered to the Turkish police. Dimitrios, the murderer, would be dead and Monsieur C. K. would be left alive to cultivate his garden. But he would require a certain amount of co-operation from Visser himself. The man would have to be lulled into feeling secure. So, Dimitrios smiled and paid up and set about getting the identity card which was to go with Visser's dead body. Nine months later, in June, he invited his good friend Visser to join him on a yachting trip.'

'Yes, but how could he have committed the murder on the yachting trip? What about the crew? What about the other passengers?'

Mr Peters looked knowing. 'Let me tell you, Mr Latimer, what I would have done if I had been Dimitrios. I would have begun by chartering a Greek yacht. There would be a reason for its being a Greek yacht: its home port would be the Piraeus.

'I would have arranged for my friends, including Visser, to join the yacht at Naples. Then I would have taken them on their cruise and returned a month later to Naples, where I would have announced that the cruise would end. They would disembark; but I would stay on board saying that I was returning with the yacht to the Piraeus. Then I would take Visser aside privately and tell him that I had some very secret business to transact in Istanbul, that I proposed to go there on the yacht, and that I would be glad of his company. I would ask him not to tell the disembarking passengers who might be angry because I had not asked them, and to return to the yacht when they had gone. To poor, conceited Visser, the invitation would be irresistible.

'To the captain I would say that Visser and I would leave the yacht at Istanbul and return overland, after we had transacted our business, to Paris. He would sail the yacht back to the Piraeus. At Istanbul Visser and I would go ashore together. I would have left word with the crew that we would send for our baggage when we had decided where we should be staying for the night. Then, I would have taken him to a *boîte* I know of in a street off the

Grande Rue de Pera, and later that night I should find myself poorer by ten thousand French francs, while Visser would be at the bottom of the Bosphorus at a place where the current would carry him, when he was rotten enough to float, out to Seraglio Point. Then I would take a room in a hotel in the name and with the passport of Visser, and send a porter to the yacht with a note authorizing him to collect both Visser's luggage and mine. As Visser, I would leave the hotel in the morning for the station. His baggage, which I should have searched overnight to see that there was nothing in it to identify it as Visser's, I would deposit in the *consigne*. Then I would take the train to Paris. If inquiries about Visser are ever made in Istanbul, he left by train for Paris. But who is going to inquire? My friends believe he left the yacht at Naples. The captain and crew of the yacht are not interested. Visser has a false passport, he is a criminal: such a type has an obvious reason for disappearing of his own free will. Finish!'

Mr Peters spread out his hands. 'That is how it would occur to me to deal with such a situation. Perhaps Dimitrios managed it a little differently, but that is what might well have happened. There is one thing, however, that I am quite sure he did. You remember telling me that some months before you arrived in Smyrna, someone examined the same police records that you examined there? That must have been Dimitrios. He was always very cautious. No doubt he was anxious to find out how much they knew about his appearance, before he left Visser for them to find.'

'But that man I told you about looked like a Frenchman.'

Mr Peters smiled reproachfully. 'Then you *were not*

quite frank with me in Sofia, Mr Latimer. You *did* enquire about this mysterious man.' He shrugged. 'Dimitrios does look like a Frenchman now. His clothes are French.'

'You've seen him recently?'

'Yesterday. Though he did not see me.'

'You know exactly where he is in Paris, then?'

'Exactly. As soon as I discovered his new business I knew where to find him here.'

'And, now that you have found him, what next?'

Mr Peters frowned. 'Come now, Mr Latimer. I am sure that you are not quite as obtuse as all that. You know and can prove that the man buried in Istanbul is not Dimitrios. If necessary you could identify Visser's photographs on the police files. I, on the other hand, know what Dimitrios is calling himself now and where to find him. Our joint silence would be worth a lot of money to Dimitrios. With Visser's fate in mind, we shall know, too, how to deal with the matter. We shall demand a million francs. Dimitrios will pay us, believing that we shall come back for more. We shall not be as foolish as to endanger our lives in that way. We shall rest content with half a million each – nearly three thousand pounds sterling, Mr Latimer – and quietly disappear.'

'I see. Blackmail on a cash basis. No credit. But why bring me into the business? The Turkish police could identify Visser without my help.'

'How? They identified him as Dimitrios and buried him. They have seen perhaps a dozen or more dead bodies since then. Weeks have gone by. Are they going to remember Visser's face well enough to justify their beginning expensive extradition proceedings against a rich foreigner because of their fourteen-year-old suspicions about a

sixteen-year-old murder? My dear Latimer! Dimitrios
would laugh at me. He would do with me as he did with
Visser: give me a few thousand francs here and there to
keep me from making myself a nuisance with the French
police and to keep me quiet until, for safety's sake, I could
be killed. But you have seen Visser's body and identified it.
You have seen the police records in Smyrna. He knows
nothing about you. He will have to pay or run an unknown
risk. He is too cautious for that. Listen. In the first place,
it is essential that Dimitrios does not discover our identities.
He will know me, of course, but he will not know my
present name. In your case, we shall invent a name. Mr
Smith, perhaps, as you are English. I shall approach Dimitrios in the name of Petersen and we shall arrange to meet
him outside Paris at a place of our own choosing to receive
our million francs. That is the last that he will see of either
of us.'

Latimer laughed but not very heartily. 'And do you
really suppose that I shall agree to this plan of yours?'

'If, Mr Latimer, your trained mind can evolve a more
ingenious plan, I shall be only too happy to . . .'

'My trained mind, Mr Peters, is concerned with wondering how best to convey this information which you have
given me to the police.'

Mr Peters' smile became thin. 'The police? What information, Mr Latimer?' he inquired softly.

'Why, the information that . . .' Latimer began impatiently and then stopped, frowning.

'Quite so,' nodded Mr Peters approvingly. 'You have no
real information to convey. If you go to the Turkish police
they will no doubt send to the French police for Visser's
photographs and record your identification. What then?

Dimitrios will be found to be alive. That is all. I have not, you may remember, told you the name that Dimitrios uses now or even his initials. It would be impossible for you to trace him from Rome as Visser and I traced him. Nor do you know the name of Madame la Comtesse. As for the French police, I do not think that they would be interested either in the fate of a deported Dutch criminal or excited by the knowledge that somewhere in France there is a Greek using a false name who killed a man in Smyrna in 1922. You see, Mr Latimer, you cannot act without me. If, of course, Dimitrios should prove difficult, then it might be desirable to take the police into our confidence. But I do not think that Dimitrios will be difficult. He is very intelligent. In any case, Mr Latimer, why throw away three thousand pounds?'

Latimer considered him for a moment. Then he said: 'Has it occurred to you that I might not want that particular three thousand pounds? I think, my friend, that prolonged association with criminals has made it difficult for you to follow some trains of thought.'

'This moral rectitude . . .' began Mr Peters wearily. Then he seemed to change his mind. He cleared his throat. 'If you wished,' he said with the calculated *bonhommie* of one who reasons with a drunken friend, 'we could inform the police *after* we had secured the money. Even if Dimitrios were able to prove that he had paid money to us, he could not, however unpleasant he wished to be, tell the police our names or how to find us. In fact, I think that that would be a very wise move on our part, Mr Latimer. We should then be quite sure that Dimitrios was no longer dangerous. We could supply the police anonymously with a dossier as Dimitrios did in 1931. The retribution would be just.' Then his face fell. 'Ah, no. It is impossible. I am afraid that the suspicions of your Turkish friends might fall upon you, Mr Latimer. We could not risk that, could we!'

But Latimer was scarcely listening. He knew that what he had made up his mind to say was foolish and he was trying to justify its folly. Peters was right. There was nothing he could do to bring Dimitrios to justice. He was left with a choice. Either he could go back to Athens and leave Peters to make the best deal he could with Dimitrios or he could stay in Paris to see the last act of the grotesque comedy in which he now found himself playing a part. The first alternative being unthinkable, he was committed to the second. He really had no choice. To gain time he had taken and lit a cigarette. Now he looked up from it.

'All right,' he said slowly. 'I'll do what you want. But there are conditions.'

'Conditions?' Mr Peters' lips tightened. 'I think that a half share is more than generous, Mr Latimer. Why my trouble and expenses alone . . .!'

'Just a moment. I was saying, Mr Peters, that there are conditions. The first should be very easy for you to fulfil. It is simply that you yourself retain all the money that you are able to squeeze from Dimitrios. The second . . .' he went on and then paused. He had the momentary pleasure of seeing Mr Peters disconcerted. Then, he saw the watery eyes narrow quite appreciably. Mr Peters' words as they issued from his mouth were charged with suspicion.

'I don't think I quite understand, Mr Latimer. If this is a clumsy trick . . .'

'Oh no. There is no trick, clumsy or otherwise, Mr Peters. "Moral rectitude" was your phrase, wasn't it? It will do. I am prepared, you see, to assist in blackmailing a person when that person is Dimitrios, but I am not prepared to share in the profits. So much the better for you, of course.'

Mr Peters nodded thoughtfully. 'Yes, I see that you might think like that. So much the better for me, as you say. But what is the other condition?'

'Equally inoffensive. You have referred mysteriously to Dimitrios's having become a person of importance. I make my helping you get your million francs conditional on your telling me exactly *what* he has become.'

Mr Peters thought for a moment, then shrugged. 'Very well. I see no reason why I should not tell you. It so happens that the knowledge cannot possibly be of any help to you in discovering his present identity. The Eurasian Credit Trust is registered in Monaco and the details of its registration are not therefore open to inspection. Dimitrios is a member of the Board of Directors.'

13

Rendezvous

It was two o'clock in the morning when Latimer left the Impasse des Huits Anges and began to walk slowly in the direction of the Quai Voltaire.

His eyes smarted, his mouth was dry and he yawned repeatedly, but his brain was working with the feverish clarity induced by too much strong coffee; the sort of clarity which makes sense of nonsense. He would, he knew, have a sleepless night. The circles of thought would become wider and wider, and more ridiculous and more ridiculous until he got up and drank a glass of water. Then, he would listen for a time to the blood beating in his head and the process would begin again. It was better to stay out.

At the corner of the Boulevard St Germain there was a café open. He went inside and was served with a sandwich and a glass of beer by the bored mute behind the zinc. When he had finished the sandwich and smoked a cigarette, he looked at his watch. Twenty minutes past two: over three hours to daybreak. A taxi returned to the rank just outside the café. Latimer hesitated for an instant, then made up his mind. Throwing away his cigarette, he left some money on the zinc and walked out to the taxi.

He paid off the driver at the Trinité Metro and walked up the Rue Blanche. Yes, there was the *Kasbah*, still there and about halfway up the hill. He could see its flickering neon sign long before he reached it.

There was a businesslike air about the street. It was like an aisle in a trade exhibition except that, instead of a double line of stands, there was a double line of nightclubs and that, instead of salesmen who peered at the visitors from the depths of hired armchairs, there were unshaven commissionaires in brightly-coloured but badly-fitting uniforms and *chasseurs* in soiled dinner jackets who fell in step beside him and talked in swift, persuasive undertones as he walked by.

Outwardly, at any rate, the *Kasbah* had changed very little from the picture Mr Peters had drawn of it. The Negro commissionaire wore a striped djibbah and a tarboosh while the *chasseur*, an Annamite, wore a red fez with his dinner jacket. The fact that the Annamite had chosen to propitiate Brahma as well as Allah by sporting a Hindu caste mark in addition to the fez, was more than offset by the life-sized portrait of a Morrocan *ouled nail* painted on, and divided neatly into two by a pair of flush doors. Inside, however, time had wrought many changes. Mr Peters' rugs and divans and amber lights had been replaced by tubular steel chairs and tables, a carpet with a vorticist pattern and indirect strip lighting. The tango band had gone too. In its place was an amplifier and loudspeaker which, when it was not reproducing French dance records, emitted a faint popping noise reminiscent of the sound of a distant motorboat. There were about twenty persons there and seating accommodation for three or four times as many. The *consommation* was thirty francs. Latimer ordered a beer and asked if the *patron* were there. The waiter, an Italian, said that he would see and went away. Then, the loudspeaker stopped popping and four couples got up to dance.

Latimer wondered what Mr Peters would say to his

Kasbah now. It was the reverse of 'cosy'. He tried to imagine what it had been like in its heyday, with the divans and the rugs and the amber lights in position, the air thick with cigarette smoke and the South Americans playing a tango for women with knee-length skirts, waistlines on their hips and *cloche* hats on their shingled heads. Mr Peters had probably spent most of his time standing just inside the entrance by the *vestiaire* or sitting in the small room marked '*Direction*' opposite it, listening to English and American voices, writing orders for more Meknes champagne and checking his partner's accounts. Perhaps he had been in there on that night ten years ago when Giraud had brought Dimitrios to see him. Perhaps . . .

The *patron* approached. He was heavy and tall with a bald head and the blank expression of a man who is used to being disliked and is undismayed by hostility.

'Monsieur wishes to see me?'

'Oh yes. I wondered if you knew Monsieur Giraud. He was the *patron* here ten years ago.'

'No, I do not know him. I have been here only two years. Why do you want to know?'

'No special reason. I should have liked to see him again, that is all.'

'No, I do not know him,' repeated the *patron*, and then, with a quick glance at Latimer's beer: 'Do you want to dance? You should wait. There will be plenty of pretty women here soon. It is early.'

'No, thank you.'

The *patron* shrugged and walked away. Latimer drank some of his beer and gazed vacantly about him like a person who has strayed into a museum for shelter from the rain. He wished that he had gone to bed after all and felt annoyed with himself for coming. The visit had been a pitifully ingenuous attempt to destroy the feeling of unreality with which he had left Mr Peters, and it had served only to accentuate this feeling. He signalled to the waiter, paid for his beer and took a taxi back to his hotel.

He was tired, of course: that was the trouble. A student given twenty-four hours to read the six volumes of Comte's *Cours de Philosophie Positive* and prepare to be examined on it could, he thought, have felt no more confused and helpless. There were so many new ideas for him to become accustomed to and so many old ones to forget, so many questions to ask and so many to answer. And brooding over the confusion there was the sinister proposition that Dimitrios, the murderer of Sholem and of Visser, Dimitrios the drug pedlar, the pimp, the thief, the spy, the white slaver, the bully, the financier, Dimitrios, whose only saving grace had seemed to be that he had allowed himself to be murdered, was alive and prosperous.

In his room, Latimer sat down by the window and gazed out across the black river to the lights which it reflected and the faint glow in the sky beyond the Louvre. His mind was haunted by the past, by the confession of Dhris, the Negro, and by the memories of Irana Preveza, by the tragedy of Bulić and by a tale of white crystals travelling west to Paris, bringing money to the fig-packer of Izmir. Three human beings had died horribly and countless others had lived horribly that Dimitrios might take his ease. If there *were* such a thing as Evil, then this man . . .

But it was useless to try to explain him in terms of Good and Evil. They were no more than baroque abstractions. Good Business and Bad Business were the elements of the new theology. Dimitrios was not evil. He was logical and consistent; as logical and consistent in the European jungle as the poison gas called Lewisite and the shattered bodies of children killed in the bombardment of an open town. The logic of Michelangelo's *David*, Beethoven's quartets and Einstein's physics had been replaced by that of the *Stock Exchange Year Book* and Hitler's *Mein Kampf.*

Yet, Latimer reflected, although you could not stop people buying and selling Lewisite, although you could do no more than 'deplore' a number of slaughtered children, there were in existence means of preventing one particular aspect of the principle of expediency from doing too much damage. Most international criminals were beyond the reach of man-made laws, but Dimitrios happened to be within reach of one law. He had committed at least two murders and had therefore broken the law as surely as if he had been starving and had stolen a loaf of bread.

It was easy enough, however, to say that he was within reach of the Law: it was not as easy to see how the Law was to be informed of the fact. As Mr Peters had so care-fully pointed out, he, Latimer, had no information to give the police. But was that an altogether true picture of the situation? He *had* some information. He knew that Dimitrios was alive and that he was a director of the Eurasian Credit Trust, that he knew a French Countess who had had a house off the Avenue Hoche and that he or she had had an Hispana Suiza car, that both of them had been in St Anton that year for the winter sports and that he had chartered a Greek yacht in June, that he had a villa on the Estoril and that he was now the citizen of a South American republic. Surely, then, it must be possible to find the person with those particular attributes. Even if the names of the directors of the Eurasian Credit Trust were unobtainable, it ought to be possible to get the names of the men who had chartered Greek yachts in June, of the wealthy South Americans with villas on the Estoril and of the South American visitors to St Anton in February. If you could get those lists, all you would have to do would be to see which names (if there should be more than one) were common to the three.

But how did you get the lists? Besides, even if you could persuade the Turkish police to exhume Visser and then apply officially for all that information, what sort of proof would you have that the man you had concluded to be Dimitrios, was in fact, Dimitrios? And supposing that you could convince Colonel Haki of the truth, would he have enough evidence to justify the French extraditing a director of the powerful Eurasian Credit Trust? If it had taken twelve years to secure the acquittal of Dreyfus, it could take at least as many years to secure the conviction of Dimitrios.

He undressed wearily and got into bed.

It looked as if he were committed to Mr Peters' blackmailing scheme. Lying in a comfortable bed with his eyes closed, he found the fact that in a few days time he would be, technically speaking, one of the worst sorts of criminals no more than odd. Yet, at the back of his mind there was a certain discomfort. When the reason for it dawned on him, he was mildly shocked. The simple truth was that he was feeling afraid of Dimitrios. Dimitrios was a dangerous man; more dangerous by far than he had been in Smyrna and Athens and Sofia, because he now had more to lose. Visser had blackmailed him and died. Now, he, Latimer, was going to blackmail him. Dimitrios had never hesitated to kill a man if he had deemed it necessary to do so, and, if he had deemed it necessary in the case of a man who threatened to expose him as a drug pedlar, would he hesitate in the case of two men who threatened to expose him as a murderer?

It was most important to see that, hesitation or no hesitation, he was not given the opportunity. Mr Peters had proposed the taking of elaborate precautions.

The first contact with Dimitrios was to be established by letter. Latimer had seen a draft of the letter and had found it gratifyingly similar in tone to a letter he himself had written for a blackmailer in one of his books. It began, with sinister cordiality, by trusting that, after all these years, Monsieur C.K. had not forgotten the writer and the pleasant and profitable times they had spent together, went on to say how pleasing it was to hear that he was so successful and hoped sincerely that he would be able to meet the writer who would be at the So-and-So Hotel at nine o'clock on the Thursday evening of that week. The writer concluded with an expression of his *'plus sincere amitié'* and a significant little postscript to the effect that he had chanced to meet someone who had known their mutual friend Visser quite well, that this person was most anxious to meet Monsieur C. K. and that it would be so unfortunate if Monsieur C. K. could not arrange to keep the appointment on Thursday evening.

Dimitrios would receive that letter on the Thursday morning. At half past eight on the Thursday evening, 'Mr Petersen' and 'Mr Smith' would arrive at the hotel chosen for the interview and 'Mr Petersen' would take a room. There they would await the arrival of Dimitrios. When the situation had been explained, Dimitrios would be informed that he would receive instructions as to the payment of the million francs on the following morning and told to go. 'Mr Petersen' and 'Mr Smith' would then leave.

Precautions would now have to be taken to see that they were not followed and identified. Mr Peters had not specified what sort of precautions, but had given assurances that there would be no difficulties.

That same evening, a second letter would be posted to Dimitrios telling him to send a messenger with the million francs, in *mille* notes to a specified point on the road outside the cemetery of Neuilly at eleven o'clock on the Friday night. There would be a hired car waiting for him there with two men in it. The two men would have been recruited for the purpose by Mr Peters. Their business would be to pick up the messenger and drive along the Quai National in the direction of Suresnes until they were quite sure that they were not being followed and then to make for a point on the Avenue de la Reine near the Porte de St Cloud where 'Mr Petersen' and 'Mr Smith' would be waiting to receive the money. The two men would then drive the messenger back to Neuilly. The letter would specify that the messenger must be a woman.

Latimer had been puzzled by this last provision. Mr Peters had justified it by pointing out that if Dimitrios came himself there was just a chance that he might prove too clever for the men in the car and that 'Mr Petersen' and 'Mr Smith' would end up lying in the Avenue de la Reine with bullets in their backs. Descriptions were unreliable and the two men would have no certain means of knowing in the dark if a man presenting himself as the messenger were Dimitrios or not. They could make no such mistake about a woman.

Yes, Latimer reflected, it was absurd to imagine that

there could be any danger from Dimitrios. The only thing he had to look forward to was the meeting with this curious man whose path he had stumbled across. It would be strange, after he had heard so much about him, to meet him face to face; strange to see the hand which had packed figs and driven the knife into Sholem's throat, the eyes which Irana Preveza and Wladyslaw Grodek and Mr Peters had remembered so well. It would be as if a waxwork in the chamber of horrors had come to life.

For a time he stared at the narrow gap between the curtains. It was getting light. Very soon he fell asleep.

He was disturbed towards eleven by a telephone call from Mr Peters, who said that the letter to Dimitrios had been posted and asked if they could have dinner together 'to discuss our plans for tomorrow'. Latimer was under the impression that their plans had already been discussed, but he agreed. The afternoon he spent alone at the Vincennes Zoo. The subsequent dinner was tedious. Little was said about their plans, and Latimer concluded that the invitation had been another of Mr Peters' precautions. He was making sure that his collaborator, who now had no financial interest in the business, had not changed his mind about collaborating. Latimer spent two hours listening to an account of Mr Peters' discovery of the works of Dr Frank Crane and a defence of his contention that *Lame and Lovely* and *Just Human* were the most important contributions to literature since *Robert Elsmere*.

On the pretext of having a headache, Latimer escaped soon after ten o'clock and went to bed. When he awoke the following morning he actually had a headache and concluded that the carafe burgundy which his host had recommended so warmly at dinner had been even cheaper

than it had tasted. As his mind crept slowly back to consciousness he had, too, a feeling that something unpleasant
had happened. Then he remembered. Of course! Dimitrios had by now received the first letter.

He sat up in bed to think about it and, after a moment
or two, came to the profound conclusion that if it were easy
enough to hate and despise blackmailing when one wrote
and read about it, the act of blackmailing itself called for
rather more moral hardihood, more firmness of purpose,
than he, at any rate, possessed. It made no difference to
remind oneself that Dimitrios was a criminal. Blackmail
was blackmail, just as murder was murder. Macbeth would
probably have hesitated at the last minute to kill a criminal
Duncan just as much as he hesitated to kill the Duncan
whose virtues pleaded like angels. Fortunately, or unfortunately, he, Latimer, had a Lady Macbeth in the person of
Mr Peters. He decided to go out to breakfast.

The day seemed interminable. Mr Peters had said that
he had arrangements to make in connection with the car
and the men to drive in it, and that he would meet Latimer
at a quarter to eight, after dinner. Latimer spent the
morning walking aimlessly in the Bois and, in the afternoon, went to a cinema.

It was towards six o'clock and after he had left the
cinema that he began to notice a slight breathless feeling in
the region of the solar plexus. It was as if someone had
dealt him a light blow there. He concluded that it was Mr
Peters' corrosive burgundy fighting a rearguard action and
stopped in one of the cafés on the Champs Elysées for an
infusion. But the feeling persisted, and he found himself
becoming more and more conscious of it. Then, as his gaze
rested for a moment on a party of four men and women

0

talking excitedly and laughing over some joke, he realized what was the matter with him. He did not want to meet Mr Peters. He did not want to go on this blackmailing expedition. He did not want to face a man in whose mind the uppermost thought would be to kill him as quickly and quietly as possible. The trouble was not in his stomach. He had cold feet.

The realization annoyed him. Why should he be afraid? There was nothing to be afraid of. This man Dimitrios was a clever and dangerous criminal, but he was far from being superhuman. If a man like Peters could . . . but then Peters was used to this sort of thing. He, Latimer, was not. He ought to have gone to the police as soon as he had discovered that Dimitrios was alive and risked being thought a troublesome crank. He should have realized before that, with Mr Peters' revelations, the whole affair had taken on a completely different complexion, that it was no longer one in which an amateur criminologist (and a fiction writer at that) should meddle. You could not deal with real murderers in this irresponsible fashion. His bargain with Mr Peters, for example: what would an English judge say to that? He could almost hear the words:

'As for the actions of this man Latimer, he has given an explanation of them which you may find difficult to believe. He is, we have been told, an intelligent man, a scholar who has held responsible posts in universities in this country and written works of scholarship. He is, moreover, a successful author of a type of fiction which, even if it is properly regarded by the average man as no more than the pabulum of adolescent minds, has, at least, the virtue of accepting the proposition that it is the business of right-thinking men and women to assist the police, should the opportunity present itself, in preventing crime and in capturing criminals. If you accept Latimer's explanation, you must conclude that he deliberately conspired with Peters to defeat the ends of justice and to act as an accessory before the fact of the crime of blackmail for the sole purpose of pursuing researches which he states had no other object than the satisfaction of his curiosity. You may ask yourselves if that would not have been the conduct of a mentally unbalanced child rather than that of an intelligent man. You must also weigh carefully the suggestion of the prosecution that Latimer did in fact share in the proceeds of this blackmailing scheme and that his explanation is no more than an effort to minimize his part in the affair.'

No doubt a French judge could make it sound even worse.

It was still too early for dinner. He left the café and walked in the direction of the Opera. In any case, he reflected, it was too late now to do anything. He was committed to helping Mr Peters. But was it too late? If he went to the police now, this minute, something could surely be done.

He stopped. This minute! There had been an *agent* sauntering along the street through which he had just come. He retraced his steps. Yes, there was the man, leaning against the wall, swinging his baton and talking to someone inside a doorway. Latimer hesitated again, then crossed the road and asked to be directed to the police *Poste*. It was three streets away, he was told. He set off again.

The entrance to the *Poste* was narrow and almost entirely concealed by a group of three *agents* deep in a conversation which they did not interrupt as they made way for him. Inside was an enamelled plate indicating that inquiries should be made on the first floor and pointing to a flight of stairs with a thin iron banister rail on one side and a wall with a long, greasy stain on it on the other. The place smelt strongly of camphor and faintly of excrement. From a room adjacent to the entrance hall came a murmur of voices and the clacking of a typewriter.

His resolution ebbing with every step, he went up the stairs to a room divided into two by a high wooden counter, the outer edges of which had been worn smooth and shiny by the palms of innumerable hands. Behind the counter a man in uniform was peering with the aid of a hand-mirror into the inside of his mouth.

Latimer paused. He had yet to make up his mind how he was going to begin. If he said: 'I was going to blackmail a murderer tonight, but I have decided to hand him over to you instead,' there was more than a chance that they would think him mad or drunk. In spite of the urgent need for immediate action, he would have to make some show of beginning at the beginning. 'I was in Istanbul some weeks ago, and was told of a murder committed there in 1922. Quite by chance, I have found that the man who did it is here in Paris and is being blackmailed.' Something like that. The uniformed man caught a glimpse of him in the mirror and turned sharply round.

'What do you want?'

'I should like to see Monsieur le Commissaire.'

'What for?'

'I have some information to give him.'

The man frowned impatiently. 'What information? Please be precise.'

'It concerns a case of blackmail.'

'You are being blackmailed?'

'No. Someone else is. It is a very complicated and serious affair.'

'Your *carte d'identité*, please.'

'I have no *carte d'identité*. I am a temporary visitor. I entered France four days ago.'

'Your passport, then.'

'It is at my hotel.'

The man stiffened. The frown of irritation left his face. Here was something that he understood and with which his long experience had enabled him to deal. He spoke with easy assurance.

'That is very serious, Monsieur. You realize that? Are you English?'

'Yes.'

He drew a deep breath. 'You must understand, Monsieur, that your papers must always be in your pocket. It is the law. If you saw a street accident and were required as a witness, the *agent* would ask to see your papers before you were permitted to leave the scene of the accident. If you had not got them, he could, if he wished, arrest you. If you were in a *boîte de nuit* and the police entered to inspect papers, you would certainly be arrested if you carried none. It is the law, you understand? I shall have to take the necessary particulars. Give me your name and that of your hotel, please.'

Latimer did so. The man noted them down, picked up a telephone and asked for *'Septième'*. There was a pause, then he read out Latimer's name and address and asked for confirmation that they were genuine. There was another pause, of a minute or two this time, before he began to nod his head and say: *'Bien, bien.'* Then he listened for a moment, said: *'Oui, c'est ca,'* and put the telephone back on its hook. He returned to Latimer.

'It is in order,' he said, 'but you must present yourself with your passport at the Commissariat of the Seventh Arrondissement within twenty-four hours. As for this complaint of yours, you can make that at the same time. Please remember,' he went on, tapping his pencil on the counter for emphasis, 'that your passport must always be carried. It is obligatory to do so. You are English, and so nothing more need be made of the affair, but you must report to the Commissariat in your arrondissement, and in future always remember to carry your passport. *Au 'voir,* Monsieur.' He nodded benevolently with an air of knowing his duty to be well done.

Latimer went out in a very bad temper. Officious ass! But the man was right, of course. It had been absurd of him to go into the place without his passport. Complaint, indeed! In a sense he had had a narrow escape. He might have had to tell his story to the man. He might well have been under arrest by now. As it was, he had not told his story and was still a potential blackmailer.

Yet the visit to the police *Poste* had eased his conscience considerably. He did not feel quite as irresponsible as he had felt before. He had made an effort to bring the police into the affair. It had been an abortive effort, but short of collecting his passport from the other side of Paris and starting all over again (and that, he decided comfortably, was out of the question) there was nothing more he could do. He was due to meet Mr Peters at a quarter to eight in a café on the Boulevard Hausmann. But by the time he had finished a very light dinner the curious feeling had returned again to his solar plexus and the two brandies which he had with his coffee were intended to do more than pass the time. It was a pity, he reflected as he went on to keep his appointment, that he could not accept even a small share of the million francs. The cost of satisfying his curiosity was proving, in terms of frayed nerves and an uneasy conscience, practically prohibitive.

Mr Peters arrived ten minutes late with a large, cheap-looking suitcase and the too matter-of-fact air of a surgeon about to perform a difficult operation. He said, 'Ah, Mr Latimer!' and sitting down at the table, ordered a raspberry liqueur.

'Is everything all right?' Latimer felt that the question was a little theatrical, but he really wanted to know the answer to it.

'So far, yes. Naturally, I have had no word from him because I gave no address. We shall see.'

'What have you got in the suitcase?'

'Old newspapers. It is better to arrive at a hotel with a suitcase. I do not wish to have to fill up an *affiche* unless I am compelled to do so. I decided finally upon a hotel near to the Ledru-Rollin Metro. Very convenient.'

'Why can't we go by taxi?'

'We shall go by taxi. But,' added Mr Peters significantly, 'we shall return by the Metro. You will see.' His liqueur arrived. He poured it down his throat, shuddered, licked his lips and said that it was time to go.

The hotel chosen by Mr Peters for the meeting with Dimitrios was in a street just off the Avenue Ledru. It was small and dirty. A man in his shirtsleeves came out of a room marked 'Bureau', chewing a mouthful of food.

'I telephoned for a room,' said Mr Peters.

'Monsieur Petersen?'

'Yes.'

The man looked them both up and down. 'It is a large room. Fifteen francs for one. Twenty francs for two. Service, twelve and a half per cent.'

'This gentleman is not staying with me.'

The man took a key from a rack just inside the Bureau and, taking Mr Peters' suitcase, led the way upstairs to a room on the second floor. Mr Peters looked inside it and nodded.

'Yes, this will do. A friend of mine will call for me here soon. Ask him to come up, please.'

The man withdrew. Mr Peters sat on the bed and looked round approvingly. 'Quite nice,' he said, 'and very cheap.'

'Yes, it is.'

It was a long, narrow room with an old hair carpet, an iron bedstead, a wardrobe, two bentwood chairs, a small table, a screen and an enamelled iron bidet. The carpet was red, but by the washbasin was a threadbare patch, black and shiny with use. The wallpaper depicted a trellis supporting a creeping plant, a number of purple discs and some shapeless pink objects of a vaguely clinical character. The curtains were thick and blue and hung on brass rings.

Mr Peters looked at his watch. 'Twenty-five minutes before he is due. We had better make ourselves comfortable. Would you like the bed?'

'No, thank you. I suppose you will do the talking.'

'I think it will be best.' Mr Peters drew his Lüger pistol from his breast pocket, examined it to see that it was loaded and then dropped it into the right-hand pocket of his overcoat.

Eric Ambler

Latimer watched these preparations in silence. He was now feeling quite sick. He said suddenly: 'I don't like this.'

'Nor do I,' said Mr Peters soothingly, 'but we must take precautions. It is unlikely, I think, that they will be needed. You need have no fears.'

Latimer remembered an American gangster picture that he had once seen. 'What is to prevent him from walking in here and shooting us both?'

Mr Peters smiled tolerantly. 'Now, now! You must not let your imagination run away with you, Mr Latimer. Dimitrios would not do that. It would be too noisy and dangerous for him. Remember, the man downstairs will have seen him. Besides, that would not be his way.'

'What is his way?'

'Dimitrios is a very cautious man. He thinks very carefully before he acts.'

'He has had all day to think carefully.'

'Yes, but he does not yet know how much we know, and if anyone else knows what we know. He would have to discover those things. Leave everything to me, Mr Latimer. I understand Dimitrios.'

Latimer was about to point out that Visser had probably had the same idea, and then decided not to do so. He had another, more personal misgiving to air.

'You said that when Dimitrios paid us the million francs that would be the last he heard of us. Has it occurred to you that he may not be content to let things rest in that way? When he finds that we don't come back for more money he may decide to come after us.'

'After Mr Smith and Mr Petersen? We would be difficult to find under those names, my dear Mr Latimer.'

'But he knows your face already. He will see mine. He

266

could recognize our faces, whatever we chose to call ourselves.'

'But first he would have to find out where we were.'

'My photograph has appeared once or twice in newspapers. It may do so again. Or supposing my publisher decided to spread my photograph over the wrapper of a book. Dimitrios might easily happen to see it. There have been stranger coincidences.'

Mr Peters pursed his lips. 'I think you exaggerate, but – ' he shrugged ' – since you feel nervous perhaps you had better keep your face hidden. Do you wear spectacles?'

'For reading.'

'Then put them on. Wear your hat, too, and turn up the collar of your coat. You might sit in the corner of the room where it is not so light. In front of the screen. It will blur the outlines of your face. There.'

Latimer obeyed. When he was in position, with his collar buttoned across his chin and his hat tilted forward over his eyes, Mr Peters surveyed him from the door and nodded.

'It will do. I still think it unnecessary, but it will do. After making all these preparations we shall feel very foolish if he does not come.'

Latimer, who was feeling very foolish anyway, grunted. 'Is there any likelihood of his not coming?'

'Who knows?' Mr Peters sat on the bed again. 'A dozen things might happen to prevent him. He might not, for some reason, have received my letter. He may have left Paris yesterday. But, if he has received the letter, I think that he will come.' He looked at his watch again. 'Eight forty-five. If he *is* coming, he will soon be here.'

They fell silent. Mr Peters began to trim his nails with a pair of pocket scissors.

Except for the clicking of the scissors and the sound of Mr Peters' heavy breathing, the silence in the room was complete. To Latimer it seemed almost tangible; a dark grey fluid that oozed from the corners of the room. He began to hear the watch ticking on his wrist. He waited for what seemed an eternity before looking at it. When he did look it was ten minutes to nine. Another eternity. He tried to think of something to say to Mr Peters to pass the time. He tried counting the complete parallelograms in the pattern of the wallpaper between the wardrobe and the window. Now he thought he could hear Mr Peters' watch ticking. The muffled sound of someone moving a chair and walking about in the room overhead seemed to intensify the silence. Four minutes to nine.

Then, so suddenly that the sound seemed as loud as a pistol shot, one of the stairs outside the door creaked.

Mr Peters stopped trimming his nails and, dropping the scissors on the bed, put his right hand in his overcoat pocket.

There was a pause. His heart beating painfully, Latimer gazed rigidly at the door. There was a soft knock.

Mr Peters stood up and, with his hand still in his pocket, went to the door and opened it.

Latimer saw him stare for a moment into the semi-darkness of the landing and then stand back.

Dimitrios walked into the room.

14

The Mask of Dimitrios

A man's features, the bone structure and the tissue which covers it, are the product of a biological process; but his face he creates for himself. It is a statement of his habitual emotional attitude; the attitude which his desires need for their fulfilment and which his fears demand for their protection from prying eyes. He wears it like a devil mask; a device to evoke in others the emotions complementary to his own. If he is afraid, then he must be feared; if he desires, then he must be desired. It is a screen to hide his mind's nakedness. Only a few men, painters, have been able to see the mind through the face. Other men in their judgements reach out for the evidence of word and deed that will explain the mask before their eyes. Yet, though they understand instinctively that the mask cannot be the man behind it; they are generally shocked by a demonstration of the fact. The duplicity of others must always be shocking when one is unconscious of one's own.

So, when at last Latimer saw Dimitrios and tried to read in the face of the man staring across the room at him the evil which he felt should be there, it was of that sense of shock which he was conscious. Hat in hand, in his dark, neat French clothes, with his slim, erect figure and sleek grey hair, Dimitrios was a picture of distinguished respectability.

His distinction was that of a relatively unimportant guest

at a large diplomatic reception. He gave the impression of being slightly taller than the one hundred and eighty-two centimetres with which the Bulgarian police had credited him. His skin had the creamy pallor which succeeds in middle age a youthful sallowness. With his high cheekbones, thin nose and beak-like upper lip he might well have been the member of an Eastern European legation. It was only the expression of his eyes that fitted in with any of Latimer's preconceived ideas about his appearance.

They were very brown and seemed at first to be a little screwed up, as if he were short-sighted or worried. But there was no corresponding frown or contraction of the eyebrows, and Latimer saw that the expression of anxiety or short-sightedness was an optical illusion due to the height of the cheekbones and the way the eyes were set in the head. Actually, the face was utterly expressionless, as impassive as that of a lizard.

For a moment the brown eyes rested on Latimer; then, as Mr Peters closed the door behind him Dimitrios turned his head and said in strongly accented French: 'Present me to your friend. I do not think that I have seen him before.'

Latimer very nearly jumped. The face of Dimitrios might not be revealing, but the voice certainly was. It was very coarse and sharp, with an acrid quality that made nonsense of any grace implicit in the words it produced. He spoke very softly, and it occurred to Latimer that the man was aware of the ugliness of his voice and tried to conceal it. He failed. Its promise was as deadly as the rattle of a rattlesnake.

'This is Monsieur Smith,' said Mr Peters. 'There is a chair behind you. You may sit down.'

Dimitrios ignored the suggestion. 'Monsieur Smith! An Englishman. It appears that you knew Monsieur Visser.'

'I have *seen* Visser.'

'That is what we wanted to talk to you about, Dimitrios,' said Mr Peters.

'Yes?' Dimitrios sat down on the spare chair. 'Then talk and be quick. I have an appointment to keep. I cannot waste time in this way.'

Mr Peters shook his head sorrowfully. 'You have not changed at all, Dimitrios. Always impetuous, always a little unkind. After all these years no word of greeting, no word of regret for all the unhappiness you caused me. You know, it was most unkind of you to hand us all over to the police like that. We were your friends. Why did you do it?'

'You still talk too much,' said Dimitrios. 'What is it you want?'

Mr Peters sat down carefully on the edge of the bed. 'Since you insist on making this a purely business meeting – we want money.'

The brown eyes flickered towards him. 'Naturally. What do you want to give me for it?'

'Our silence, Dimitrios. It is very valuable.'

'Indeed? How valuable?'

'It is worth at the very least a million francs.'

Dimitrios sat back in the chair and crossed his legs. 'And who is going to pay you that for it?'

'You are, Dimitrios. And you are going to be glad to get it so cheaply.'

Then Dimitrios smiled.

It was a slow tightening of the small, thin lips; nothing more. Yet there was something inexpressibly savage about it; something that made Latimer feel glad that it was Mr

Peters who had to face it. At that moment, he felt, Dimitrios was far more appropriate to a gathering of man-eating tigers than to a diplomatic reception, however large. The smile faded. 'I think,' he said, 'that you shall tell me now precisely what you mean.'

To Latimer, who would, he knew, have responded promptly to the menace in the man's voice, Mr Peters' bland hesitation was maddeningly reckless. He appeared to be enjoying himself.

'It is so difficult to know where to begin.'

There was no reply. Mr Peters waited for a moment and then shrugged. 'There are,' he went on, 'so many things that the police would be glad to know. For instance, I might tell them who it was who sent them that dossier in 1931. And it would be such a surprise for them to know that a respectable director of the Eurasian Credit Trust was really the Dimitrios Makropoulos who used to send women to Alexandria.'

Latimer thought that he saw Dimitrios relax a little in his chair. 'And you expect me to pay you a million francs for that? My good Petersen, you are childish.'

Mr Peters smiled. 'Very likely, Dimitrios. You were always inclined to despise my simple approach to the problems of this life of ours. But our silence on those matters would be worth a great deal to you, would it not?'

Dimitrios considered him for a moment. Then: 'Why don't you come to the point, Petersen? Or perhaps you are only preparing the way for your Englishman.' He turned his head. 'What have you to say, Monsieur Smith? Or is neither of you very sure of himself?'

'Petersen is speaking for me,' mumbled Latimer. He

wished fervently that Mr Peters would get the business over.

'May I continue?' inquired Mr Peters.

'Go on.'

'The Yugoslav police, too, might be interested in you. If we were to tell them where Monsieur Talat . . .'

'*Par example!*' Dimitrios laughed malignantly. 'So Grodek has been talking. Not a sou for that, my friend. Is there any more?'

'Athens, 1922. Does that mean anything to you, Dimitrios? The name was Taladis, if you remember. The charge was robbery and attempted murder. Is that so amusing?'

Into Mr Peters' face had come the look of unsmiling, adenoidal viciousness that Latimer had seen for a moment or two in Sofia. Dimitrios stared at him unblinkingly. In an instant the atmosphere had become deadly with a naked hatred that to Latimer was quite horrible. He felt as he had once felt when, as a child, he had seen a street fight between two middle-aged men. He saw Mr Peters draw the Lüger from his pocket and weigh it in his hands.

'You have nothing to say to that, Dimitrios? Then I shall go on. A little earlier that year you murdered a man in Smyrna, a moneylender. What was his name, Monsieur Smith?'

'Sholem.'

'Sholem, of course. Monsieur Smith was clever enough to discover that, Dimitrios. A good piece of work, don't you think? Monsieur Smith, you know, is very friendly with the Turkish police; almost, one might say, in their confidence. Do you still think that a million francs is a lot to pay, Dimitrios?'

Dimitrios did not look at either of them. 'The murderer of Sholem was hanged,' he said slowly.

Mr Peters raised his eyebrows. 'Can that be true, Monsieur Smith?'

'A Negro named Dhris Mohammed was hanged for the murder, but he made a confession implicating Monsieur Makropoulos. An order was issued for his arrest in 1924. The charge was murder, but the Turkish police were anxious to catch him for another reason. He had been concerned in an attempt to assassinate Kemal in Adrianople.'

'You see, Dimitrios, we are very well informed. Shall we continue?' He paused. Dimitrios still stared straight in front of him. Not a muscle of his face moved. Mr Peters looked across at Latimer. 'Dimitrios is impressed, I think. I feel sure he would like us to continue.'

When Latimer thinks of Dimitrios now it is that scene which he remembers: the squalid room with its nightmare wallpaper, Mr Peters sitting on the edge of the bed, his wet eyes half closed and the pistol in his hands, talking, and the man sitting between them, staring straight in front of him, his white face as still as that of a waxwork and as lifeless. The droning of Mr Peters' voice was punctuated by silences. To Latimer's overwrought nerves those silences were piercing in their intensity. But they were short, and after each one Mr Peters would drone on again: a torturer mumbling the repetition of his questions after each turn of the screw.

'Monsieur Smith has told you that he saw Visser. It was in a mortuary in Istanbul that he saw him. As I told you, he is very friendly with the Turkish police, and they showed him the body. They told him that it was the body of a criminal named Dimitrios Makropoulos. It was foolish of them to be so easily deceived, was it not? But even Monsieur Smith was deceived for a while. Fortunately I was able to tell him that Dimitrios was still alive.' He paused. 'You do not wish to comment? Very well. Perhaps you would like to hear how I discovered where you were and who you were.' Another silence. 'No? Perhaps you would like to know how I knew that you were in Istanbul at the time poor, silly Visser was killed; or how easily Monsieur Smith was able to identify a photograph of Visser with the dead man he saw in the mortuary.' Another silence. 'No? Perhaps you would like to be told how easy it would be for us to arouse the interest of the Turkish police in the curious case of a dead murderer who is alive, or of the Greek police in the case of the refugee from Smyrna who left Tabouria so suddenly. I wonder if you are thinking that it would be difficult for us to prove that you *are* Dimitrios Makropoulos, or Taladis, or Talat, or Rougemont, after such a long time has elapsed. Are you thinking that, Dimitrios? You do not wish to answer? Then let me tell you that it would be quite easy for us to prove. I could identify you as Makropoulos, and so could Werner or Lenôtre or Galindo or the Grand Duchess. One of them is sure to be alive and within reach of the police. Any of them would be glad to help to hang you. Monsieur Smith can swear that the man buried in Istanbul is Visser. Then there is the crew of the yacht you chartered in June. They knew that Visser went with you to Istanbul. There is the concièrge in the Avenue de Wagram. He knew you as Rougemont. Your present passport would not be a very good protection to a man with so many false names, would it? And even if you submitted to a little *chantage* from the French and Greek police, Monsieur Smith's Turkish friends would not be so accommodating. Do you think that a million francs is too much to pay for saving you from the hangman, Dimitrios?'

He stopped. For several long seconds Dimitrios continued to stare at the wall. Then at last he stirred and looked at his small gloved hands. His words, when they came, were like stones dropped one by one into a stagnant pool. 'I am wondering,' he said, 'why you ask so little. Is this million all that you are asking?'

Mr Peters sniggered. 'You mean, are we going to the police when we have the million? Oh, no, Dimitrios. We shall be fair with you. This million is only a preliminary gesture of good will. There will be other opportunities for you. But you will not find us greedy.'

'I am sure of that. You would not want me to become desperate, I think. Are you the only ones who have this curious delusion that I killed Visser?'

'There is no one else. I shall want the million in *mille* notes tomorrow.'

'So soon?'

'You will receive instructions as to how you are to give them to us, by post, in the morning. If the instructions are not followed exactly you will not be given a second chance. The police will be approached immediately. Do you understand?'

'Perfectly.'

The words were spoken levelly enough. To a casual observer they might have been concluding an ordinary business deal. But neither of their voices was quite steady. To Latimer it seemed as if it were only the Lüger that prevented Dimitrios from attacking and killing Mr Peters and only the thought of a million francs that prevented Mr

Peters from shooting Dimitrios. Two lives hung by the thin, steel threads of self-preservation and greed.

As Dimitrios stood up an idea seemed to occur to him. He turned to Latimer. 'You have been very silent, Monsieur. I wonder if you have been understanding that your life is in your friend Petersen's hands. If, for example, he decided to tell me your real name and where you might be found, I should very likely have you killed.'

Mr Peters showed his white false teeth. 'Why should I deprive myself of Monsieur Smith's help? Monsieur Smith is invaluable. He can prove that Visser is dead. Without him you could breathe again.'

Dimitrios took no notice of the interruption. 'Well, Monsieur Smith?'

Latimer looked up into the brown anxious-seeming eyes and thought of Madame Preveza's phrase. They were certainly the eyes of a man ready to do something that hurt, but they could have belonged to no doctor. There was murder in them.

'I can assure you,' he said, 'that Petersen has no inducement to kill me. You see . . .'

'You see,' put in Mr Peters quickly, 'we are not fools, Dimitrios. You can go now.'

'Of course.' Dimitrios went towards the door, but at the threshold he paused.

'What is it?' said Mr Peters.

'I should like to ask Monsieur Smith two questions.'
'Well?'

'How was this man whom you took to be Visser dressed when he was found?'

'In a cheap blue serge suit. A French *carte d'identité*, issued at Lyons a year previously, was sewn into the lining.

The suit was of Greek manufacture, but the shirt and underwear were French.'

'And how was he killed?'

'He had been stabbed in the side and then thrown into the water.'

Mr Peters smiled. 'Are you satisfied, Dimitrios?'

Dimitrios stared at him. 'Visser,' he said slowly, 'was too greedy. You will not be too greedy, will you, Petersen?'

Mr Peters gave him stare for stare. 'I shall be very careful,' he said. 'You have no more questions to ask? Good. You will receive your instructions in the morning.'

Dimitrios went without another word. Mr Peters shut the door, waited a moment or two, then, very gently opened it again. Motioning to Latimer to remain where he was, he disappeared on to the landing. Latimer heard the stairs creak. A minute later he returned.

'He has gone,' he announced. 'In a few minutes we, too, shall go.' He sat down again on the bed, lit one of his cheroots and blew the smoke out as luxuriously as if he had just been released from bondage. His sweet smile came out again like a rose after a storm. 'Well,' he said, 'that was Dimitrios about whom you have heard such a great deal. What did you think of him?'

'I didn't know what to think. Perhaps, if I had not known so much about him, I should have disliked him less. I don't know. It is difficult to be reasonable about a man who is obviously wondering how quickly he can murder you.' He hesitated. 'I did not realize that you hated him so much.'

Mr Peters did not smile. 'I assure you, Mr Latimer, that it was a surprise to me to realize it. I did not like him. I did not trust him. After the way he betrayed us all, that was understandable. It was not until I saw him in this room just now that I realized that I hated him enough to kill him. If I were a superstitious man, I would wonder if perhaps the spirit of poor Visser had entered into me.' He stopped, then added '*Salop!*' under his breath. He was silent for a moment. Then he looked up. 'Mr Latimer, I must make an admission. I must tell you that even if you had agreed to the offer I made you, you would not have received your half million. I would not have paid you.' He shut his mouth tightly as if he were prepared to receive a blow.

'So I imagine,' said Latimer dryly. 'I very nearly accepted the offer just to see how you would cheat me. I take it that you would have made the real time for delivery of the money an hour or so earlier than you would have told me, and that, by the time I arrived on the scene, you and the money would have gone. Was that it?'

Mr Peters winced. 'It was very wise of you not to trust me, but very unkind. But I suppose that I cannot blame you.' He rubbed salt in the wound. 'The Great One has seen fit to make me what is known as a criminal, and I must tread the path to my Destiny with patient resignation. But it was not to abase myself that I admitted to having tried to deceive you. It was to defend myself. I would like to ask you a question.'

'Well?'

'Was it – forgive me – was it the thought that I might betray you to Dimitrios that made you refuse my offer to share the money with you?'

'It never occurred to me.'

'I am glad,' said Mr Peters solemnly. 'I should not like you to think that of me. You may dislike me, but I should not care to be thought cold-blooded. I may tell you that the thought did not occur to me either. There you see Dimitrios! We have discussed this matter, you and I. We have mistrusted one another and looked for betrayal. Yet it is Dimitrios who put this thought in our heads. I have met many wicked and violent men, Mr Latimer, but I tell you that Dimitrios is unique. Why do you think he suggested to you that I might betray you?'

'I imagine that he was acting on the principle that the best way to fight two allies is to get them to fight each other.'

Mr Peters smiled. 'No, Mr Latimer. That would have been too obvious a trick for Dimitrios. He was suggesting to you in a very delicate way that *I* was the unnecessary partner and that you could remove me very easily by telling him where I could be found.'

'Do you mean that he was offering to kill you for me?'

'Exactly. He would have only you to deal with then. He does not know, of course,' added Mr Peters thoughtfully, 'that you do not know his present name.' He stood up and put on his hat. 'No, Mr Latimer, I do not like Dimitrios. Do not misunderstand me, please. I have no moral rectitude. But Dimitrios is a savage beast. Even now, though I know that I have taken every precaution, I am afraid. I shall take his million and go. If I could allow you to hand him over to the police when I have done with him, I would do so. He would not hesitate if the situation were reversed. But it is impossible.'

'Why?'

Mr Peters looked at him curiously. 'Dimitrios seems to have had a strange effect on you. No, to tell the police afterwards would be too dangerous. If we were asked to explain the million francs – and we could not expect

Dimitrios to remain silent about them – we should be embarrassed. A pity. Shall we go now? I shall leave the money for the room on the table. They can take the suitcase for a *pourboire*.'

They went downstairs in silence. As they deposited the key, the man in his shirtsleeves appeared with an *affiche* for Mr Peters to complete. Mr Peters waved him away. He would, he said, fill it in when he returned.

In the street he halted and faced Latimer.

'Have you ever been followed?'

'Not to my knowledge.'

'Then you will be followed now. I do not suppose that Dimitrios has any real hope of our leading him to our homes, but he was always thorough.' He glanced over Latimer's shoulder. 'Ah, yes. He was there when we arrived. Do not look round, Mr Latimer. A man wearing a grey mackintosh and a dark soft hat. You will see him in a minute.'

The hollow feeling which had disappeared with the departure of Dimitrios jolted back into its position in Latimer's stomach. 'What are we to do?'

'Return by Metro, as I said before.'

'What good will that do?'

'You will see in a minute.'

The Ledru-Rollin Metro station was about a hundred yards away. As they walked towards it the muscles in Latimer's calves tightened and he had a ridiculous desire to run. He felt himself walking stiffly and self-consciously.

'Do not look round,' said Mr Peters again.

They walked down the steps to the Metro. 'Keep close to me now,' said Mr Peters.

He bought two second-class tickets and they walked on down the tunnel in the direction of the trains.

It was a long tunnel. As they pushed their way through the spring barriers, Latimer felt that he could reasonably glance behind him. He did so, and caught a glimpse of a shabby young man in a grey raincoat about thirty feet behind them. Now the tunnel split into two. One way was labelled: '*Direction* Pte. de Charenton', the other: '*Direction* Balard'. Mr Peters stopped.

'It would be wise now,' he said, 'if we appeared to be about to take leave of one another.' He glanced out of the corners of his eyes. 'Yes, he has stopped. He is wondering what is going to happen. Talk, please, Mr Latimer, but not too loudly. I want to listen.'

'Listen to what?'

'The trains. I spent half an hour here listening to them this morning.'

'What on earth for? I don't see . . .'

Mr Peters gripped his arm and he stopped. In the distance he could hear the rumble of an approaching train.

'*Direction* Balard,' muttered Mr Peters suddenly. 'Come along. Keep close to me and do not walk too quickly.'

They went on down the right-hand tunnel. The rumble of the train grew louder. They rounded a bend in the tunnel. Ahead was the green automatic gate.

'*Vite!*' cried Mr Peters.

The train was by now almost in the station. The automatic door began to swing slowly across the entrance to the platform. As Latimer reached it and passed through with about three inches to spare, he heard, above the hiss and screech of pneumatic brakes the sound of running feet. He looked round. Although Mr Peters' stomach had suffered some compression, he had squeezed himself through on to the platform. But the man in the grey rain-coat had, in spite of his last-minute sprint, left it too late. He now stood, red in the face with anger, shaking his fists at them from the other side of the automatic gate.

They got into the train a trifle breathlessly.

'Excellent!' puffed Mr Peters happily. 'Now do you see what I meant, Mr Latimer?'

'Very ingenious.'

The noise of the train made further conversation impossible. Latimer stared vacantly at a Celtique advertise-ment. So that was that. Colonel Haki had been right after all. The story of Dimitrios had no proper ending. Dimitrios would buy off Mr Peters and the story would merely stop. Somewhere, at some future time, Dimitrios might happen to find Mr Peters and then Mr Peters would die as Visser had died. Somewhere, at some time, Dimitrios himself would die: probably of old age. But he, Latimer, would not know about those things. He would be writing a detective story with a beginning, a middle and an end; a corpse, a piece of detection and a scaffold. He would be demon-strating that murder would out, that justice triumphed in the end and that the green bay tree flourished alone. Dimi-trios and the Eurasian Credit Trust would be forgotten. It had all been a great waste of time.

Mr Peters touched his arm. They were at Chatelet. They got out and took the Porte d'Orléans *correspondance* to St Placide. As they walked down the Rue de Rennes, Mr Peters hummed softly. They passed a café.

Mr Peters stopped humming. 'Would you like some coffee, Mr Latimer?'

'No, thanks. What about your letter to Dimitrios?'

Mr Peters tapped his pocket. 'It is already written. Eleven o'clock is the time. The junction of the Avenue de la Reine and the Boulevard Jean Jaurès is the place. Would you like to be there, or are you leaving Paris tomorrow?' And then, without giving Latimer a chance to reply: 'I shall be sorry to say goodbye to you, Mr Latimer. I find you so sympathetic. Our association has, on the whole, been most agreeable. It has also been profitable to me.' He sighed. 'I feel a little guilty, Mr Latimer. You have been so patient and helpful and yet you go unrewarded. You would not,' he enquired a trifle anxiously, 'accept a thousand francs of the money? It would help to pay your expenses.'

'No, thank you.'

'No, of course not. Then, at least, Mr Latimer, let me give you a glass of wine. That it is! A celebration! Come, Mr Latimer. There is no taste in nothing. Let us collect the money together tomorrow night. You will have the satisfaction of seeing a little blood squeezed from this swine Dimitrios. Then we will celebrate with a glass of wine. What do you say to that?'

They had stopped at the corner of the street which contained the Impasse. Latimer looked into Mr Peters' watery eyes. 'I should say,' he said deliberately, 'that you are wondering if there is a chance that Dimitrios might decide to call your bluff and thinking that it might be a good idea to have me in Paris until you have the money actually in your pocket.'

Mr Peters' eyes slowly closed. 'Mr Latimer,' he said bitterly, 'I did not think . . . I would not have thought that you could have put such a construction on . . .'

'All right, I'll stay.' Irritably, Latimer interrupted him. He had wasted so many days: another one would make no difference. 'I'll come with you tomorrow, but only on these conditions. The wine must be champagne; it must come from France, not Meknes, and it must be a vintage *cuvée* of either 1919, 1920 or 1921. A bottle,' he added vindictively, 'will cost you at least one hundred francs.'

Mr Peters opened his eyes. He smiled bravely. 'You shall have it, Mr Latimer,' he said.

15

The Strange Town

Mr Peters and Latimer took up their positions at the corner of the Avenue de la Reine and the Boulevard Jean Jaurès at half-past ten, the hour at which the hired car was due to pick up the messenger from Dimitrios opposite the Neuilly cemetery.

It was a cold night, and as it began to rain soon after they arrived, they stood for shelter just inside the *porte cocher* of a building a few yards along the Avenue in the direction of the Pont St Cloud.

'How long will they be getting here?' Latimer asked.

'I said that I would expect them by eleven. That gives them half an hour to drive from Neuilly. They could do it in less, but I told them to make quite certain that they were not followed. If they are in doubt they will return to Neuilly. They will take no chances. The car is a Renault *coupé-de-ville*. We must have patience.'

They waited in silence. Now and again Mr Peters would stir as a car that might have been the hired Renault approached from the direction of the river. The rain trickling down the slope formed by the subsidence of the cobbles formed puddles about their feet. Latimer thought of his warm bed and wondered if he would catch a cold. He had booked a seat in the Athens slip-coach of the Orient Express due to leave the following morning. A train would not be the best place to spend three days nursing a cold.

He remembered that he had a small bottle of cinnamon extract somewhere in his luggage and resolved to take a dose before he went to bed.

His mind was occupied with this domestic matter when suddenly Mr Peters grunted: '*Attention!*'

'Are they coming?'

'Yes.'

Latimer looked over Mr Peters' shoulder. A large Renault was approaching from the left. As he looked it began to slow down as if the driver were uncertain of the way. It passed them, the rain glistening in the beams of the headlights, and stopped a few yards farther on. The outline of the driver's head and shoulders were just visible in the darkness, but blinds were pulled down over the rear windows. Mr Peters put his hand in his overcoat pocket.

'Wait here, please,' he said to Latimer, and walked towards the car.

'*Ca va?*' Latimer heard him say to the driver. There was an answering '*Oui*'. Mr Peters opened the rear door and leaned forward.

Almost immediately he withdrew a pace and closed the door. In his left hand was a package. '*Attendez,*' he said, and walked back to where Latimer was standing.

'All right?' said Latimer.

'I think so. Will you strike a match, please?'

Latimer did so. The package was the size of a large book, about two inches thick and was wrapped in blue paper and tied with string. Mr Peters tore away the paper at one of the corners and exposed a solid wad of *mille* notes. He sighed. 'Beautiful!'

'Aren't you going to count them?'

'That pleasure,' said Mr Peters seriously, 'I shall reserve

for the comfort of my home.' He crammed the package into his overcoat pocket, stepped on to the pavement and raised his hand. The Renault started with a jerk, swung round in a wide circle and splashed away on its return journey. Mr Peters watched it go with a smile.

'A very pretty woman,' he said. 'I wonder who she can be. But I prefer the million francs. Now, Mr Latimer, a taxi and then your favourite champagne. We have earned it, I think.'

They found a taxi near the Porte de St Cloud. Mr Peters enlarged on his success.

'With a type like Dimitrios it is necessary only to be firm and circumspect. We put the matter to him squarely; we let him see that he has no choice but to agree to our demands, and it is done. A million francs. Very nice! One almost wishes that one had demanded two million. But it would have been unwise to be too greedy. As it is, he believes that we shall make fresh demands and that he has time to deal with us as he dealt with Visser. He will find that he has deceived himself. That is very satisfactory to me, Mr Latimer: as satisfying to my pride as it is to my pocket. I feel, too, that I have, in some measure, avenged poor Visser's death. It is at moments like these, Mr Latimer, that one realizes that if it sometimes appears as if the Great One has forgotten His children, it is only that we have forgotten Him. I have suffered. Now I have my reward.' He patted his pocket. 'It would be amusing to see Dimitrios when at last he realizes how he has been tricked. A pity that we shall not be there.'

'Shall you leave Paris immediately?'

'I think so. I have a fancy to see something of South America. Not my own adopted fatherland, of course. It is one of the terms of my citizenship that I never enter the country. A hard condition, for I would like for sentimental reasons to see the country of my adoption. But it cannot be altered. I am a citizen of the world and must remain so. Perhaps I shall buy an estate somewhere, a place where I shall be able to pass my days in peace when I am old. You are a young man, Mr Latimer. When one is my age, the years seem shorter and one feels that one is soon to reach a destination. It is as if one were approaching a strange town late at night when one is sorry to be leaving the warm train for an unknown hotel and wishing that the journey would never end.'

'Doesn't your philosophy cover that point?'

'Philosophy,' said Mr Peters, 'is for explaining that which has already happened. Only the Great One knows what will happen in the future. We are just human. How can our poor minds hope to understand the infinite? The sun is one hundred and sixty million kilometres from the earth. Think of it! We are insignificant dust. What is a million francs? Nothing! Useful, no doubt, but nothing. Why should the Great One concern Himself with such small matters? It is a mystery. Think of the stars. There are millions of them. It is remarkable.'

He went on to talk about the stars while the taxi traversed the Rue Lecourbe and turned into the Boulevard Montparnasse.

'Yes, we are insignificant,' Mr Peters was saying. 'We struggle for existence like the ants. Yet, had I my life to live over again, I would not wish it any different. There have been disagreeable moments and the Great One has seen fit that I should do some unpleasant things, but I have made a little money and I am free to go where I wish. Not every man of my age,' he added virtuously, 'can say as much.'

The taxi turned left into the Rue de Rennes.

'We are nearly home. I have your champagne. It was, as you warned me, very expensive. But I have no priggish objections to a little luxury. It is sometimes agreeable and, even when it is disagreeable, it serves to make us appreciate simplicity. Ah!' The taxi had stopped at the end of the Impasse. 'I have no change, Mr Latimer. That seems odd with a million francs in one's pocket, does it not? Will you pay, please?'

They walked down the Impasse.

'I think,' said Mr Peters, 'that I shall sell these houses before I go to South America. One does not want property on one's hands that is not yielding a profit.'

'Won't they be rather difficult to sell? The view from the windows is a little depressing, isn't it?'

'It is not necessary to be always looking out of the windows. They could be made into very nice houses.'

They began the long climb up the stairs. On the second landing Mr Peters paused for breath, took off his overcoat and got out his keys. They continued the climb to his door.

He opened it, switched on the light, and then, going straight to the largest divan, took the package from his overcoat pocket and undid the string. With loving care he extracted the notes from the wrappings and held them up. For once his smile was real.

'There, Mr Latimer! A million francs! Have you ever seen so much money at once before? Nearly six thousand English pounds!' He stood up. 'But we must have our little celebration. Take off your coat and I will get the champagne. I hope that you will like it. I have no ice, but I put it in a bowl of water. It will be quite cool.'

He walked towards the curtained-off part of the room.

Latimer had turned away to take off his coat. Suddenly he became aware that Mr Peters was still on the same side of the curtain and that he was standing motionless. He glanced round.

For a moment he thought that he was going to faint. The blood seemed to drain away suddenly from his head, leaving it hollow and light. A steel band seemed to tighten round his chest. He felt that he wanted to cry out, but all he could do was to stare.

Mr Peters was standing with his back to him, and his hands were raised above his head. Facing him in the gap between the gold curtains was Dimitrios, with a revolver in his hand.

Dimitrios stepped forward and sideways so that Latimer was no longer partly covered by Mr Peters. Latimer dropped his coat and put up his hands. Dimitrios raised his eyebrows.

'It is not flattering,' he said, 'for you to look so surprised to see me, Petersen. Or should I call you Caillé?'

Mr Peters said nothing. Latimer could not see his face, but he saw his throat move as if he were swallowing.

The brown eyes flickered to Latimer. 'I am glad that the Englishman is here, too, Petersen. I am saved the trouble of persuading you to give me his name and address. Monsieur Smith, who knows so many things and who was so anxious to keep his face hidden, is now shown to be as easy to deal with as you are, Petersen. You were always too ingenious, Petersen. I told you so once before. It was on the occasion when you brought a coffin from Salonika. You remember?

Ingenuity is never a substitute for intelligence, you know. Did you really think that I should not see through you?' His lips twisted. 'Poor Dimitrios! He is very simple. He will think that I, clever Petersen, will come back for more, like any other blackmailer. He will not guess that I may be bluffing him. But, just to make sure that he does not guess, I will do what no other blackmailer ever did. I will tell him that I *shall* come back for more. Poor Dimitrios is such a fool that he will believe me. Poor Dimitrios has no intelligence. Even if he finds out from the records that, within a month of my coming out of prison, I had succeeded in selling three unsaleable houses to someone named Caillé, he will not dream of suspecting that I, clever Petersen, am also Caillé. Did you not know, Petersen, that before I bought these houses in your name they had been empty for ten years? You are such a fool.'

He paused. The anxious brown eyes narrowed. The mouth tightened. Latimer knew that Dimitrios was going to kill Mr Peters and that there was nothing that he could do about it. The wild beating of his heart seemed to be suffocating him.

'Drop the money, Petersen.'

The wad of notes hit the carpet and spread out like a fan.

Dimitrios raised the revolver.

Suddenly, Mr Peters seemed to realize what was about to happen. He cried out: 'No! You must . . .'

Then Dimitrios fired. He fired twice and with the ear-splitting noise of the explosions Latimer heard one of the bullets thud into Mr Peters' body.

Mr Peters emitted a long drawn-out retching sound and

sank forward on to his hands and knees with blood pouring from his neck.

Dimitrios stared at Latimer. 'Now you,' he said.

At that moment Latimer jumped.

Why he chose that particular moment to jump he never knew. He never even knew what prompted him to jump at all. He supposed that it was an instinctive attempt to save himself. Why, however, his instinct for self-preservation should have led him to jump in the direction of the revolver which Dimitrios was about to fire is inexplicable. But he did jump, and the jump did save his life; for, as his right foot left the floor, a fraction of a second before Dimitrios pressed the trigger, he stumbled over one of Mr Peters' thick tufts of rug and the shot went over his head into the wall.

Half dazed and with his forehead scorched by the blast from the muzzle of the revolver, he hurled himself at Dimitrios. They went down together with their hands at each other's throats, but immediately Dimitrios brought his knee up into Latimer's stomach and rolled clear of him.

He had dropped his revolver, and now he went to pick it up. Gasping for breath, Latimer scrambled towards the nearest movable object, which happened to be the heavy brass tray on top of one of the Moroccan tables, and flung it at Dimitrios. The edge of it hit the side of his head as he was reaching for the revolver and he reeled, but the blow stopped him for barely a second. Latimer threw the wooden part of the table at him and dashed forward. Dimitrios staggered back as the table caught his shoulder. The next moment Latimer had the revolver and was standing back, still trying to get his breath, but with his finger on the trigger.

Eric Ambler

His face sheet-white, Dimitrios came towards him. Latimer raised the revolver.

'If you move again, I shall fire.'

Dimitrios stood still. His brown eyes stared into Latimer's. His grey hair was tousled; his scarf had come out of his coat; he looked dangerous. Latimer was beginning to recover his breath, but his knees felt horribly weak, his ears were singing and the air he breathed reeked sickeningly of cordite fumes. It was for him to make the next move, and he felt frightened and helpless.

'If you move,' he repeated, 'I shall fire.'

He saw the brown eyes flicker towards the notes on the floor and then back to him. 'What are you going to do?' said Dimitrios suddenly. 'If the police come we shall both have something to explain. If you shoot me you will get only that million. If you will release me I will give you another million as well. That would be good for you.'

Latimer took no notice. He edged sideways towards the wall, until he could glance quickly at Mr Peters.

Mr Peters had crawled towards the divan on which his overcoat lay, and was now leaning against it with his eyes half closed. He was breathing stertorously through the mouth. One bullet had torn a great gaping wound in the side of his neck from which the blood was welling. The second had hit him full in the chest and scorched the clothing. The wound was a round purple mess about two inches in diameter. It was bleeding very little. Mr Peters' lips moved.

Keeping his eyes fixed on Dimitrios, Latimer moved round until he was alongside Mr Peters.

'How do you feel?' he said.

It was a stupid question, and he knew it the moment the

words had left his mouth. He tried desperately to collect his wits. A man had been shot and he had the man who shot him. He . . .

'My pistol,' muttered Mr Peters; 'get my pistol. Overcoat.' He said something else that was inaudible.

Cautiously, Latimer worked his way round to the overcoat and fumbled for the pistol. Dimitrios watched with a thin ghastly smile on his lips. Latimer found the pistol and handed it to Mr Peters. He grasped it with both hands and snicked back the safety catch.

'Now,' he muttered, 'go and get police.'

'Someone will have heard the shots,' said Latimer soothingly. 'The police will be here soon.'

'Won't find us,' whispered Mr Peters. 'Get police.'

Latimer hesitated. What Mr Peters said was true. The Impasse was hemmed in by blank walls. The shots might have been heard, but unless someone had happened to be passing the entrance to the Impasse during the few seconds in which they were fixed, nobody would know where the sounds had come from.

'All right,' he said. 'Where is the telephone?'

'No telephone.'

'But . . .' He hesitated again. It might take ten minutes to find a policeman. Could he leave a badly wounded Mr Peters to watch a man like Dimitrios? But there was nothing else for it. Mr Peters needed a doctor. The sooner Dimitrios was under lock and key the better. He knew that Dimitrios understood his predicament and the knowledge did not please him. He glanced at Mr Peters. He had the Lüger resting on one knee and pointed at Dimitrios. The blood was still pouring from his neck. If a doctor did not attend to him soon he would bleed to death.

'All right,' he said. 'I'll be as quick as I can.'

He went towards the door.

'One moment, Monsieur.' There was an urgency in the harsh voice that made Latimer pause.

'Well?'

'If you go he will shoot me. Don't you see that? Why not accept my offer?'

Latimer opened the door. 'If you try any tricks you will certainly be shot.' He looked again at the wounded man, huddled over the Lüger. 'I shall be back with the police. Don't shoot unless you have to.'

Then, as he made to go, Dimitrios laughed. Involuntarily, Latimer turned. 'I should save that laugh for the executioner,' he snapped. 'You will need it.'

'I was thinking,' said Dimitrios, 'that in the end one is always defeated by stupidity. If it is not one's own it is the stupidity of others.' His face changed. 'Five million, Monsieur,' he shouted angrily. 'Is it not enough, or do you want this carrion to kill me?'

Latimer stared at him for a moment. The man was almost convincing. Then he remembered that others had been convinced by Dimitrios. He waited no longer. He heard Dimitrios shout something after him as he shut the door.

He was halfway down the stairs when he heard the shots. There were four of them. Three cracked out in quick succession. Then, there was a pause before the last one. His heart in his mouth, he turned and ran back up to the room. It was only later that he found anything curious in the fact that, as he raced up the stairs, the fear uppermost in his mind was for Mr Peters.

Dimitrios was not a pleasant sight. Only one of the

bullets from Mr Peters' Lüger had missed. Two had lodged in the body. The fourth, evidently fired at him after he had fallen to the floor, had hit him between the eyes and almost blown the top of his head off. His body was still twitching.

The Lüger slipped from Mr Peters' fingers and he was leaning, with his head on the edge of the divan, opening and shutting his mouth like a stranded fish. As Latimer stood there he choked suddenly and blood trickled from his mouth.

Scarcely knowing what he was doing, Latimer blundered through the curtain. Dimitrios was dead; Mr Peters was dying; and all he, Latimer, could think about was the effort required not to faint or vomit. He strove to pull himself together. He must do something. Mr Peters must have water. Wounded men always need water. There was a washbasin and beside it were some glasses. He filled one and carried it back into the room.

Mr Peters had not moved. His mouth and eyes were open. Latimer knelt down beside him and poured a little water into the mouth. It ran out again. He put down the glass and felt for the pulse. There was none.

Latimer got quickly to his feet and looked at his hands. There was blood on them. He went back to the washbasin, rinsed them and dried them on a small, dirty towel which hung from a hook.

He should, he knew, call the police immediately. Two men had killed each other. That was a matter for the police. Yet . . . what was he going to say to them? How was he going to explain his own presence there in that shambles? Could he say that he had been passing the end of the Impasse and had heard the shots? But someone might have noticed him with Mr Peters. There was the taxi driver who had brought them. And when they found that Dimitrios had that day obtained a million francs from his bank . . . there would be endless questionings. Supposing they suspected him.

His brain seemed to clear suddenly. He must get out at once and he must leave no traces of his presence there. He thought quickly. The revolver in his pocket belonged to Dimitrios. It had his fingerprints on it. He took it out of his pocket, put on his gloves and wiped it all over carefully with his handkerchief. Then, setting his teeth, he went back into the room, knelt down beside Dimitrios and, taking his right hand, pressed the fingers round the butt and trigger. Removing the fingers and holding the revolver by the barrel, he then put it near the body on the floor.

He considered the *mille* notes strewn over the rug like so much wastepaper. To whom did they belong – Dimitrios or Mr Peters? There was Sholem's money there and the money stolen in Athens in 1922. There was the fee for helping to assassinate Stambulisky and the money of which Madame Preveza had been cheated. There was the price of the charts Bulić had stolen and part of the profits from the white slave and drug traffics. To whom did it belong? Well, the police would decide. Best to leave it as it was. It would give them something to think about.

There was, however, the glass of water. It must be emptied, dried and replaced with the other glasses. He looked round. Was there anything else? No. Nothing at all? Yes, one thing. His fingerprints were on the tray and the table. He wiped them. Nothing more? Yes. Fingerprints on the doorknobs. He wiped them. Anything else? No. He carried the glass to the washbasin. The glass dried and replaced, he turned to go. It was then that he noticed the champagne which Mr Peters had bought for their celebration standing in a bowl of water. It was a Verzy 1921 – a half bottle.

★

No one saw him leave the Impasse. He went to a café in the Rue de Rennes and ordered a cognac.

Now he began to tremble from head to foot. He had been a fool. He ought to have gone to the police. It was still not too late to go to them. Supposing the bodies remained undiscovered. They might lie there for weeks in that ghastly room with the blue walls and gold stars and rugs, while the blood congealed and hardened and collected dust and the flesh began to rot. It was horrible to think of. If only there were some way of telling the police. An anonymous letter would be too dangerous. The police would know immediately that a third person had been concerned in the affair and would not be satisfied with the simple explanation that the two men had killed each other. Then he had an idea. The main thing was to get the police to the house. Why they went was unimportant.

There was an evening paper in the rack. He took it to his table and read it through feverishly. There were two news items in it which suited his purpose. One was a report of the theft of some valuable furs from a warehouse in the Avenue de la Republique; the other was an account of the smashing of the shop window of a jeweller in the Avenue de Clichy and the escape of two men with a tray of rings.

He decided that the first would suit his purpose best, and, summoning the waiter, ordered another cognac together with writing materials. He drank the brandy at a gulp and put his gloves on. Then, taking a sheet of the letter paper, he examined it carefully. It was ordinary, cheap café notepaper. Having satisfied himself that there was no distinguishing mark of any kind on it, he wrote across the middle of it in capital letters: '*FAITES DES ENQUETES SUR CAILLÉ – 3, IMPASSE DES HUITS ANGES.*' Then he tore the report of the fur robbery out of the paper, folded it inside the note and put the two in an envelope, which he addressed to the Commissaire of Police of the Seventh Arrondissement. Leaving the café, he bought a stamp at a tobacco kiosk and posted the letter.

It was not until four o'clock that morning, when he had lain awake in bed for two hours, that the nerves of his stomach succumbed at last to the strain which had been put upon them and he was sick.

Two days later a paragraph appeared in three of the Paris morning papers saying that the body of a South American named Frederik Peters, together with that of a man, at present unidentified, but believed to be a South American also, had been found in an apartment off the Rue de Rennes. Both men, the paragraph continued, had been shot and it was thought that they had killed one another in a revolver fight following a quarrel over money, a considerable sum of which was found in the apartment. It was the only reference to the affair, the attention of the public being divided at the time between a new international crisis and a hatchet murder in the suburbs.

Latimer did not see the paragraph until several days later.

Soon after nine o'clock on the morning of the day on which the police received his note, he left his hotel for the

Gare de l'Est and the Orient express. A letter had arrived for him by the first post. It had a Bulgarian stamp and a Sofia postmark and was obviously from Marukakis. He put it in his pocket unread. It was not until later in the day, when the express was racing through the hills west of Belfort, that he remembered it. He opened it and began to read:

My Dear Friend.

Your letter delighted me. I was so pleased to get it. I was also a little surprised, for – forgive me, please – I did not seriously expect you to succeed in the difficult task which you had set yourself. The years bury so much of our wisdom that they are bound to bury most of our folly with it. Some time I hope to hear from you how a folly buried in Belgrade comes to be unearthed in Geneva.

I was interested in the reference to the Eurasian Credit Trust. Here is something that will interest you.

There has been recently, as you may know, a great deal of tension between this country and Yugoslavia. The Serbs, you know, have reason to feel tense. If Germany and vassal Hungary attacked her from the north, Italy attacked her through Albania from the south and by sea from the west, and Bulgaria attacked her from the east, she would be quickly finished. Her only chance would lie in the Russians outflanking the Germans and Hungarians with an attack launched through Rumania along the Bukovina railway. But has Bulgaria anything to fear from Yugoslavia? Is she a danger to Bulgaria? The idea is absurd. Yet, for the past three months or four, there has been here a stream of propaganda to the effect that Yugoslavia is planning to attack Bulgaria. 'The menace across the frontier' is a typical phrase.

If such things were not so dangerous one would laugh. But one recognizes the technique. Such propaganda always begins with words, but soon it proceeds to deeds. When there are no facts to support lies, facts must be made.

Two weeks ago there took place the inevitable frontier incident. Some Bulgarian peasants were fired upon by Yugoslavs (alleged to be soldiers), and one of the peasants was killed. There is much popular indignation, an outcry against the devilish Serbs. The newspaper offices are very busy. A week later the Government announces fresh purchases of anti-aircraft guns to strengthen the defences of the western Provinces. The purchases are made from a Belgian firm with the help of a loan negotiated by the Eurasian Credit Trust.

Yesterday a curious news item comes into this office.

As a result of careful investigations by the Yugoslav Government, it is shown that the four men who fired on the peasants were not Yugoslav soldiers, nor even Yugoslav subjects. They were of various nationalities and two had previously been imprisoned in Poland for terrorist activities. They had been paid to create the incident by a man about whom none of them knows anything more than that he came from Paris.

But there is more. Within an hour of that news item reaching Paris, I had instructions from the head office there to suppress the item and send out a *démenti* to all subscribers taking our French news. That is amusing, is it not? One would not have thought that such a rich organization as the Eurasian Credit Trust would be so sensitive.

As for your Dimitrios: what can one say?

A writer of plays once said that there are some situations that one cannot use on the stage; situations in which the audience can feel neither approval or disapproval, sympathy or antipathy; situations out of which there is no possible way that is not humiliating or distressing and from which there is no truth, however bitter, to be extracted. He was, you may say, one of those unhappy men who are confounded by the difference between the stupid vulgarities of real life and the ideal existence of the imagination. That may be. Yet, I have been wondering if, for once, I do not find myself in sympathy with him. Can one explain Dimitrios, or must one turn away disgusted and defeated? I am tempted to find reason and justice in the fact that he died as violently and indecently as he lived. But that is too ingenuous a way out. It does not explain Dimitrios; it only apologizes for him. Special sorts of conditions must exist for the creation of the special sort of criminal that he typified. I have tried to define those conditions – but unsuccessfully. All I do know is that while might is right, while chaos and anarchy masquerade as order and enlightenment, those conditions will obtain.

What is the remedy? But I can see you yawning and remember that if I bore you you will not write to me again to tell me whether you are enjoying your stay in Paris, whether you have found any more Bulićs or Prevezas and whether we shall see you soon in Sofia. My latest information is that war will not break out until the spring, so there will be time for some skiing. Late January is quite good here. The roads are terrible, but the runs, when one gets to them, are quite good. I shall look forward eagerly to learning from you when you will come.

    With my most sincere regards

      N. Marukakis.

Latimer folded the letter and put it in his pocket. A good fellow, Marukakis! He must write to him when he had the time. But just at the moment there were more important matters to be considered.

He needed, and badly, a motive, a neat method of committing a murder and an entertaining crew of suspects. Yes, the suspects must certainly be entertaining. His last book had been a trifle heavy. He must inject a little more humour into this one. As for the motive, money was always, of course, the soundest basis. A pity that wills and life insurance were so outmoded. Supposing a man murdered an old lady so that his wife should have a private income. It might be worth thinking about. The scene? Well, there was always plenty of fun to be got out of an English country village, wasn't there? The time? Summer; with cricket matches on the village green, garden parties at the vicarage, the clink of teacups and the sweet smell of grass on a July evening. That was the sort of thing people liked to hear about. It was the sort of thing that he himself would like to hear about.

He looked out of the window. The sun had gone and the hills were receding slowly into the night sky. They would be slowing down for Belfort soon. Two more days to go! He ought to get some sort of a plot worked out in that time.

The train ran into a tunnel.